On The Banks of The Chestatee

A Novel By

Robert Carruth

Table of Contents

Dedication

To Nelwyn Turk, my Senior English Teacher – who never in a million years would have expected this

About the Author

After a successful career as a military officer, public servant, and business leader, Robert has embarked on a new venture involving his first love, history, and a hidden talent, writing. On the Banks of the Chestatee is his debut novel.

Out of the hills of Habersham,

Down the valleys of Hall,

I hurry amain to reach the plain,

Run the rapid and leap the fall,

Split at the rock and together again,

Accept my bed, narrow or wide,

And flee from folly on every side.

With a lover's pain to attain the plain

Far from the hills of Habersham,

Far from the valleys of Hall.

Song of the Chattahoochee

William Sidney Lanier

Chapter 1

Dawson County, Georgia

March 1904

A decade had passed since he laid his dear wife Cissy in her final resting place in the nearby. He visited her grave almost every day until it got too hard to walk the half mile to the cemetery. He had little left now. His eyesight was about gone, and when he could no longer care for himself, he knew the time was drawing close to join his family on the other side.

They had been more than accommodating. In passing the torch to the next generation, it was easier said than done. So much he wanted to share, so much he wanted to say, having bottled it all up over the last 60 years. He had witnessed all three of his sons marching off to war together while only having two to return. The oldest had taken a bullet at Antietam, and he had outlived the other two as well. A daughter was married and moved to Montana. They had received a few letters, but they stopped coming after a few months, and he soon learned of her passing as well. The only ones left were his grandson's family and the widow of his youngest son, Hezekiah. She now sat by his side and provided for his care.

After Hezekiah's death two years ago, it was inevitable that Sophie would become his caregiver. She really had nowhere else to go, so it only made sense she would take on this role. In addition, his grandson and wife were busy with their family, trying to keep the old mill running and raising their kids. Although they had returned here with the promise of taking care of him, they soon showed they had little time for the half-blind, frail old man that they had barely known.

He had taken ill about 10 months ago. The doctor said it was cancer. The family was told there was little hope. The best thing to do was to try and keep him comfortable. At first, he was able to sit on his porch and watch the day pass by. Sophie would busy herself with chores, but as time went along, she found herself drawn to the stories that Jacob wanted to tell. Many times, young Tom would sit nearby, listening intently as Jacob told of his sons going off to war, surviving the aftermath, and how much times had changed during his almost 90 years of life.

Family members and friends had stopped by throughout the day, and his papa, who had maintained a sharp mind up until a few days earlier, was mumbling nonsensical things now.

There was now a constant vigilance by his bed. Most of the time, it was Sophie or Michael, his oldest grandson. All the children were gone, waiting for him to join them. He had outlived them all.

Sophie looked up as Michael quietly entered the room. The boy noticed as Michael motioned for Sophie, and they left the room for a moment, leaving the boy alone with the old man.

Jacob roused, and then he called for Tom. "Son, come over here where I can talk to you. My voice is weak, and I want you to hear me."

The boy approached the bedside as Jacob was now fully awake and more coherent than he had been in days.

"Boy, don't ever tell anyone what I am about to tell you. Take care of your momma. There's a lot of folks that want her out of here, you understand?"

The boy slowly nodded his head. Jacob continued. "Your momma has something very valuable. She is sworn to keep everything just between us." There's more to this story that I ain't telling anyone the details of. I've decided to take it to my grave."

The old man, having used the last of his strength, started muttering, "I didn't mean to kill him….I'm sorry God…." He then turned again and looked at the boy. "Its there….its all there…." His eyes fluttered a couple of times, then he let out a deep sigh and laid there. He took another deep breath, and as the boy held his hand, he could feel it getting colder.

"I didn't mean to do it; I really didn't mean to do it. He's there – all of it is there." He stopped, almost as if he realized something he shouldn't have said. There was almost a look of terror in his eyes as if he was back at that point in time. Then, in a small, quiet whisper, he uttered, "Please, No one has to know this. Please tell me you will keep this a secret between us."

He sank back on the pillow and slept, at peace that he had finally said it.

Sometime around late afternoon, as the shadows were getting long, several other people, mostly church folk, had arrived at the home as word of the vigil had reached the community. Michael sat on one side of the bed, while Sophie sat on the other side, with the boy hugged up against her, hoping that the angels the older folks kept talking about wouldn't grab him, too. Then, he let out a small whimper…"I didn't mean to do it. Have mercy on me, Jesus." He then whispered "goodbye" and breathed his last. Michael checked for a pulse, then gently closed his eyes. He then announced to the group, choking back tears… "He's gone."

August 1954

He wiped his eyes as his eyes adjusted to the light illuminating the room. The lights through the dingy window cast a pasty light across the small cabin he called home. His bed, or what passed as a bed, took up one corner of the room. He sat up, clearing his mind. The place looked like something out of another century, and in some ways it was. The chestnut logs that made up its structure were a testament to its age. He looked around the room. A solitary picture of his mom hung on the wall. There was little furniture other than a small table sitting next to the fireplace. There was an old lantern sitting on the mantle, which provided the only light for the place. Besides no electricity, he also had no running water, still relying on the old well out back. A hundred yards or so beyond it sat the outhouse.

He lived simply.

Standing up and stretching, he could touch the ceiling flat-footed. His tall, lanky posture looked even more pronounced when he slipped on the ever-present bib overalls he wore everywhere. This was like this every morning. He would walk the half mile to the local store, where coffee and a biscuit would be waiting. After that, he went to the cemetery, where he would check on the graves, make sure no one had bothered anything, and check on his grandpappy and granny.

Once back home, he would then visit with her. He hoped today would be the day… the day she would tell him more secrets.

The routine had been the same for the past ten years. The store, the cemetery, the morning conversation. Just him and her. Some days, she was more talkative than others. Some days, he forgot about her. Some days, he looked for something, he was not sure what. And most other days, everything was as foggy as the bottomland that provided the moat for his castle. On the good days, he was everybody's buddy. On the bad days, he was not to be dealt with. Some dealt with their fear by teasing, making him the butt of their jokes. They called him names such as Beanpole, String-Bean, or Tom-Tom, which seemed most fitting.

Recently, he has become more reclusive as he descended into the world his own mind had created. Crazy? A lot of people thought so, but it wasn't always this way. When first moving into the cabin, he seemed to be okay but always busy as on a mission. After the storm, life was a mess.

Other than the ever-present limp and the scar that ran along the side of his head above his ear, you would have never thought anything was wrong. But then, not all wounds are visible. As time went along, his mind began to play tricks. It was as if that part of his brain had been turned off, only to, at times, to come back to life. For a while, he had been quiet, living his life in peace. One day, he started chattering – about crazy stuff. The first time it happened, he was sitting on a bench outside the neighborhood store. What he said didn't make sense. Sometimes, he claimed he was an Indian. Other times, he was looking for his lost gold. Sometimes, both. Of course, no one took him seriously; however, his dark features did cause one to wonder.

Over the next few years, the legend of Tom Tom grew. He was a local novelty, a nuisance to some, a kook to others, and to the stranger, scary. Even with his quirks, everyone, even if they would not admit it, loved ole Tom Childers.

On most days, he lived in a fog. Today was one of those days.

He walked out to the small garden patch he had planted. The few vegetables that had sprouted were mainly from the vegetables that were not picked last year or the year before that. Had it not been for a few strangers showing up periodically to bring him the periodic meal or box of food, he would probably starve.

Times, they were changing. The community was one of the contrasts– on one hand, the place reflected the hard-scrapple, rural folk that tilled its land, going to church on Sundays and working hard to make sure their children would have a better life than them. Several of them, having scratched out a meager life off the land, now could use their land to grow chickens and sell them and their eggs for a regular income. On the other hand, there were those that took full advantage of being right across the county line. This really helped give them the chance to meet the increasing entertainment demands of a more "sophisticated" crowd. Paving that road from Gainesville a few years ago really made a difference.

Now, in a few short months, the landscape would change forever. After a decade of planning and construction, the water would soon arrive and cover the rocks in the riverbed, then would continue to rise, flooding everything in its path. The fertile bottomland was about to see its final crop before the waters turned them into lake bottom. It was coming. All those juke joints down by the river would disappear, and this community, in some ways, would return to its sleepy nature from decades before.

For some, they would be paid to move. For others, their land would suddenly be worth a fortune, creating a weekend escape for those from miles and miles away. The lake would change everything.

The morning wore on. His world was this hilltop, this cabin or better yet, the shack he called home. But today, he was uneasy. Very little breeze stirred in the large hickories surrounding the place. The heat was oppressive, but this was Georgia, and it was August. But his apprehension had more to do with what the newcomers would find when they arrived. Especially afraid they would find HER. He wiped the sweat from his brow as he cut a few sticks of wood for his stove. Hard to believe it was 1954 because he lived like it was 1854.

Tom sat in what was left of an old rocker that sat under a tree in the front yard. He had held out to the end. They weren't going to take her away. He would fight them every step of the way. Something was going to happen today. He could feel it. The air hung heavy over the hillside, and he could smell trouble. She wasn't as talkative the last few days. Yesterday, she was sullen and upset about something; he could not determine why. It must be the lake. When she was upset, he was upset. When she was happy, he was happy.

He heard the truck pull up to the road near the house. People talking. They must be bringing him something to eat. He glanced through the leaves. These people were different. They had tools with them. The strange men started walking down the path toward the river. What were they here for? Were they going to take her away from him? Did they know about IT?

This can't be happening, he thought. *They can't find her.* There was only one option. He had to stop them. It was time to act. He went into the cabin and quickly re-emerged with the shotgun in his hands.

He walked down the hill toward the men, being careful not to make a sound. Gently, step by step, he walked. For a moment, he felt every bit of the Indian he believed he was. *They can't find her. They can't...* He kept muttering quietly to himself. They could not find out. It would be bad for him and especially for HER.

He continued to watch. There were three of them. One was an older man who was writing things down in a book as they walked slowly along the slope, looking, measuring, and marking the trees as they went. They were talking and joking. *If they only realized what they are doing to us, he thought.*

He crept slowly along, doing his best to remain concealed as he moved from tree to tree. "What are you doing? Get out of here!" He stepped out from behind a giant oak tree, shouting at the men. "Cain't you see this is my place? You cain't have it!"

The two men were startled, dropping the tablet they were working from. "My friend, we don't want any trouble now. We are just trying to do our job." He turned and spat a long line of tobacco juice on the ground. We won't be long now. We don't mean no harm." Tom could see he had them scared. They were visibly shaken.

They all stood there silent for several moments until he heard a voice over his shoulder. "Tom-Tom! Put that thing down!"

Tom turned to the voice of another man; his friend, the lawman, had stepped in. Maybe he was there to help him get rid of the new intruders. "Tom, now calm down. You know this has been coming. We talked about it last week." The three intruders were staring down the barrel of his Winchester.

The lawman took a step toward him. "It will be okay. Put the gun down. Somebody's gonna get…"

The blast exploded across the hollow where they all stood. The lawman fell, hit in the leg. Tom turned and re-cocked the gun with a quick pump, then pulled the trigger again. One of the intruders clutched at his chest, trying to stem the flow of blood, then fell over to the ground. Tom fired again. The other intruder ran a few more feet, then collapsed face-first into a pile of leaves. Tom paused. *I need to finish them all off, he thought. He* pointed his gun again, and just as he was about to pull the trigger, the fog in his brain cleared. He looked around at the carnage, at his friend, the deputy, trying desperately to stand up on a leg that just didn't work anymore.

"Tom, can you hear me? Put the gun down." The deputy had given up trying to walk and just sat back down, leaning up against a tree, with the pain beginning to take its toll and the dark stain beginning to darken the leg of his khaki trousers.

Tom stared innocently at the man lying on the ground in front of him and began to shake and wail; then, giant sobs wracked his very being. "What have I done? What have I done?" He cried out. Then, the loud crack of a rifle echoed across the holler they stood in.

Tom fell like a tree and was gone. He kept his grandpappy's wishes secrets til his death.

Three days later, they laid him to rest with the rest of the Childers that had gone before.

June 1971

He crouched behind the monument, peering around the edge very carefully to avoid detection. He reached up to wipe a trickle of sweat that was getting into his eyes. The small stones which covered the grave were digging into his knees, but somehow, he didn't care. He had crawled across this part of the cemetery, looking for a good place to fire in case of a counterattack. He was both excited and emboldened as he awaited the imminent onslaught of the enemy lurking out there somewhere. "Bang! You're dead! I got you!" Came the excited cry, startling the boy out of his supposed alerted status. "Timmy, I told you that was against the rules!! You were not supposed to come that way! That's not fair!" the boy exclaimed. He threw down the stick that moments ago had been his rifle. Soon, other boys were popping up everywhere around the graveyard. This time, since the war games they were playing were boring them, their attention turned to a new pursuit – grasshoppers. These weren't just any grasshoppers – these were genuine, big, black monsters that filled up the palm of your hand and would send any girl into a frenzy when confronted with one. For some reason, at the ripe old age of 7, this cemetery, of all places in the world, was the hunting ground. They were everywhere – and it took some skill to catch one. Compounding the fact that when you got within two feet of the monster, it would hop away was the heat that reflected off the white gravel that seemed to cover all the graves in the cemetery, along with all the steps and corners that beckoned to gash open any shin or knee that was unlucky to come in contact with it. The plan was simple– One boy, usually the fastest one, would catch the grasshopper, then while another boy distracted the targeted girl, the first boy would drop the grasshopper down her dress, sending her off running in a screaming fit. For an eight-year-old, this was heaven. Soon, the boys found themselves in an older section of the cemetery. The fancy graves, with their sculpted gravel covers and finely carved gravestones, gave way to darker, grayer stones, with more grass, hence more grasshoppers. Someone pulled out a bag – with it, they could capture lots of grasshoppers, and boy did they. Within just a few minutes, they had at least a dozen of the creatures hopping around in the bag. For some, they were a nuisance. For others, fish bait is to be used on the nearby lake. For the boys, it was like they had been on an elephant hunt and had bagged the big one.

The boys' play was interrupted by the solemn tolling of the chimes that sat on top of the olde arbor next to the church, which towered over the upper end of the cemetery in its eternal overlook. The music wafted through the graveyard like a refreshing summer breeze. Almost at the same time, a car horn sounded three times. This was the signal for the boys to come to eat. The six boys, who had only met an hour earlier, took off, gallivanting arm and arm up the small road that sliced through the cemetery. That's when it happened. The boy lingered, then stopped as his friends continued their journey back to civilization. He thought he heard something, almost as if someone was calling his name. He walked toward the noise. It may have been a mid-summer breeze or maybe an echo, but he stopped as he heard it again, only more faint this time.

It was strange. There were several gravestones in the plot, but three in particular drew his attention. The first two were much older. He looked closely. As he walked over toward the gravestone, a strange sensation wafted through him. It was not fear but a strange presence and peace that seemed to reach out and touch him.

"Hey, Handsome– going my way?" It was his mom, Meg, coming to retrieve him. "What's wrong? You look like you've seen a ghost!" She laughed as she scooped him up. "You are getting almost too bid to carry!"

"Here, I'll take him from here." It was Colin's granddad joining them. "I see you are over here checking out our Childers family– good learn. When you are a little older, I will tell you all about them. You ready to eat? Come on, I'll give you a ride." The three of them walked up the gravel path that took them back up to the church. Although there was a lot of worry and concern, everyone tried their best to keep Colin insulated from it. As for now, things were right with the world, even if he did miss his dad.

Since their arrival that morning, the place had transformed. The long table capped with a large slab of granite seemed to stretch forever and was covered with every food known to man. Underneath the table, every style of the picnic basket and box was garaged, waiting like stray dogs to claim the leftovers. There were plates of fried chicken, roast beef and ham– any combination you would want. Next came the vegetables– green beans, green peas, butter beans, fried okra and what seemed like hundreds of ears of fresh corn. Tomatoes, cantaloupes, cucumbers. Bowls of sweet pickles. Casseroles– not exactly the boy's favorites. But oh, nirvana– next to this was the macaroni & cheese. This morning early, he was awakened to the sounds of his mom and grandma, busy in the kitchen as they prepared the food they brought with them. He had been tortured all morning long with the smell as it baked in the oven, as he had to share the back seat of his granddad's car with it, and as he helped his paw-paw carry the picnic basket with its precious contents over to the table upon their arrival.

Of course, the food was not the only thing that was there– there were also people, from all over, of every size and age. Other than his mom, grandma, and paw-paw, there were some familiar faces, but none that he really knew. All of them seemed to be related in one way or another– after all, the families that settled in this corner of Appalachia two centuries before had married, intermarried, and then intermarried again. It seemed that if you talked to someone long enough, you would "strike up kin" with them. The women were fussing over the food, shooing away the flies that seemed incessant in their aerial attacks on the food. A group of older men were sitting in a loose gaggle around the base of an old oak tree, which provided some shade to the table and the group. Other kids, including his newly found friends, were scampering about, only marginally successful in avoiding the clutching hands of an adult, eager to snatch them and tell them who they were and how they were related to the particular kid. Like they cared at 8 or 9 years old…

Their cemetery was long forgotten, and others were too far away to think or care about. He ate dinner under the big arbor with the rest of the extended Childers family.

As the afternoon wore on, the food was put away, and the crowd gathered around for a group photo– he sat next to cousins he probably wouldn't see again, and after what seemed to be an eternity, the afternoon was done. They were the last to leave, and as they at last drove out of the churchyard, the strange encounter he had with the tombstone was forgotten, at least for now.

Tired and worn out, Colin slept soundly that night, sharing the big feather bed in his grandparents' house with his mom.

Early the next morning, after a quick breakfast, Colin and his mom, Meg, began the long journey home to Ft. Benning. Colin rarely saw his other grandparents, as they were never very supportive of his mom marrying "a serviceman" and, even more so, the fact that he was an officer. Colin's dad and mom met soon after his dad had been commissioned. Colin's dad had attended the college in nearby Dahlonega, where he graduated in 1963. After commissioning and his initial training, he found himself on his first all-expense paid trip to Vietnam.

The other thing he found while at Fort Benning – the girl he would eventually marry. After returning from Vietnam in 1965, they were married, and not surprisingly, within the year, Colin was born.

Although there was plenty of tension over Billy's second tour, which began in early 1971, Meg tried her best to shield Colin from the stress that his departure and absence meant to their young family.

The rolling hills began to flatten out as Meg drove south on through Cumming, Alpharetta, and Roswell. Soon, the two-lane road they were on was transitioned to a busy city street, and Colin got to gaze at the tall buildings of downtown Atlanta as they made their way along the interstate. South of town, the hills and tall buildings gave way to flat, monotonous farmland dotted occasionally by a pine thicket. Following a stop at a rest stop to eat from the picnic basket his grandmom had prepared for them that morning, they were back on their way and arrived soon at the one-level duplex in the small housing area they lived on just inside the main gate to the sprawling base called Fort Benning.

Being the "man of the house" gave you special responsibilities. Even though the bags were heavy, he helped his mom as much as he could to unload the car. Since they had been gone almost a week, there was plenty of mail to go through, toys to play with, and things to check up on. His mom hurried him out the door to play with the other kids in the small cul-de-sac several families shared and sat down on the small front porch to sort through the mail.

It was not clear how much time had passed, but Colin's attention was diverted from the construction project the other boys and he had started. He saw the rather plain sedan that had pulled up to the curb in front of the house, from which two men in uniform emerged.

Colin leapt to his feet and started running full speed toward the front yard. All he could think was his daddy was home!!! As he ran, though, he noticed something strange happening. His mom, who should have been elated, was standing frozen in the middle of the front yard like a statue, with her hand over her mouth. As they got to her and started talking to her, she slowly sank to the ground, crumpled up in a ball, not able to move.

By the time Colin got her, the men had helped her to her feet and were supporting her on each side as she slowly walked to the house. Neighbors began to step outside to see the commotion and, in some perverse sort of way, were thankful they did not have visitors that sweltering summer afternoon. Mary, Steve's mom from next door, took Colin to her house, trying to stifle the tears that were beginning to flow down her face.

Life for Colin changed forever that day.

Chapter 2

Dawson County, Georgia - Present Day

It was a magical time of the morning when the birds were first waking up, and the sun was just beginning to light the sky in the east. It would still be another 30 minutes or so until sunrise, when the ribbon of light would burst forth across the water, and the sun would share its warmth with the awakening world below.

Colin sat down in his favorite chair to watch the show begin. With his favorite coffee mug, he relished this daily opportunity. The last two days, heck, the last dozen years had been a whirlwind. He often thought of how far he had come and what he had been through, then sighed a deep sigh as he quietly prayed, thanking God for all that had transpired.

"Mornin' Hon. Hope you rested well." Linda had walked up behind him, hugging him around his shoulders and planting a kiss on the top of his head. "Special day yesterday, can't but think today will be just as good." She moved over to the chair beside him and took a seat.

"Have you seen Luke this morning? He mentioned something about going fishing early," She asked.

"I have not, but that must have been him I saw out on the water earlier. In fact, here he is now."

The boy had reached that magic age where he was half man and half child. He had only recently reached the age where he was showing interest in his world beyond what would normally entertain a young boy of his age. Other than being adopted five years ago, he didn't know a lot yet bout how his current world had been constructed. When all that had gone on the last couple of days, it was time he knew.

"Son, I know there are some things going on here that may cause you to have some questions…"

"Are we about to have THAT talk? Dad, please…"

Colin grinned. "Not unless you want to have the talk, but I do have something I want to tell you about."

Linda appeared with a big plate full of muffins. Colin and Luke both took the time to grab one.

"So, let me begin at the beginning…"

Chapter 3

Chicago

2010

The gathering that took place had been replayed thousands of times over the years. A gentle spring breeze wafted across the hilltop, ruffling the scalloped edges of the tent, which was emblazoned with the name WINTER across the side. The sweet smell of carnations lay heavy in the air. Off in the distance, the purple ribbon of the Blue Ridge provided a frame to the clear blue sky. It had rained the day before, and where the trap did not cover, red specks of Georgia clay were waiting to adhere to any shoe that trudged outside the safe area set aside for the family. On the small gravel road next to the cemetery sat a lonely hearse empty now of its precious cargo. A dozen or so cars trailed along the road and in the adjacent parking lot.

The cemetery was not a lot, unlike others that dotted these rural hills. Some were small, holding only a few reminders of some family who had come and gone, fading into the horizon on their journey to their promised land. Some were large cemeteries, growing and expanding over time to house each generation of some town or city. And others, like this one, were here because the church was here, ever keeping a watch over the long-departed souls of its flock.

If this cemetery could talk, oh, the stories it could tell - Young and old, rich or poor, sinner or saint – they were all buried here. Some were recent. Most were old. The chronicle of this small community, most of which lay under the surface of this red clay hilltop. Today, it would gain its newest resident.

A lot of people say that living past 90 has one problem – there are not a lot of people left that were part of your world. This was true for the old man. Most of the 50 or so people standing around the gravesite with the flower-draped coffin are the newest residents of this square mile of land. His siblings and almost all of his cousins were already lying in their place of eternal rest. He would be interred today next to his wife of sixty years, who had also bore her several years before. Resting next to her was their only son – who had anchored this plot of land, keeping it safe for his parents for the last four decades.

What was remaining of the old man's family were seated under the tent, in a line of chairs across the front row – among them was the old man's nurse, who had taken care of him in his final years, who now could move on to other things in her life. Also, there were a couple of nieces, all from out of state, who made the trek here to pay their last respects. Outside of these folks were fellow church members, a handful of neighbors, the pastor of the church and the stoic attendants from the funeral home.

He looked on from a distance, standing close enough to see what was going on but far enough away not to be noticed. It hadn't gotten any easier. They were all hard.

He suddenly heard the music. Taps? More people appeared. Before his very eyes, the scene was changing. He saw the young boy huddled next to what was likely his mom, trying to crawl inside her. Then, he was sitting in that boy's seat……The music became deafening. People were crying and laughing.

Colin jolted awake. Apparently, someone next door was making a late night of it, or better yet, an early morning. He blinked his eyes and looked at the clock on the nightstand - 5:00. *Great,* he thought, *I actually slept to 5 this morning.* The dream was back with a vengeance. Some nights, he hardly slept at all, dreading what the night would bring. *Burying three people in the last six months will do that to you,* he thought as he lay there in the early morning darkness. It had been a little different each time. *At least I wasn't the one being buried this time,* he thought.

They had died down somewhat, but since getting the latest news, the dream had come back with a vengeance. *Thank goodness for Uncle Jim and Aunt Mel, and* Colin thought as he lay there, getting over the latest rerun, rolled out of bed.

First, there was Henry, his long-time mentor and closest colleague. The dirt hadn't had time to settle on his grave when he lost his mom suddenly. She wanted to keep it for himself. Then, he had to deal with the death of his grand-dad in Georgia – although they had only spoken a few times over the last ten years – they really weren't that close – his death seemed to act as some sort of trigger.

Between the dreams and trying to deal with all the memories – not all good – that were popping up from having to deal with his mom's junk, he had started seeing a therapist to help him wade through all the emotions. He kept trying to piece together the full story – his story – but it was as if his own mind had sealed it off. It was hard to do, but the therapist stressed the importance of bringing out the memories – some way, somehow, something inside him didn't want to deal with it. *I wish I had never heard the news,* Colin thought as he walked into the kitchen to grab breakfast before going to the office.

He sat down with his usual – two pieces of toast, with butter and jam, and washed down a cup of black coffee. He had essentially eaten the same breakfast for years, and it would fuel him for the next few hours. He ate quietly, then nodded off briefly, a combination of the bad night's sleep and the lag of the caffeine kicking in. He woke up when Truman, the cranky old tom cat he had taken in a few months ago, jumped up in his lap. As he slowly stroked the old orange tabby, his mind began to mull over the upcoming day and what it was likely going to bring. It wasn't going to be fun.

Although this rented condo was his home most of the time, the home had still been where his mom was on the north side. They settled there 30 years ago earlier when settling in Chicago. He will go there later today to meet with the realtor who will be selling it for him. Fortunately, the same realtor was working with the owner of the condo he was currently renting. His plan was to buy this one, plus three more in the building. With a little luck, he would have the deal nailed down by the end of the week.

He finished the toast, then gulped down the last of the coffee. *Time to start another day.*

Chapter 4

An hour later, there was no appearance of any turmoil as Colin Childers, CEO of Matthews Software, stepped off the elevator with his game face on. The dream and the rough night were but a memory now. He worked hard at keeping his world separated, and very few, if any, of his co-workers knew of the cauldron of turmoil that simmered deep in his soul. Nobody would care anyway, he had told himself. Besides, today, he had bigger things to deal with.

"Mr. Childers, Mr. Williams has already called this morning to confirm he would be here at 10:00. Also, you received another message from Jack Smith – he needed to talk to you about a personal matter. There is a note on your desk with his number." She talked fast, trying to get everything in before he disappeared into his office.

"Yep, 10:00. Got it." Sitting down at his desk, Colin glanced at the note – Jack Smith. Who was that? Not having time to dwell on it, he stuck the note in his pocket. He would deal with that later.

Although he was trying to remain calm on the exterior, he was growing more nervous about the meeting this morning, which had been scheduled the day before on rather short notice.

Colin took a moment to look around at the office. He had gotten so familiar with it that he no longer saw it. It had all the trappings of what a CEO of a blossoming company would have – from 20 years ago. He had really done nothing to add his personal touches to the place other than find a couple of plants and add a couple of photos – mainly of himself with some of the local movers and shakers he had met over the years.

He was recently promoted to the position after Henry's death. Although he helped start the company, his main focus had been on the software side, so managing the entire operation had been somewhat of a challenge. His tendency to be a loner didn't help. Things were looking up when they were awarded a large federal contract, which boosted Colin's confidence, and it appeared that he was going to succeed in his new role.

Then, the glitch – not sure how it happened, but some of the more controversial features of the software leaked to the public, and in the firestorm that followed, the whole program funding the contract was cut, and the company lost the contract. With that, they had little choice but to entertain an offer from a much larger software firm, who offered to buy the company while continuing to allow it to operate independently. But it did. The leak. It started small but soon became a torrent. The civil libertarians were having a fit. He voiced his suspicions to the board, but the decision had already been made.

Within two weeks of the sale, his suspicions played out - most of the board members had been either let go or provided with a seat on the large Humantix board. It was like moving from driving a Volkswagen to a Mercedes. To Colin's dismay, most of his supporters on the board were not asked to stay on.

This morning, he was to meet with the new Chairman, Larry Williams, and the board's general counsel, Phillip Rosen. At exactly 10 AM, Joan knocked softly on the door. "Colin, Larry Williams is here."

"Show them in," Colin said as he turned away from the door, catching sight of a small boat fighting the current as it made its way alone along the river to the outlet at Lake Michigan in the distance.

Colin had been expecting the two visitors but did not expect to see a third. Accompanying Larry and Phillip, he was soon to learn, was the Chief HR Officer at Humantix.

I know what this is about, thought Colin. *Whatever you are planning, let's just get it over with.* "Joan, if you will excuse us. Would any of you like some coffee? Water?" Colin tried to appear gracious as he seethed inside.

"No, thank you. We haven't a lot of time this morning," Larry said rather curtly.

Although Larry had generally been supportive of Colin since the acquisition and still had confidence in his leadership, he also knew that there was no way that he could continue after the way things had gone over the past week. Philip was the first to speak.

"Colin, these things are never easy, but we are here to talk about your future with the organization…."

"Cut the bullshit," Colin snapped, cutting off the short, dumpy attorney mid-sentence. "You can save all the legal mumbo-jumbo. The tension reached the boiling point. "I'm a big boy. I can understand what is about to happen. And, as long as we treat each other right, there won't be a problem, if you know what I mean."

"Hold on, Colin," Larry chimed in. "I think you are kind of jumping to conclusions here."

Colin stared at the four people seated around the table. Maybe he had screwed up. He thought he knew, but why were they here this morning? After the blow-up at the board meeting last week, Colin figured he was done. Plus, the micro tantrum he had didn't help, either. After all, who would want a short-tempered, out-of-control CEO who continues to be part of the company?

"The board, as you know, had a rather testy meeting yesterday… I must admit that when we started the meeting, you were as good as gone; however, after an hour of debate, the board voted 7-2 to offer you the following package…"

Chapter 5

Chicago

Although mid-May, and even with a bright, warm sun, the breeze blowing off Lake Michigan made it feel like March. It has been said that Chicago has two seasons – winter and the Fourth of July. This adage certainly holds true today. He sat on a bench, looking out over the water, oblivious to the few brave souls out on the beach this morning.

After the events the week before, he realized how much his role at Matthews had defined who he was. As long as he was engaged in his business pursuits, he was important. Without them, he was a nobody. He didn't like being a nobody. Letting go of his position was very difficult, but there was really no choice in the matter. After another sleepless night and consultation with his financial advisor and attorney, Colin had decided to take the severance and walk away, free and clear. He did not want any part of the board of directors unless he was still running things. He managed to convert his severance into a combination of stock options, six months' severance, and royalties on future sales of the various software packages he had developed while at the company.

For the first couple of days, he was filled with hope. After all, he should be in high demand, given his position and stature in the downtown business community. "Should have been" was the operative term. Now, six weeks later, it was as if he had fallen off the face of the earth. No one called. He had quickly learned something about life in Chicago – the world would go on without Colin Childers. Without his position, he was really a nobody.

He had contemplated many things these past few weeks. After he had made his decision, he spent the rest of the day packing up his personal belongings in the office, giving Williams a quick phone call, signing the paperwork they had left, and walking out the door, never to return. *That will show them,* he thought. But had he done the right thing??

Now, every day was practically the same. He found himself sitting on this park bench by the lake. The biting wind blowing off the water nipped at his nose but was nothing compared to the coldness and emptiness he felt deep in his soul. His work had kept his mind off dealing with things and covered over the emptiness that dwelt there. With his mind not occupied with work, the loneliness, resentment, and even fear had crept back in. The busy nature of each day, the façade he had so carefully built, had crumbled. He didn't like what was there when he woke up each morning, which is why he was there. Every day, he got one step closer to his goal – walking into the expanse of water in front of him and starting swimming until he ran out of energy. Maybe they would find his body, maybe not. It wasn't his problem. He had to do something.

The odd thing was something kept stopping him. Most mornings, he just sat there. But on those mornings following the dreams the night before, He would find himself walking toward the water, only to stop, then walk slowly back and sit down again.

He was jolted out of his funk by the vibration of his phone lying beside him on the bench. The number showed was work - who would be calling? Maybe they had realized how much they needed him and were calling to beg him to come back.

He tried to sound as professional as possible, but given his dark mood, he picked up the phone, flipping it open.

"Hello, this is Colin Childers."

"Colin, are you okay?" came the voice of concern on the other end. "I haven't heard from you in a couple of weeks, and just checking on you." It was Matt Sweeney, one of his few colleagues, who stuck with him through this mess.

"I'm doing… okay, I guess," Colin answered half-heartedly.

"Jean's cousin is in town, and we've tickets to the Blackhawks tonight. You up to it?"

"Sure…I guess so." Even though he and Matt had been friends for years, he didn't know about Colin's inner struggles. He put back on the mask of stability. "Is this another one of Jean's matchmaking schemes?"

"No, why do you ask? You know that is never the intent." Matt replied with a slightly sarcastic laugh.

Matt and Jean were probably the two closest people right now to Colin. They had met not long after Colin had returned to Chicago 20 years ago and had remained friends, even as their particular roles at the company diverged, with Tom never progressing much beyond being a senior software developer. Over the years they had been friends, it had become almost a joke about Jean's attempt to match

Colin to one of her several "cousins" – she must have about a thousand, Colin thought to himself. Jean was the only person who knew both sides of him, but he didn't seem to mind.

In spite of his sometimes eccentric ways, Colin was also seen as one of the most eligible bachelors in Chicago and had a string of short-lived romances to show for it. It did not take very long for most women to see that Colin was a much more complicated character than what appeared on the surface and that his first love was his work.

The hockey match was a good diversion. Matt and Jean were their usual chatty selves, and Colin even had a good time talking with Jean's "Cousin" Beth. Beth was from Colorado and had recently moved to Chicago. She had begun attending the same church with Matt and Jean, and she and Colin both had a good laugh or two over Jean's favorite past-time of trying to find him his soulmate.

The time passed quickly, and after a nightcap at the bar around the corner from the arena, Colin bid them all adieu and took the train back home to the small bungalow that would soon be sold. He looked around at the few things that remained. He was alone again, and it wasn't a bad thing, except it was always with him.

He reached into the mail basket on the back of the door. There was the weekly coupon mailer that usually found its way quickly to the trash. The other mail was a combination of credit offers and car advertisements. Colin couldn't help but chuckle. *Who would give me credit now?*

As he thumbed through the small bundle of envelopes, he came across one that was different than the others. It was a standard envelope, with no return address, addressed to him.

Probably some kid wanting a donation, he thought as he started to drop it in the trash, but then noticed something hard inside. Curious, he tore the envelope open, and sure enough, taped to a small note-sized slip of paper was a key, apparently to a closet or file cabinet. There was also a message written on the paper, obviously from someone who was having issues. All it said was, "You will need this," with the initial W at the bottom. *This is weird,* he thought, as he looked at the note, then slipped the key into his pocket.

He was awakened early the next morning with the phone ringing. Glancing at it, he could see it was a local number, but the number wasn't familiar to him.

"Mr. Childers, this is Joan. Where have you been? I have been worried about you and haven't been able to get in touch with you since you left."

"I've been around," Colin said guardedly. "Is that you that has been calling?"

"Yes, sir, things happened so quickly that I did not get the chance to say goodbye. I felt like that with the new boss; he wouldn't like me to call you on the company phone, so I have been calling you from home. How have you been doing?"

"Okay, I guess." After working with him for years, Joan could read him like a book. Or so she thought, anyway. She knew what this had done to him.

"The biggest reason I am calling – that gentleman -- Jack Smith – remember, he called you that morning of the meeting with Mr. Williams. He - he has been calling me almost every day, about to drive me…"

"Crap!" Colin interrupted her. "Let me call him."

"And, by the way, I enjoyed the years we worked together – sorry the way things turned out. Maybe one evening, we can have you over for dinner?" She asked.

"That sounds good. Let's do that." Of course, Colin had no intention of following through. Why would he? Why did everyone want to help him? He wasn't a charity case, after all. And besides, he wasn't really interested unless it meant him getting his job back.

"Oh, and one more thing, Joan."

"Yes-Sir?"

"You can call me Colin from now on."

"Yes, Sir, will do – you take care. Bye for now." Joan replied with a hint of sadness in her voice.

"Same to you." One more formality of the workplace he could wash out of his system, Colin thought as he disconnected the call.

As soon as he hung up, he dialed the number he had quickly scrawled on the paper. The first time, the phone rang and rang. The second time, it went to voice mail. *Probably just as good,* Colin thought. *I am not in the mood to talk right now, anyway.*

An hour later, his phone rang.

"Hello, how can I help you?"

"Mr. Childers – this is Jack Smith calling. Not sure if you recall, I was the one who notified you of your grandfather's death several weeks ago.

Now Colin remembered who he was.

"I remember you – what can I help you with? Do you need some more money to help take care of his final arrangements? "

"No, and thank you again for taking my call. Your grandfather had pretty much gone through most of his cash during the final few months, and even though you shared that you had little contact with him over the years, Your contribution was just what was needed to help say the proper goodbye. Your grandfather was a good man, and he and I have become pretty close over the years. He spoke very highly of you."

"Okay, great. I am sure you didn't call just to chit-chat. What do you need?" Colin was already growing impatient.

"So, you have been calling here just to tell me how much my grandfather thought of me? It would have been great if I actually had a relationship with him," *If This guy only knew the whole story.*

"There is one other matter. In addition to assisting your grand-dad over the years with legal matters, he also asked me to handle his final affairs, including the disbursement of his assets." Jack said. "That's why I have been calling – to notify you that you are named in his will as the sole heir to his assets.”

“Is this where you tell me I get the tractor?” Colin remarked rather sarcastically.

Jack chuckled. “No, it is a little more than that.”

“Okay, two tractors.”

“Boy, you are quite the comedian. No, there is a small bank account with less than $1,000 in it, as well as the land and residence. As I said, he had gone through most of his cash in his final years, but there are also several personal items in the house that you have also inherited. All in all, if you want to sell the property, you would live pretty comfortably.

“Okay,” Colin replied, “I probably don’t need anything he has, so it is simple as far as I am concerned, just donate the personal effects, sell the property and then send me the final check. Have a good day sir. He hung up the phone.

Ten seconds later, the phone rang again.

“You are a persistent cuss, aren’t you?” Colin said as he answered the call.

“Colin, trust me, I wish it were that easy. There is only one stipulation in regard to the estate – your grandfather insisted, or better yet *demanded,* that you had to be here come here in person to finalize the estate settlement before making any move to sell it.”

"Well, that is one of the stupidest things I have heard. So you are telling me that in this modern age when millions are transferred daily with a touch of a button, I have to get on a plane, fly all the way to some backwater town in Georgia just so I can receive the proceeds of an estate, which pretty much is nothing but an old broken down farm? What century are you people from? This sounds too much like the making of a Hollywood movie plot – or a very expensive practical joke."

Of course, he didn't mention that he had all the time in the world to go there…no need to disclose that at this point. After all, he was still worth millions despite acting like a street bum the last few weeks.

"Mr. Childers, now, no need to get upset. I am sorry, but when your grandfather first sat down with me a couple of years ago, he insisted it be done this way. I even recommended that I be allowed to liquidate it all, as you are suggesting, then just send you a check, but he would have nothing of it."

He could hear the attorney flipping through his day planner. Can you be here next Tuesday at 1:30? That will give you enough time to fly in that morning. You should expect to stay a couple of nights this first trip."

"First trip? What do you mean by the first trip? Do you mean this is not just signing some papers? I guess not…"

"No, we will need to do several other things, and depending on what you want to do with the personal effects, it could take another trip. Then, there is the land."

"Okay, I will call you back with my travel plans." Colin hung the phone up and sat there, contemplating what was about to happen. Colin looked around at the few mementos his mom had that decorated the place. She never was one for clutter. She had also had a hard life, and the struggles she had on and off over the years with the bottle didn't help. Colin also knew that he had to deal with the pain that came with going through her stuff but had been putting it off. The excuse of being too busy was always a good one.

After moving back to Chicago 20 years earlier, it only seemed logical that he would move back in with his mom, who was living alone after the disappearance and death of his stepdad. The arrangement worked well - a few years later, she made the decision to transfer ownership of the house to him. Having this place was good - it provided a place of escape by separating his personal life from his public persona. He had been touted as one of Chicago's most successful young entrepreneurs, as well as one of its most eligible bachelors. Publicly, the story was about how he was too busy to have much of a social life and what little he had revolved around his business pursuits. Privately, he knew differently. His personal life sucked. His whole persona was built around the image he had built up, and he spent a great deal of energy maintaining it. Very few people knew the real Colin. The darkness – the loneliness – was always there, and his chosen remedy was work. Stay busy, and don't think about it. Surround yourself with activity, and the darkness is covered up. Now, that cover was gone, and Colin was scared for the first time in a long time.

His attention was diverted by a scratch at the door. Truman was purring, looking up at him, obviously out of food. "You are a hunter – why don't you just go find a mouse or something?" Colin muttered as he put down a dish of food for the ragged old excuse for a cat. *Oh well, I guess at least one person still needs me…*

After settling back into his seat, Colin began to consider the events that had happened over the last several weeks. The deaths of his mother and then the passing of his grand-dad - although not as troubling, as he hardly knew him, still had taken its toll. Add to that the sudden ouster and disruption of his career, and it was about too much. *Maybe next time, I won't stop and turn around at the water's edge,* he thought, as a huge lump swelled up in his chest, the tears welled up in his eyes, and in spite of his ability to hold a check on his emotions, he couldn't hold back the torrent of emotions racking his soul.

Now, there was this phone call – why would his grand-dad, who he only saw twice in the past 20 years, want to leave his estate to *him*, of all people? Surely, there was some other relative that was much more – connected – or deserving than him.

Colin sighed deeply as he grabbed another beer out of the refrigerator. Maybe it was time to think about the next adventure – after all, he had re-invented himself a couple of times, and maybe getting away for a few days would help clear his mind and get him back to where he should be or where he *thought* he should be.

He picked the phone up again and quickly dialed the number that was first on the call list. The phone at the other end rang several times, and just as Colin was about to hit the end of the call, there came a sing-sing voice at the other end of the call – "Smith & Rogers, can I assist you?"

Colin stated simply – "I'll be there next week."

Later that evening, after a quick meal of Chinese takeout, he set in once again, going through his mom's final possessions. She didn't own much when she died other than her clothes and a few personal items. He had donated her clothes and most of her other possessions to a local charity. Alt that remained were a few personal items, including a small jewelry box sitting on the dresser in her room.

I guess no time is quite like the present, he thought. The box was locked, but after a couple of minutes of fiddling with it, it snapped open. There wasn't really anything in there other than a few earrings and a bracelet that his stepfather had given her. There were also several necklaces that, over the years, had managed to tangle themselves into one large ball. None of it was really worth anything, so he figured he might as well donate it all as well and let someone else deal with it. He went to close the lid when something else caught his eye.

Tangled up with the necklaces was a small pendant that looked as if it had been broken in half. He stopped for a moment; he picked up the paper clip he had used to jimmy the lock earlier. It wasn't just any pendant, it was THE pendant. Within a couple of minutes of untangling the stringy ball, the necklace came free. He held it in his hand, flipping it over a couple of times. He hadn't seen it in years – ever since it went missing from his dresser drawer. They had tried to purge all of that out of his life. He had searched valiantly for it and had given it up for loss. Even his mom told him she didn't know what had happened to it. Alongside the sadness and grief, anger flared as he realized the lies he had been told, even if they were overall for his own good.

Colin was sobbing uncontrollably as Meg held him close, her own heart broken, trying to hold it together. The phone call to Billy's parents had already been made; they were enroute. Neighbors were a steady stream in and out of the house. Colin held on to the small stuffed bear and the pendant his dad had given him some months ago...

His dad had given it to him days before he left for the last time. It was a keepsake. The pendant had two halves, with a simple Bible verse written on its face: "May the Lord watch between me and thee while we are absent one from another." It was cut in two pieces, with the complete verse only visible when they were put side by side. His dad put one half of the necklace around his neck; he, in turn, had put the other half on the chain that held his dog tags. As he did it, with tears rolling down his cheek, he promised one day he and Colin could put the two halves back together – but that day never came.

Colin looked at it closely, suddenly feeling his emotions welling up again; he quickly swallowed the lump he felt in his throat and diverted his mind. He had gotten pretty good at that over the years. *Well. At least they didn't get rid of everything,* he thought. He started to put the necklace on, but being afraid the aging chain would break, he remembered the key he had received unexpectedly in the mail. Something deep down inside of him made him sense that, somehow, these two discoveries were connected in some way. Finding an old key ring hanging by the back door, he put it and the key together for safekeeping. What he intended to do with either one of them, he wasn't quite sure at this point.

Chapter 6

Gainesville, Georgia

Colin had not been seated long; the plane had just started taxiing for the runway - when he dozed off. Amazing how that happens when you aren't getting enough sleep. He woke up in a start about 15 minutes later when the clunk of the landing gear folded itself in its own graceful way into the plane's fuselage. Now wide awake, He found his mind fully occupied with the treasure he had just found and the memories and emotions it had conjured up.

Colin sighed as he looked out the window at the ground far below. Life had been hard for an 8-year-old boy who had lost his dad. In the years since that day, the memories had churned around in his mind, mixing with the stories he had been told about that eventful time. As a result, everything melted together and was then buried as much as possible. Things were a blur; he could remember the yard, then the visitors, and watching his mom crying as she clutched him and the folded flag she had been given since most of his life had occurred SINCE that day. Their new life really began a few weeks afterward, as his mom and he drove away from Fort Benning for the final time, following the moving van with all their stuff.

Meg worked very hard to make a new life for them, getting a small place not too far from Columbus, close enough to stay associated with the area but far enough to get the Army out of their systems. She was able to get a job as a production planner at a local textile mill, and although the pay wasn't great, between it and the money they got from the VA, they were able to live a comfortable life, and things began to settle down for them, at least to the outside world. Even for a nine-year-old boy, Colin could still see that things weren't the same for either of them. Almost every night, Colin could hear the sobs coming from her bedroom as his mom cried herself to sleep. The truth was, if a third person had been there, most nights would have been said the same way about Colin. Sometimes, he would pad softly to his mom's side, where they would keep each other safe for the rest of the night. They were a team. That's what made this latest discovery about the pendant so hard to process - it was like the wound kept coming back. Grief is a funny thing. It is hard enough for someone old enough to understand such things, but it was harder still for a young boy who couldn't quite grasp the pangs of sadness that would suddenly overtake him at times when he was least expecting it.

Their relationship began to take a subtle shift with his mom. It didn't take long to figure out what had happened. First, there was Russ. Russell Cantrell - the man who would end up becoming his stepfather. Colin's mom was introduced to Russ by a neighbor when he was in town on business, and his mom and Russ hit it off from the very beginning. His mom seemed happy again. He was happy for her, but not for himself, for two reasons. First of all, it started creating distance between his mom and his dad's parents. Although they had tried to remain close after his dad's death, they had slowly drifted apart, and her new relationship seemed to be the final straw in their relationship. Secondly, Colin saw him as an intruder – Meg and him were a team – and Russ was a threat. Colin was suspicious from the start.

One day, after dating for about six months, they announced they were getting married. A month later, they had a simple ceremony at the courthouse. They did it during the day while Colin was at school. He wasn't even invited. That didn't help matters any.

Russ tried his best, or so it seemed, to win Colin over, but it didn't work. Yeah, they had fun together, but he still wasn't his dad. Colin's mom even took him to see a therapist but to no avail. The tension grew between him and Russ.

Things really came to a head about a year later. Coming home from school, he went to his room as he always had done, to find everything had changed. Anything and everything that he had in his room to remind him of his dad had all been taken away. All the things… the pictures, the flag he had sent, everything… was all gone.

Colin was naturally upset, and when he asked about it, Meg told him, "Russ took the stuff away. I told him to. It is time for you to move on with your life."

Upset, Colin hardly spoke to anyone for three days, and he sure didn't speak to Russ much after that. He had grown in his dislike for Russ, who was trying too hard to replace his dad. He also didn't like the fact that when Russ got drunk, he got abusive and even one time threatened to take a board to his mom. Russ had even hit him once when he tried to defend his mom from one of his drunken tirades.

Having dozed off again, the message to fasten his seatbelts came on, awakening him from his brief nap. He hoped to avoid seeing anyone he knew by catching the late flight. He didn't like talking to anyone about his recent career change or crash as he really thought about it.

Colin walked through the airport, which was mainly empty at this time of day but still busy. He longed for the days when he would be part of this monolithic mass of business, hyped up on caffeine and energy drinks. Having no checked bags, it only took about 30 minutes to get his rental car and hit the interstate.

The last thing he wanted to do was to go to Georgia. He had worked very hard over the years to build an image of the sophisticated Chicago businessman and had not traveled there since he was young. He didn't know what to expect other than where he was going, which was in the backwoods.

All he knew at this time was that his granddad had required him to do this for some strange reason. Not sure why he was even doing this, but here he was. To be truthful, what else was occupying his time right now? Besides, it would make what he thought of as a ridiculous, unnecessary trip a little more palatable. On the other hand, he knew that returning here could dredge up memories he would rather be kept buried.

Although his granddad and he had reestablished contact the past few years, including exchanging letters every six months or so, they had not really been close since he grew apart from them in the years after his mom remarried, and things got so tense with Russ.

Things really got testy when he was getting ready to graduate high school, and his grandfather had laid out a plan for him to come back and attend the same college his dad had. It would be easy if he didn't want to be a member of the corps and work toward an army career; he could live with them, and it would be close enough to commute. Although he probably meant well, his mom opposed it from the beginning and did not seem to savor it, rekindling the pain that she had lived with since that fateful summer day so many years before. Plus, why would she let the only thing she had from that life go down the same path? The fight was bad enough, and such tension was created that he had no contact with his grandparents for many years. He had the last laugh, however, when soon after turning 18, in an act of defiance to his mom and Russ, he quietly enlisted in the Army as a systems automation specialist, a job he knew very little about when he had signed his name on the contract.

He arose early the next morning, leaving the hotel in plenty of time to get to his appointment in Gainesville, an hour's drive north – on a good day. This was not one of those good days, however. The traffic just crept along as a tractor-trailer had decided to try and create another lane in the median. The longer he waited, the more impatient he became.

It took almost 45 minutes to clear the accident downtown. He also had to fight his way through two more accidents on the interstate. When he finally saw the exit sign for Gainesville, he was already running 5 minutes late to the meeting.

The law offices – Smith, Rogers & Cline – were in an older office building on the north edge of downtown. The building's best years were apparently behind it – the Art Deco design stuck out prominently among several other smaller buildings, mixed in with a scattering of older Victorian homes that had been converted to various offices.

Sighing deeply, glancing at his watch as he stepped off the elevator, frustrated that he was 15 minutes late, he opened the door to the small office suite.

"May I help you?" asked the older, grey-haired lady whose obvious accent gave her German ancestry away.

"I am here to see Jack Smith," Colin explained. "I have an appointment."

"Yes, you did," the lady explained, "and you were late, so I had to let the next person go ahead. Time is money. You will just need to take a seat. Mr. Smith will be with you in a moment."

That was it. No offer of coffee, no water, nothing. Whatever happened to southern hospitality, Colin thought. She didn't know him, obviously, or she would not have treated him like that. At least he wasn't **used** to being spoken with in this manner.

And then, as if she had just read his mind, she asked, "I'm sorry, rough day today. Would you like a bottle of water or coffee while you wait?"

Colin got comfortable in the small waiting room with an ice-cold bottle in his hand and allowed the self-pity and melancholy to invade again. Here he was, having been let go as CEO of one of the fastest growing software companies in the country, then having to go through this labyrinth of nonsense in order to close out his granddad's estate, that is having to travel 900 miles to get it done. For someone who had an army of accountants and attorneys at his disposal, this was quite an adjustment – now, like everything also had been the last few weeks. He wasn't used to doing things for himself, details that he hadn't had to worry about for a long time, and then getting jerked around, and now sitting in this little backwater town, about to hear God knows what from some backwoods southern lawyer.

As the minutes passed, however, Colin's melancholy mood began to be eclipsed by the ever-growing fatigue. The stress of the last three weeks had taken its toll, and this was really the first time he had the opportunity to simply relax. He was just about to drift off when he awoke with a start.

"Mr. Childers? Jack Smith." The short, stocky attorney stuck out his hand, which appeared to look like 4 sausages stuck on a spit.

"How was your flight? Sorry for keeping you waiting, but I had to take care of Mrs. Patterson. Her husband died last month, and.."

"I couldn't give a shit about Mrs. Patterson." Muttered Colin under his breath, trying to hold his cool. "For what it took to get here, it had better be worth it. Let's get this show on the road. I have work waiting for me back home, and I need to get back to it. Do you have all the documents ready?"

"It's not quite that easy… you must not have understood me clearly. It may take a couple of days to get all of this done." Explained the attorney. We have to have the will probated, and there is the issue of having the property all surveyed."

"You mean I won't fly back out this afternoon? And why wasn't this taken care of earlier? Could you not have taken care of this *before* I got here? Did that ever cross your mind??" By now, Colin was really beginning to get steamed. The frustrations of the last few days, including the traffic, all started to boil over. He remembered the guidance from his therapist – and took a couple of deep breaths.

"I'm sorry, just a rough trip and quite the unusual circumstances…"

"No, Mr. Childers, please accept my apologies, but my last conversation with your granddad was very explicit. He even wrote it down that you were to be present for all activities related to the settlement of his estate."

The attorney then proceeded to open up the manila folder and pulled out two documents – one was the last will and testament for William Childers, Sr, his granddad, and the other was a listing of the estate's assets, which included about $10,000 in a checking account, all of the furnishings in his home, and the property. By the time he had finished perusing the documents, Colin's demeanor was much calmer, and the frustration of having to deal with his granddad's things was strangely beginning to intrigue him a bit.

It took about an hour to go through the documents, and at the end of the discussion, Jack offered to buy dinner, which gave them a chance to talk. A couple of beers later, Colin began to relax a little as he learned a little more about what was now his new place.

"I hope you brought something else other than what you have on to wear," said Jack as he swallowed the last bite of his baked potato. "This ain't Chicago, and where we will be going tomorrow is a little more rustic…"

"Okay, cut the crap. I did not pack anything for an excursion, but if you will humor me, I can get something to wear."

Chapter 7

Dawson County

He finally found a department store at the local mall, and after parting with a hundred bucks, he outfitted himself with a shirt, jeans, and some boots. He started buying a straw cowboy hat, too, but decided that maybe that would push things a bit.

Once he was settled in his room, he was able to get on his laptop, where, out of pure habit, he signed on to check his emails. Other than the usual spam and junk mail, he had a couple of emails from former colleagues, most of whom were just receiving the news. An interesting one was a link to the press release that announced his decision to leave the company and a pithy quote about how he wished his successor well. What was so bad was that he never said anything. Growing peeved at the thought that they would make this look so sweet. He started thinking of ways to retaliate, even contacting an attorney to address the issue. Then a quote from an old army boss rang out in his mind; "Sometimes you just have to say 'The Bitch Ain't Worth it.'" With that, he shut the laptop and turned out the lights on what had been a very long day.

But, as was often the case these days, sleep was elusive. Colin's mind was running in a hundred different directions. *This place is like a foreign country.* His desire was to do what it took to get this settled as quickly as possible and get back to Chicago. After all, there was the next opportunity awaiting him there, and the longer he stayed here, the greater the likelihood he would miss out on it.

The money from the severance was nice, but he needed to work. Boredom scared him. Being out of his comfort zone allowed the demons that haunted him to rise up. He wanted to be in Chicago, around the things that had been familiar. But, also then, as he thought more about it, just *why* would his grandfather force him to come down here anyway to settle the estate? Despite all the chaos of the meeting earlier, why did he feel a strange curiosity about all of this? It was as if there was a tug-of-war going on between two unseen forces, with his soul as the prize. As he mulled over this, Jack was sitting at his conference room table, having a conversation with his mom. Huh? The thoughts became more muddled, and Colin drifted off quietly with the fatigue of the last few days. He slept soundly for the first time in days.

He woke up with his phone buzzing. Rolling over, he looked at the clock that he had forgotten to set. Jack was calling. He had overslept.

"Give me 15 minutes," Colin said as he quickly put on the clothes he had bought the night before.

Walking out the door, Jack was waiting on him, parked under the hotel's awning, driving what had to be the ugliest Cherokee Colin had ever seen.

"You dress up pretty good," Jack said, "But you may want to remove the tag from your sleeve."

"Damn boots don't fit right, and I would give you an answer that would be more appropriate for how I still feel about this whole situation. But I reserve my comments since my mom told me to talk nice," Colin was still a little angry that he had to waste extra time dealing with this situation when he was clearly needed back in Chicago, or so he thought. "How about some coffee?"

Jack walked over to a vacant table in the small diner that sat next to the hotel and proceeded to unroll a rather large map. *Good thing nothing was on it,* Colin thought, shaking his head. *I just hope this guy didn't forget to put on his head this morning...*

"I remembered after you left last night that this map was in the office. Billy had given it to me a couple of years ago after your grandmother died. At the time, he was thinking of selling or developing it, but for some reason, he backed out at the last moment. Not sure why that happened, but that is beside the point."

Jack quickly oriented Colin to the map. The main feature was a jagged body of water that looked like a small "y" tilted at an angle. Lake Lanier was one of the most popular lakes in the region, near enough to Atlanta to provide a source of endless entertainment and leisure. The other large feature was the built-up areas east of the lake, which were Gainesville and its surrounding communities.

Jack then pointed to a highlight on the west side of the lake, crudely outlined in red. "There is the property. You can see that it was originally a rectangle, but whe the lake was built decades ago, part of it was sold to the Army for the construction of the lake itself. Other than that, the original tract, which was actually four lots, is still in its original form from when it was first laid out over 150 years ago."

Lakefront. This is a new twist, Colin thought. He was not familiar with the property size, nor as a young boy when last here, cared then about stuff like this. So this was ON the lake, not just NEAR the lake.

"Why didn't you tell me that this was lakefront property?"

"I assumed you knew."

"You assume too much. I was 15 years old the last time I saw this place, and I hardly cared then. Where did you say you went to law school?"

"Okay, so I was not aware you had not been on the property since you were 15. I guess since that time, you have forgotten a lot."

A lot, but not everything, Colin thought as a response to Jack's quip.

"Let's take a drive. We have the day to burn anyway, as we can't get the other stuff done until tomorrow, anyway."

"Boy. You folks really know how to plan…"

During the half-hour drive to the property, Colin looked for landmarks, but other than the lake itself, there was not much he recognized until they turned off the main road by what Colin remembered as the only store in the community and headed down to what the locals called "War Hill." No one really knew how that name came to be. According to legend, two Indian tribes had apparently battled it out there. No one had ever found any evidence of a battle, but the name sounded good, anyway. Five minutes later, Jack slowed and turned onto a narrow gravel road that had become overgrown. *It's obvious no one has taken care of this place in a while,* Collin thought to himself. After another 10 feet or so, they came to what had been a recently installed gate, which blocked any further access to the property. At least easy access. Opening the leather satchel Jack had placed in the back seat, he soon produced a key to unlock the gate.

"Can't be too careful," said Jack as he climbed back into the Jeep. "Lots of people get nosy and especially want to find a shortcut to get to the water."

Not far down the road, the trees opened up into a clearing, and for the first time since that day as a teenager, he knew exactly where he was at. The weathered old farmhouse sat humbly in a grove of pecan trees, its view of the surrounding landscape obscured by the overgrowth that now almost enveloped it. There was a small barn to the right of the front porch and several small planting beds around the house, all in some level of neglect, many overgrown with weeds. The house itself was a white frame with green shutters. At each end of the house was a rock chimney, and there were three dormer windows on the second floor. A long, wide porch stretched across the front. The road they were on created somewhat of a semicircle around the house before disappearing into the dark woods on the other side. Even though it seemed like they were a long way off the road, the house actually commanded a good view of the road in front of the house in both directions.

"That road there leads down to the lake…"

Colin cut him off with a glare.

"That's right, I guess you were able to figure that one out."

For Colin, he had been here before. That was part of the problem. The last time he left here, it was under less than good terms. He had little to say about it, as his mom and granddad had a huge blowup, and they had thrown their stuff in the car, leaving never to return again. Soon after, she and Russ married. No doubt, the discussion she and his granddad had was over her decision to remarry.

Overall, the house was well kept, with the exception of standing empty for the last 3 months. His grand-dad was always somewhat of a neat freak, which played well since he had pretty much lived by himself for the last 5 years until he got sick and needed in-home care.

They walked around the place, and with each step, Colin's mind began to open up more to things he didn't care to think about. Soon, they stopped at the front steps, and Jack pulled a key out of his pocket and started up the steps. "Let's take a look inside." He said to Colin.

Colin stopped him. "That's okay, Jack. No need to go in there." Colin said with a hint of apprehension in his voice, the cockiness was gone, and his heart was pounding out of his chest. *This is going to be harder than I thought.* Even after so much time, he just couldn't do it.

"Colin, you okay?" Jack asked.

"Yeah, I'll be okay." Colin swallowed hard. "This is going to be tougher than I realized."

For the next 20 minutes or so, they looked around at the other buildings, through the house, without disturbing anything. *There will be plenty of time later to go through this stuff.*

Back in the car, they started down the dirt road to check out the rest of the property.

"I remember coming down this road – once," noted Colin, being rather reflective. It was right before he…"

Suddenly, they took a lurch to the left, completely interrupting Colin's train of thought.

A doe and her fawn had run right out in front of them, forcing Jack to take evasive action.

"Whew! That was a close one!" he exclaimed. "I guess I better keep my eyes open."

"Since you reminded me you have been here before and also told me you haven't been here since you were 15, you are going to have to tell me when I start to explain something you may know about."

The deeper they went into the woods, the less Colin could remember. When he was here last, it was only for a short visit, so he didn't get to explore much.

"You see, back after WWII, the idea was developed to build the lake. It took over ten years to get the project approved. Once construction of the dam began in the early 50s, land had to be acquired. This meant that several hundred farmers had to relocate off of what they thought to be valuable bottom land. The Childers were lucky; they only lost a small portion of their land to the water."

"So you don't remember hearing the legend of ole 'Tom-Tom.' He was a local character. Was living here when the lake was built, but died right here on this property. Not sure of the exact details, but it had something to do with the sale of the property to the government. It was a big story, a Wild West shootout and all that stuff… He was a little touched in the head. Some say he still walks around this place, still chasing people away he doesn't want here. Anyway, more about that later. That is the old cabin he lived in, out in the woods behind the house. Not sure how old it is. Just another one of the mysteries about this place."

The next morning, Colin left town, heading back to the airport. Although he was longing to get back to Chicago and explore new opportunities there, deep down in his soul, there was a spark of something different. Maybe it was time for a new start somewhere else, and he might have just found it.

Chapter 8

Chicago

"So, living with the hillbillies is to your liking, eh?" Matt quipped sarcastically.

"Not really, but I have seen my first pair of overalls…" Both men chuckled softly. "But I realized it did me some good to get out of town, a change of scenery, so to speak," Colin said, hoping he could also convince himself.

"This time, it looks like I will be gone for a while," Colin told his friend Matt as he swallowed the last of the steak he had been attacking. They had met at the usual place near the office, but it seemed sort of surreal. After all, here was the former CEO, who, in spite of the fact that his life had been turned upside down for the last month. His life right now was a paradox. Despite the initial grief of losing his career and, in a lot of ways, his identity, he was beginning to enjoy the freedom that had been given him from the constant stress he had been under. He told himself that anyway and made sure that was the story he told everyone else. But, at inopportune times, loneliness and fear would almost overwhelm him. He was trying to rebuild his castle of protection before the demons discovered the vacuum of time in his life and took the opportunity to creep in.

"As I have considered it, the property has quite a bit of potential. Right now, not sure what I am going to do with it. Part of me wants to sell it quickly and get back here to Chicago, but there is this-- Colin whipped out a small sheet of paper on which he had drawn a crude copy of the tract. He also had an envelope of photos that he had made during the tour with Jack a few weeks earlier.

"Matt, I am torn. It only makes sense, you know, as I really have no need for all of this, so I might as well make some more money on it. But, at the same time, maybe I should just sell it, take the money, and try to get things going here again," said Colin, as he paused between bites, knowing that if anyone could read him like a book, it was Matt.

"Yep, the old Colin is back," said Matt as he sat back in his chair, watching his friend's face light up for the first time in weeks. "I know you are torn about what to do… just remember to think through. What makes you think it will work?"

Colin flipped the page over and picked up the map he had drawn. "As you can see here, the property is less than 5 minutes from the interstate and an hour from downtown Atlanta." If I market this right, I can make a lot of money off it. Besides, the area is booming, and with the lake, well…"

Both men were interrupted by a familiar voice. "I hope you aren't trying to steal away my help." Colin turned around to see Jim Montgomery, his successor, seated two tables over. Colin quickly folded away the papers he had on the table as Jim invited himself and moved over to their table to sit with them.

"No, Jim, just showing him my new plans. You never know; I may go into business against you guys." Colin winked at Matt, who was appearing increasingly uncomfortable.

"Well, hope it doesn't jeopardize that severance you got. Hate to have to take it back."

"Trust me, you don't have anything to worry about," replied Colin.

The three gentlemen sat there for about another ten minutes, discussing if the Black Hawks had any chance for the upcoming season. Colin stood up, "Well, gentlemen, if you will excuse me, I have a few things I need to tend to this afternoon. Even us unemployed guys have things to do," he cracked.

With that, Colin left the two other men standing there in awkward silence.

A few minutes later, Colin's phone rang. It was Matt. "I really appreciate you leaving me there with him. That was a whole lot of fun. Just got away from him."

Colin laughed. "You better learn how to like him; you have work for him now."

"I never did finish telling you, but I am leaving for Georgia again this weekend. Plan to get this deal going and then will be back in a few weeks. Until then, you take care and give Jean a hug from me..."

After hanging up, Colin paused for a moment to realize how conflicted he was. Part of him was not even considering leaving Chicago permanently. This place had been his home for three decades. If he intended to return, he should get everything settled, sell the property quickly, and get back here. There seemed to be a hundred things to get done, but his end-game was simple – finish disposing of his grandparent's personal effects, then work with a developer to start carving up and selling the land, which would no doubt bring a small fortune. *This shouldn't take more than a few weeks,* he thought.

At first, a little apprehensive voice told him he was crazy, but another soft voice seemed to override his fears. *I've got this; you will make it and see what I have for you.* It was almost audible, close enough so that Colin whipped his head around to see where it was coming from.

I need to stop eating such heavy lunches, Colin thought as he reached for his suitcase and grabbed it out of the closet.

Three hours later, he passed by a sign on the interstate that said, "Welcome to Indiana." He looked at the skyline of Chicago getting smaller in his rear-view mirror. Little did he realize he wouldn't be coming back.

Chapter 9

Dawson County

He woke with a start. The dream was back. The funeral, the flag-draped coffin, the little boy - they were all there. Although the room was quite cool, he was still drenched in sweat. As hard as he tried, he couldn't shake the gloom that hung over his empty soul when he awoke every morning. For years, that had been quickly replaced by his escape - work. That had been replaced with the whole bouquet of activity he experienced in making the transition from CEO to just a nobody. Now that the transition was complete for the most part, the pangs of both loneliness and grief had crept back in. Why was he here, at this place, at this time? He looked around the lifeless hotel room, then fixed a cup of coffee from the small coffee pot in the room. Besides the usual morning gloom, there was also something else - a small spark of something that was drawing him in. There was also the anticipation of the unknown. "Oh well, showtime," he said as he laced up his shows, grabbed his bag and walked out the door of the relative confinement of the room. If he only knew that the fun was just beginning.

Fifteen minutes later, his gloom was put back into its box; he was on the road. The blanket of fog that had not only covered his soul but the landscape as well had quickly burned off, and the day was beautiful. The fast pace of the interstate he had been on gave way to the pastoral scenes of the rolling Georgia hills. As he pushed his BMW around the curves, hills, and dips that defined the highway he was on, his mind pondered what needed to get done first. The drive was hypnotic, with the late summer wildflowers and lush trees covering the hilltops providing a green carpet that framed the highway he was on. He pulled over a couple of times at a scenic overlook, then decided to lower the top on the small convertible.

With traffic thinning out, Colin decided to see what this little roadster would do. As he revved the engine higher, he began to dwell on his new adventure. *Why ME? What am I even doing here?* The same voices that kept breaking through were creating doubt. What if no one wants this place? He thought. Are you crazy? Part of him wanted to turn around and avoid what he faced. His last trip had somehow triggered this last round of dreams, and he never even visited the cemetery, even to see his granddad's grave. If just one brief visit triggered this dream, then what would being around this place for weeks do to him? Even when he made the first trip down as he drove along. He was sure there was some other cousin, niece, or nephew his grandfather could have left it to, sparing him the need to leave Chicago to come down here, just to get rid of this place – or start a new life.

Colin was jolted back into the real world around the next curve. He had to slam on his brakes to avoid hitting the large truck that had pulled out onto the highway right in front of him. The truck was creeping along, obviously hauling a pretty heavy load. Colin thought of passing, but the road at this point was full of curves, and even with the BMW, it was too great a risk; then, he realized it was probably one worth taking. Colin had seen livestock trailers before, but this one was different. The truck looked as though it could barely stay on the road. The trailer looked to be stacked high with what looked like wire crates or cages, and as he surveyed it closer, each cage was full of chickens. Not only were feathers flying everywhere, but sprinkles began to dot his windshield with God only knows what. On top of this, the stench was worse than any stockyard that Colin had ever smelled. It was almost as if a cloud of ammonia was hanging in the air over his car. He was trapped as more and more sprinkles hit the windshield. He tried backing off a little, not following as close, but it seemed the more distance he gave up, the worse the feathers were. The curves seemed endless, as they seemed to never end. Finally, the road straightened out, and Colin saw his chance. 10 minutes later, he was at the end of his patience. Colin created some distance between his vehicle and the truck, wanting to know when it was time to pass. His car was now coated with small white and black dots all over it.

Then he saw the straightaway, and the road ahead was clear. He flipped on his blinker, moved the car to the left, and stomped it. As long as nothing was coming, he would be okay...

Then, the bump. It didn't really seem like much, but it was enough for the truck, as one of the crates was not shut well and popped open. At least 5 birds came flying right at his car. Instinctively, Colin swerved to try to avoid the birds, but one hit his windshield, spiderwebbing it. Colin was now driving down the left shoulder of the road and ground to a halt inches from propelling himself off a 20-foot drop.

The truck disappeared into the distance, not even knowing what happened. He sat quietly for a moment, collecting his wits.

"You okay, buddy?" came a voice out of nowhere. "I thought for sure you were a goner."

Colin turned to the voice. "I'm fine. Not sure if my car is, though." Standing beside the car was probably the biggest man Colin believed he had ever seen, well, other than the few times he had been introduced to a couple of Chicago Bears.

He slowly got out of the car. He stood for a moment, then stretched slowly, while all the while paying attention to any new aches and pains.

"That was a purty good bit of driving. By the way, Junior's name is Junior Bryant." he stuck out a hand that looked like it could hold a watermelon unassisted. The man was at least 6"5 and probably weighed well over 300 pounds; he had on a pair of overalls with some remnants of a sweatshirt underneath. His head was capped with a faded-out baseball cap, and he was attached to the ground by a worn pair of work boots. He had at least three days of growth in his beard, and a brown streak trailed out of one side of his mouth, with a bulge of tobacco riding shotgun in his jaw. For a moment, Colin could have sworn he heard banjo music.

"Colin Childers." He wasn't too much in the mood to be talking to anyone right now. Now feeling okay, he walked around the car to see if there was any damage. Other than a cracked windshield from where the chicken smacked it, there was not a lot of other damage, other than the car was coated all over with white and black specks, and the tires and fenders were now matching the red clay that seemed to be everywhere he looked.

"Looks like I may need a tow truck to get my car out of this mud. Know where I can get one?"

"Aww, no need for that. I got a winch right here on my truck." Junior pointed back at the truck, which surprisingly looked almost brand-new. Sure enough, mounted to the front was a winch.

"I don't think you want this." Junior reached over in the backseat of Colin's car and picked up the mangled body of the chicken that had performed the avian gymnastics a few minutes earlier. Picking it up like a twig, he hurled it off in the woods to be a treat for a buzzard or coyote.

"Childers, let's see, you wouldn't be connected to Billy Childers, would you? He just passed away a few weeks ago."

"William Childers was my grandfather. How did you know him?" replied Colin.

"Why, he lived over close to some relatives at the lake. Never got to know him that well. So what brings you to town?" asked the suddenly inquisitive stranger in front of him.

"Well, I sorta inherited the place from him," replied Colin.

"Whatta a small world!" a big grin broke out on the big man's face. "Looks like we gonna be neighbors… if you don't get scared and sell the place."

Colin didn't know quite what he was talking about. He looked at his watch. "Well, if you will excuse me, I need to get on about my trip. How far is it from here?" Colin was really in less of a mood to talk now and just wanted to get where he was going.

"Oh, only about 10 minutes from here, and when you first get into town, there is a carwash right beside the gas station and a place to get a bite to eat. I would join you, but I need to take a look at some land I plan to hunt on later. Think you can find your way?" the big man finally hushed.

"Well, thanks again; maybe we will cross paths again," said Colin as he got back in his car.

"Oh, I'm about certain we will. By the way, tell the gal in the store that Junior Bryant sent you, and the car wash is on me. Welcome to town." the big man winked at him as he walked back to his truck.

Dawsonville, Georgia, was just like Dawson County as a whole - the old and the new, the simple and the complex, a small nugget of the past, sitting inside an ever-creeping spread of growth and development, similar to the ever-present kudzu that covered the red hills and gullies of this corner of the state.

In a lot of ways, this old and new is divided by the narrow ribbon of a street that runs down the center of the downtown. Many years ago, this ribbon tied the hustle and bustle of Atlanta with the quiet comfort of the mountains. Every weekend, it would be filled with travelers, stopping at a wayside peanut shack or fruit stand. After dark, the ribbon took on a different role. It became the economic livelihood for those who would make their living from liquid corn - moonshine - by selling it to waiting patrons in far-away Atlanta. That road, like the downtown, was quiet now. Thirty years earlier, it was felt that the Atlanta crowd needed to get to the quietness faster, so the interstate was built. Now, the peanut stands were quiet; the street was just a remnant of its past, and replacing it was the bustling interchange on the interstate, five miles east of town.

In spite of being left behind, Dawsonville was a survivor. The early residents saw it fit to make this the county seat, so for over 150 years, the citizens needing to do business with their government would make the trek here to pay their taxes, go to court, get married, and do whatever else had to be done. In addition to this, the moonshine that flowed so freely in these parts adapted itself to another endeavor: racing. Along with that came a long line of legends, the latest being a tall, lanky redhead that catapulted stockcar racing onto the national stage. Soon, tourists were returning. Growth also brought new people with funny-sounding names, and for that matter, even funnier-sounding dialects, to this sleepy little corner of the north Georgia hills.

So, smelling like God knows what, Colin arrived. He found the car wash, and sure enough, the young girl working at the store, who looked like she would give birth any day, gave him a passcode to use. Ravenous, after not eating for most of the past two days, quickly rinsed the chicken shit and red mud off his car, then walked across the street to the small diner. It was typical, not a lot, unlike the diners and restaurants that dotted rural America, even in his more familiar places of Illinois and Wisconsin. There were several pickups parked outside, along with a mixture of old and new. Flanking the glass front door were two large plate glass windows where the patrons could sit and watch the world go by over two eggs, bacon, and a cup of coffee. There were several signs, most hand-lettered, taped to the inside of the windows. Most were advertising something for sale, announcing a kids' bake sale, or seeking to find a lost dog. The small bell on a spring mounted to the door was there to alert the staff that someone had entered; however, there was enough activity at this time of the day that one could barely hear it when the door was opened.

The inside of the diner was a blend of 5 decades of decorating. It looked as up-to-date as an antique shop. There was little artwork on the walls but plenty of photos of various racecars and drivers that left little doubt as to the town's most famous resident.

Colin waited briefly at the door until a well-seasoned, matronly woman behind the counter invited him to sit wherever he liked. Before he sat down, he looked around. Even though there was no one there, he knew it was just a habit he had developed over the years, even though no one had in mind to do him harm. A couple of gentlemen in suits appeared to be headed to court. An older couple on their daily excursion to town, and a mixture of construction workers and farmers getting a late breakfast or early lunch now that the early morning work had been done.

Colin slid quietly into a booth, grabbed a menu from behind the napkin holder, and then suddenly felt self-conscious and out of his league. It was as if everyone in the restaurant was staring or thinking of him.

"Morning dear, coffee?" the young waitress said, smiling at Colin.

"Sure… Thanks." Colin was rather taken aback by the forwardness. No one had called him dear in a long time. "I will take two eggs over easy, bacon, and potatoes. I'm starving."

"Then you have come to the right place. I think you might want to wash up," she said, with a rather sly grin on her face. He had planned to do that. "The bathroom is around the corner of the counter to the left."

The bathroom was basically a closet, which was generous. He looked in the mirror and saw why she was so adamant about his washing up. Covering his face and neck was a nice spattering of the same thing that coated the car earlier, and little white feathers were scattered throughout his hair. *No wonder I thought they were staring*, he thought. He spent the next several minutes picking the feathers out of his hair and proceeded to wash his face and hands. After finding the roll of paper towels stashed on top of a dispenser that hadn't been used in years, he opened the door, ignoring the hand-written sign to open it SLOWLY.

The waitress was standing on the other side, and as if in a movie, the door caught her elbow perfectly, sending a steaming cup of coffee across the floor, splattering everyone seated near it.

"Aaaargh," the waitress screeched as she and a well-dressed woman began to wipe the coffee from the table where the cup landed. They both glared at Colin since he had obviously ignored the sign warning to open the bathroom door SLOWLY. The rest of the place had grown quiet.

"What a day this is turning out to be." She muttered. "I have a meeting in less than an hour and will need to change when I get to work."

"I am so sorry; I didn't see the sign… Let me help…" Colin reached over, trying to help restore some calmness to the situation.

The waitress, who was so eager to please before, now took on the vestige of a prison guard. "Why don't you just go back to your seat, and we can handle this."

Colin slinked back to his seat, where his plate of food had been waiting. By this time, the food had started to get cold, but being hungry, Colin wolfed it down, hoping to clear out as quickly as possible without causing any more mayhem. Maybe because he hadn't eaten a real meal in a couple of days, but the food was divine, right down to the four triangles of toast he used to wipe up the last of his eggs.

"You must have been hungry. Sorry about my reaction earlier. Been a rough morning. Hope all was well." She punched in the items from the tab on the old-fashioned cash register.

"That will be $5.65," she said.

Colin reached into his wallet and handed her his AMEX card. The waitress shook her head incredulously and pointed at the hand-lettered sign above the register:

CASH ONLY!

NO CREDIT/DEBIT CARD OR CHECKS ACCEPTED.

Colin reached back into his wallet and realized he only had a couple of dollars. *You should have thought of this, you idiot.* He was so used to Chicago, where everything was pretty much cashless. You also didn't walk around with a pocketful of cash, anyway.

"Uh, is there an ATM close by? I seemed to be a little short of cash..." Colin said.

"Boy, you are having some day today. There is one at the bank on the other side of the courthouse. How do I know you won't just take off? I've seen your type before," she looked at him with a sarcastic grin on her face.

"I've got it," came a voice behind Colin. It was the lady from the booth. "Besides, it looks like our friend here is having a rough first day in town."

"You don't have to do this; I am capable of paying myself." Colin felt as though he was suddenly some bum looking to pick up a free meal. Well, he may have looked like a chicken catcher, but he wasn't.

"No, it's okay; I know where to find you," she said with a slight smile on her face.

"Okay, thanks." Colin waited until she had paid, then thanked her again for "rescuing" him from the situation.

"No problem. The name is Linda – Linda Simmons," she said, sticking out her hand.

"I'm Colin – Colin Childers. I'm puzzled. You said you knew where to find me. That's rather creepy. I've just arrived in town. My family owns some property here..."

She chuckled. "Childers – so you are the one that got that place. Good luck with it. You will need it. I am sure I will see you around." Her phone began to ring. "Excuse me, I need to take this."

Colin turned and walked over and got in his car. *That's twice now someone has commented about the place. As for the past hour, it turned out better than I thought it would, but what a way to make a first impression,* he thought as he drove away.

Chapter 10

Colin placed a call to Jack Smith to let him know he had arrived as he pulled into the hotel parking lot. He usually made reservations but figured this time, there was no need to - there would likely be a vacancy anyway. He had planned to spend a few nights here until he could get settled in and familiar with the area. Also, he could make sure the house was ready before he moved in. At least, that was his story. After the experience a couple of weeks earlier, he was anxious about how things would go and dreaded having to face waht many would see would be an irrational fear.

"What do you mean there is no room? Can anything go right in this town?" He didn't feel like in a small town like this, in the backside of nowhere, that a reservation would be necessary after all that had transpired this morning – getting chicken whatever covering his car, to the incident at the diner, and now this. He even surprised himself that he hadn't blown a gasket.

"No, sir, I don't have anything at all this weekend," said the young girl meekly as she tried to smooth things over.

"I wish I could help you, but it's that time of the year; half of Atlanta comes this way. We have an alumni weekend in Dahlonega; there is a bass tournament on the lake. There is nothing open in a 20-mile radius. In fact, you are not the first one to have this issue. I have called around, and all the hotels in the area are booked solid. We may have something by Tuesday the next week."

Colin stood for a few seconds, staring at her, "So, what am I supposed to do? Camp out?" He paused for the dramatic effect as if it would do any good, "I'm sorry, I should have made advanced arrangements, but getting out of Chicago--" he stopped. She didn't want to hear his sob story.

"Sir, there is really nothing I can do. Let me do this: I will write your name down, and if someone cancels, I can call you." She truly seemed nice and wanted to help out.

Colin could see that she was frustrated, and after giving her his contact information, he pivoted out of the small office, pulling the door shut behind him. *I guess my only option is to stay there, he thought, or maybe Jack could help.*

When he saw the place three weeks ago, he was with Jack Smith, and he had an unexpected panic attack. Not wanting to repeat that, he also knew that the first time he saw the place after many years was with Jack Smith a few weeks earlier. Then, everything was sort of surreal, and he really, at the time, didn't do too much processing, and it was easy to avoid the memories that flooded his brain. After all, simply returning the first time for the funeral had unleashed a torrent of nightmares and near panic attacks.

He pulled up the gravel drive, hearing the crunch of the gravel under his tires, as he was already hyper-aware of his surroundings. After shutting the car off, he sat there for a few minutes, heart pounding in his chest. He sat there for a few minutes and, surprisingly, found himself beginning to calm down. *Maybe this won't be too bad after all,* he thought as he looked out across the front yard. Two squirrels were scampering around one of the big hickory trees that provided an umbrella of shade across the front yard. *Not a care in the world,* Colin thought. His mind briefly flashed back 40 years, playing Hide & Seek with his mom and dad in the yard.

He reached over, picked up the manila envelope he had laid in the seat, and fished out the keys he had been given a few weeks before. He got out of the car slowly, as if being held back by something deep in his soul. He took a deep breath and began walking the 20 feet or so to the front steps.

Grass and moss were growing in the cracks of the huge granite blocks that had been there since the house was built more than a century before. The front porch creaked as he walked across the boards that served as their own old-school sort of alarm system against intruders. He noticed there were two rusty hooks still in the ceiling that secured a porch swing that was gone long ago. Two large pots that once held flowers sat on either side of the front door. Now, they grew nothing but weeds.

He was doing fine up to this point. He had done a good job of holding it together; it had come with years of practice. He remembered his therapist's advice and coaching. Avoiding the things that triggered the "spells," really anything that exposed the memories he had tried to bury so hard. Even though he had calmed down, the emotions started welling inside him despite his best efforts. Between two deaths, the loss of his career, the messes he was involved in today, being covered with feathers, and a car with a busted windshield finally broke through the rough exterior he had kept in check for weeks. He sat down on the steps that he hadn't sat on in 40 years, and what started as a lump in the throat became misty eyes before breaking loose in a torrent of sobs. Exhausted from the day, he laid back on the porch, not caring if he lived or died. He slept.

He was awakened by his phone vibrating beside him. It was a local number. *Probably some crank call,* he thought.

"Mr. Childers? This is Sherry. The clerk at the hotel. We had a cancellation for the weekend. We have that room for you if you still want it."

"Thank you. I will be there in a few minutes." Realizing he had just been granted a reprieve for at least another day, Colin laid the phone back down. Happy that he could wait a couple more days before dealing with the house gave him a sense of relief.

The return trip to the car was much easier, but the closer he got to it, the more he thought about what he was doing. He was avoiding the inevitable. He would have to battle his demons at some point. A battle began in his mind. The emotional Colin wanted to avoid the pain and leave. The logical Colin knew that each day he avoided this would be another day to dread it. He placed his hand on the door handle, and before he could open the door, in a moment's hesitation, he stopped. *It might as well be now.*

He picked up his phone and, searching, found the number. "Hello, Sherry? Yes, I've had a change of plans. I won't need the room after all," and stuck the phone back in his pocket. He stood there for a few minutes, knowing now there was no option, as he walked back to the front door and put the key in the deadbolt.

The front door creaked as it swung open slowly. *Time to get this done,* he thought, as he took a deep breath. He could almost hear his own heartbeat. He walked through the door.

He didn't hear music, and no ghosts were waiting. It was eerily quiet; the afternoon sun was shown through the front windows, illuminating the room. He admitted to himself that he was at a different place than a few weeks ago when he was last here when he declined to even go in. For not having been occupied for months, everything appeared to be in good order, although it was as if a time capsule had just been opened. The place looked almost the same as it had the last time he had been there, or at least as he could remember after 4 decades. He had entered the front room, which was the main gathering space for the home. Colin took it all in. This was the main room in the family's house until an additional two rooms were added to the place at some point after he was last here.

Walking through the newer part of the house, he felt a little more impressed with the house overall. On the left of the hallway was a formal dining room, which probably hadn't been used in years. The hallway emptied into a rather large room. In one corner was a modern, or at least more modern, kitchen with its own dining area. The rest of the room was anchored by a hulking relic of a wood stove in the corner. There was a stack of what looked to be fresh-cut firewood stacked in a cradle next to the stove.

"That's weird," Colin said out loud. Things were too neat, too perfect. Someone had recently been here. His attention was drawn to a set of built-in bookshelves along the opposite wall. They were no longer holding any books but had become a landing space for family mementos and photos. The only other things sitting there were two framed photos. One of them was his own graduation photo from high school. The other was of his dad. He stared for a moment before laying them face down on the shelf. *Too much to process right now.* He then turned and quickly walked out of the room.

The rest of the tour was pretty uneventful, or so it seemed. To the front room's right was a staircase leading to two upstairs bedrooms. Beyond that was the largest bedroom, which had a large bed. Someone had taken the time to make the bed and turn the sheets down like someone had been expecting him. There was also a towel folded and lying on the bed. *This gets weirder by the minute.* Colin thought as he walked back up the short hall. There was one other room. He stopped and looked at the door. *That door would stay shut for now, maybe one day.*

Whatever anxiety he felt about seeing the house for the first time had now been replaced with an uneasiness. After the comments made to him earlier, then seeing that someone had obviously been in the place recently, he was curious as to what was going on here. But, that urge to overthink was overwhelmed with the fatigue of the day that was beginning to overtake him.

It didn't take long to satisfy his curiosity. He looked out the window just in time to see Jack Smith walking up on the front porch, toting several plastic bags.

"What the heck are you doing here?" Colin asked, both surprised and perturbed at the same time.

"Sorry to pop in unexpectedly like this. I figured you would need something to eat, so I bought a few things. I didn't think you would be this early - I planned to spruce things up a bit more. I had my cleaning lady come over yesterday and give it a good cleaning. I planned to get the refrigerator stocked, too, but after I called the hotel, they said you had made other plans…" Jack paused with a grin on his face.

"Whew! I was beginning to wonder. By the way, how did you know that I was going to stay at the hotel, anyway? I guess this is a small town." Colin replied. Although this explained why the house looked the way it did, it still gnawed at him about the hotel.

"Come on," said Jack, let me show you how to use that stove later. "Let's go grab a bite. Dinner's on me."

An hour later, having dispatched a couple of steaks, Jack drove Colin back to the house. He hated to admit it, but Jack's gesture had helped to somewhat soften the impact on his psyche that house could have been. They had not said a lot other than typical small talk. Colin soon learned that he and Jack shared a common love for baseball, and between the Braves and Cubs, they had plenty to talk about. The conversation went on for several minutes, and then Jack sat up straighter in his chair. "Colin, I need to ask you about the property. Obviously, it's yours to do with what you wish, but I know you had told me earlier that you had thought about selling the place. Is that something you still desire to do?"

Colin sat there for a moment before replying. "Don't you think you are jumping the gun a bit? Didn't you tell me I was to hold onto the property for at least 90 days before I could sell it?"

The 90-day thing had been puzzling. Why would anyone restrict it like that…

Colin was already beginning to realize, as he looked at the sun beginning to set, that the idea of returning to Chicago was going to get pushed further to the back of his mind with each day he started here. He had a short window to get this stuff settled and get back to

Chicago, where he belonged. As for this very moment, however, having a full belly was the last straw; all he wanted to do was sleep.

"Well, now that you mention it, I do have a realtor who would like to talk with you about the property," a smirky grin broke out on his face.

"Mary is a local realtor, and I think you will want to hear what she has to say."

"Is this something we have to do now? Right now, I am exhausted. This is not something we need to discuss right now." Colin was actually a little emphatic, a little put out that Jack was being so aggressive. The whole evening had seemed to take on a manipulative air.

"Well, I didn't imply that we had to do it TOMORROW, but… She and I were talking the other day, and with you obviously wanting to get back to Chi…"

Colin was getting steamed. "Jack, you are assuming a lot. Give me a couple of days; then we can talk about it."

"I just don't know who may be interested today, but who may not be around in 90 days. You can get everything ready, and then when you satisfy the 90-day req--"

"Nope. The only thing I am interested in right now is going to bed." He opened the door and turned to get out.

"You being a sophisticated businessman from Chicago, you ought to know this." Jack continued to press the point, almost as if he had some deep interest in getting this done.

Colin ignored the snarky comment.

"Sorry for getting short with you through all of this. Thanks for handling it. Not sure where I would be without you being here," Colin said. "Goodnight."

Okay, now let the fun begin, thought Colin as Jack pulled away. Now, it was just him, alone in the house. Home alone in this house. Only his name wasn't Kevin.

It is amazing how, in the cool of the evening, a house starts to talk. Literally, in its own unique language, and if there were other houses in the neighborhood, it would be quite certain they all would be talking to each other as the heat of the day dissipated, causing the skeletons to creak, pop, and generally complain as the cool breezes of the evening helped the conversation come forth.

It would have been difficult enough to sleep in a strange place for the first time, but now, add on his past history, trying to keep his memories at bay. He went to sleep almost immediately, but an hour later, he was jolted out of a dead sleep. He lay there for a moment. All was quiet. He started to doze again when he heard it again. Then, he heard a shuffling noise that seemed to come from right above his head... *What was that?* After a few minutes of laying there, regretting he had given up on the hotel room earlier, he just got up. He turned on the light next to the bed and slipped on his shoes. *I've got to find this,* he thought.

He walked slowly down the hall, pausing every few steps to see if the sounds were still there. He soon found his way to the den, having turned on every light he could find between the bedroom and where he now stood. He heard the shuffling again. It was coming from the den itself. As he reached to turn on a lamp, he thought he saw movement out of the corner of his eye… Maybe he was dreaming again? He flipped the switch on the lamp and then saw it. Having frozen itself like a stick, the long black snake lay stretched out across the large oval rug in the middle of the room, with a large lump just below his head, having just finished off whatever other prey was in the room. It lay there like it owned the place.

Colin shrieked, though no one could hear him; it was so loud, everyone in that part of the county could… Well, except for the snake, which just lay there. Looking around for something to capture it, Colin grabbed the trash can sitting in the kitchen, which was obviously empty, and after a few harrowing moments, got the snake to cooperate. He stepped outside the back door, then dumped the can over the banister into the flower bed below. "That is where you BELONG."

Feeling like Spartacus, Colin walked back through the house, the adrenaline coursing through him, wiping out any vestiges of sleepiness. Then, he heard it: more scraping, more noise like tapping. Then, the voices began. They were unintelligible, faint. But he could hear them, mixed in with sobs… His heart began to pound, "Who's there? Hello? What are you doing here? What do you want?"

His heart pounded. Were the voices from the house, or just in his head? He was getting more frantic, trying to stop them. They kept going. He had to get away.

Grabbing his keys, he bolted for the door, down the steps, and into the safety of his car. Slinging gravel, he tore out of the driveway, then not knowing where to go, he ended up in a small parking lot at a park near the lake. He stopped the car. The voices were silent. He just sat there, breathing easier, staring at the moonlight bouncing off the water in front of him. Specks of rain began to pepper the windshield. It began to rain. Colin slept.

He woke up with the tapping. It was back. He roused; it was daybreak.

He was startled to see a somewhat elderly man staring at him through the window. "Are you okay? Do I need to call someone?"

He called Jack when he got back to the house. "So what do you have in mind? Just listing with a realtor?"

"I actually have someone in mind. There is a local realtor in Gainesville I have known for a while – Mary Conner. She is very knowledgeable about selling family property and the sensitivities that go with it."

"What sensitivities? That I might cry when we sell this place? Go ahead and call her. After last night, I am as ready as I will ever be. Tell her we can be there in an hour."

An hour later, he walked into Jack's office. He took one look at Colin and remarked, "You look like you just slept in your car."

"If you only knew."

They took the short 10-minute walk to the realtor's office. The walk did Colin good. After he had been awakened at the park this morning, Colin had returned to the house and hurriedly changed clothes, not even bothering to get a shower. He wanted to get in and out as quickly as possible. But he noticed all the anxiety he had experienced from the night before was gone. It was as if nothing had happened.

The realtor was located in a small storefront on the town square and, as typical, had plastered the front windows with advertisements for various properties that were for sale in the area. They were quickly ushered to a small conference room in the back of the building.

"Colin Childers, it is a pleasure to finally be able to meet you. My name is Mary Conners," as she stuck out her hand. "I trust you are doing well."

"Well, I have been in town for less than 48 hours, been hit with a chicken, dumped coffee out on a total stranger, got turned away from the inn, and topped the day off by trying to sleep in a snake-infested, possibly haunted house. Plus, slept for about 3 hours last night in my car. So, I'm doing just fine. What do you have to show me?" Colin asked, as he had no use for the canned small talk that realtors were so good at dishing out.

They all sat there for a few moments as Mary began, suddenly flustered but also very stoic at the same time. "You need to realize, Mr. Childers, how valuable the property is that you own. When I heard that the owner, your grandfather, had passed and you would be the sole heir, I contacted Jack. People have had their eyes on it for years, and I know your grandfather was offered quite a large sum of money for it on numerous occasions but refused to sell it. No one could understand why or what was holding him back. Selling it would have made him quite a wealthy man."

"Since the lake was built over 50 years ago, the demand has continued to grow and has only accelerated in the last 20 years with the ease of access to Atlanta."

"So, I take it you want to represent me by selling the property?

The confused realtor glanced over at Jack, then back at Colin.

"You don't understand; I am not asking to represent you. I am already representing the potential buyer, who is very motivated…"

Colin sat back down. "So, how much is this buyer willing to pay?"

"Now we are talking…" She opened a folder on her desk. Here is a proposed purchase price. If you agree to it, then I will draw up the formal offer paperwork, and we will be on our way to closing." She pushed the folder across the desk to Colin.

Colin was interested but was also interested in a little theater. "At this time, not interested. No deal. Let your buyer know that it's going to take more than a slick sales pitch to change my mind. Besides, if I decide to sell it, I won't need a realtor. I have enough contacts to sell it myself. You know I do have a pretty big network of folks that could write a check tomorrow." Colin knew he really didn't, but it gave for good theater. He winked at Jack.

Colin opened the folder and was silent for a moment. "So, $5 million, eh?

"When do they need an answer?"

"I would say the sooner, the better, but at least in the next 2-3 days."

"I will let you know. I am very aware of how valuable this property is. But, again, I own it. And I may have other plans for what I do with it, which may not include selling it to your 'motivated' buyer." Colin stood up, "Thanks, Ms. Conner. As we used to say in Chicago, 'Don't call us, we'll call you.' Now, if you will excuse me for a moment, I assume you have a bathroom in this place?"

When Colin was out of sight, Jack asked quietly, "Do you think he will take the offer?"

"I certainly hope so. You and I both know that Bryant is not used to hearing no. I hope your client realizes that."

"Realizes what?" Colin asked, walking back into the room.

"Oh, nothing. We can talk about it later." What do you say? "Just give me a quick moment."

Jack stepped off to the side and quietly checked the text message he had just received. The reply he sent back would not make some folks happy.

Chapter 11

Colin sat on the front porch. A week had passed since his whirlwind arrival. He had put the realtor off twice, knowing he needed to decide. All he had to do was to say yes, and within a couple of weeks, he could sign the closing documents, collect a hefty check, return to Chicago, and treat this little trip to the Boonies as nothing more than an extended vacation. On the other hand, however, even though the first couple of days here had been chaotic, things settled down. The episode he had experienced the first night was chalked up to just being exhausted. It had not repeated itself, although he could hear the occasional popping & cracking throughout the night.

He was already starting to restore connections to the place. He had finally come to a decision earlier today, he had come to a decision. For now, he would stay right here. He had been kidding himself to think that he had anything left in Chicago, anyway. With that, he picked up his phone and called.

"So, have you decided anything yet? Mary's been about to drive me crazy!" Jack's frustration came through.

"Let Mary know. I am not going to sell, at least for now. Thanks." He sat his phone back down. Within seconds, Jack called back.

"Are you sure this is what you want to do? So does this mean you are staying put?"

"You got it. Now, let me get back to what I was doing. Talk to you later."

Later that day, Colin drove to town to take care of changing over the utilities to his name. It came as no surprise that most of the folks he met with not only knew he had arrived in town but were also eager to point out their concern with the place that had been his family's home for generations. "So YOU'RE the one that moved into the old Childers place," quickly followed by, "Why, you're Bill Childers's grandson, aren't you?" especially for those really old-timers that had known his family. He even ran into an older couple that had gone to HIGH SCHOOL with his dad.

One of the quirky joys of moving into a small town. It started the first morning. It seemed like everyone, and everywhere he went, everybody already knew who he was or knew the family. Everyone, it seemed, knew he was here. It seemed like every day, he had been introduced to another "cousin," all of whom had a story to tell about the family. If they weren't related, they knew all about his arrival. "You are in the old Childers place, aren't you?" they would often say, right after discovering where he lived, as if somehow him telling his address granted some sort of special permission for them to start prying. After about two weeks of going to various places to handle his granddad's affairs, he pretty well got the picture – The Childers had all been crazy, the property was haunted, and that's where ole' Tom-Tom used to live!

"So you got the old Childers place..." This had become the standard phrase. Going to eat. At the bank. At the post office. Even at the local hardware store, it seemed everyone had a strange glance or some level of disbelief that someone would actually WANT to live there.

At first, it was creepy. He was not used to this level of openness and almost comical lack of privacy. He would smile politely, but deep down, he was unsettled that so much could be known so quickly about someone. He was beginning to understand why people either loved or hated living in a small town. As for the town's fascination with his place, he had no clue. Once he got to know some folks in the town better, maybe he would ask.

As much as he would have loved to let his thoughts remain fixated on what was his family's and this community's quirky past, he had to begin to think about the day ahead. Business.

Colin slowly began to sift through the things that remained from his grandparent's lives. Between them and his mom, it seemed like all he did was sort. Pause to reminisce, then put stuff back he wanted to keep. The dining room table became the repository for the latter this time. It has been much easier going through his grandparent's things, as there were not many things that provoked memories or that had any value to him. It's hard to believe how much stuff two human beings need in this life. He felt a sense of accomplishment when the pickup & trailer slowly pulled away a couple of weeks later, black smoke belching out of its exhaust as it growled to life. This was the final load of stuff, most of which he had little attachment to.

Although there was much he had not brought with him, there were still some things back in Chicago that he would need, but for now, since he hadn't put the house up for sale there, he would let things sit for the moment; besides, he hadn't fully made his mind up on how long he would stay here, anyway.

As strange as it may have seemed, now that Colin had rejected the offer to sell the place, and with it deciding to remain here for the time being, he had come to a real peace about his decision. Although most of everything was gone with the last load that just left, all that remained was a file cabinet full of stuff, a box of old photographs, and the obvious – THE room. His dad's old room literally became a museum after his death. He finally got the courage to crack the door and at least look inside, but not until he had spent an hour talking himself into it. There were plenty of reminders around the place, but the room was too much to bear. He would just have to deal with it later. Although the door was not locked, and Colin could enter anytime he pleased, there was an excuse for everything, and in this situation, there were many. Bottom line, Colin did not want to go in that room, it was still just too hard at this point.

From His vantage point on the front porch, he could see the road snaking its way in front of the house, a hundred yards or so away. The old pickup slowed down in front of the house as if to turn in the drive. Instead of turning, however, it kept its slow pace until it disappeared from his view. Not thinking anything about it, Colin returned to reading the dime-store novel he had found in the stuff he was getting rid of. Then, he looked up to see the truck coming the other way, once again as if casing the place. Then, almost as if the driver could sense he had Colin's attention, he accelerated quickly, leaving a cloud of smoke as the only evidence it had been there. Colin shook his head, figuring it was someone who had used his drive for access to the lake, but saw that someone was living here now. He went back to reading.

With the move-in complete, it was now time to do a little more exploring and, in the process, let his creative juices begin to imagine what he could do with this place. For him to have an offer to buy the place as soon as he arrived meant that others also saw the potential in this place. He planned to discover for himself what was so special about the place.

There were strange things here. First, the place was covered with evidence of the farm's past. Besides the old barn that was slowly being absorbed into the ground it sat upon, down at the waterfront, half submerged, were the foundation stones for an old structure. He would have to do some research on what was once there. All that was left were a few foundation stones, which were constantly massaged by the waters of the lake, whose shoreline absorbed part of the structure and the small inlet it sat upon. It was about to fall in when he visited here as a kid, and they were forbidden to enter it. *I guess Papa must have finished tearing it down,* he thought. On the other side of the house, practically covered with Kudzu, was the remnant of the roadbed that led over to the old campground. Colin wondered if it was still there.

Then there was the cabin. The most interesting structure on the property is on the other side of the barn, at the top of the hill overlooking the lake below. This was the oldest standing structure on the property and was the source of all the mystery. It had been pretty much left to the elements, with the weeds and small trees growing around it, almost choking it out. Someone in the past had covered the place with wood siding, some of which had fallen off, leaving a glimpse of the original log structure it had hidden. According to Jack's account, this is where "Tom-Tom" had lived. He were not sure why that was such a big deal, but he was sure to find out, given how everyone knew everyone else's business, or so it seemed.

Ever curious, he yanked on the door until the hasp and old padlock that had been installed on the door fell off, and he was able to squeeze into the opening. The kudzu and wisteria had about taken over the place. It took a moment for his eyes to adjust, but soon he could see around. The light shining through the two small windows cast an eerie glow on the furnishings. The cabin had two rooms, with a fireplace along one end. The roof was in better condition than he thought, and then he remembered Jack Smith telling him that his grand-dad had started fixing the place up to be a rental or fishing cabin.

The inside was like a time capsule. Colin was not sure what was put there by earlier residents vs. what had recently been placed. Regardless, he walked gingerly on the floor, which felt like it could give way at any moment.

There was an old rocker which sat by the fireplace. A small table also sat near it. The place was spooky.

With the sun beginning to set and the shadows getting longer, Colin decided to head back to the house with the crate. There would be plenty of time to explore the rest later.

Chapter 12

Colin woke with a start. He looked over at the clock on the nightstand; the flashing 12:00 told him that the power had gone out sometime in the night. He reached and picked up his watch, to see it read 3:30. Awake again, he thought. Same time as yesterday… and the day before. Likely, going through all the stuff had triggered the dreams again. Even though he had gotten settled in here, the demons, if he believed in them, would return even stronger, trying to convince him he was crazy or something. It was the same every time – there was the funeral, everyone was there, and it always ended with the little boy crying, holding on to his mom, who had no one she could hold onto. He turned on the lamp by the bed and got up.

Might as well get a snack, he thought, as he grabbed a banana and poured a glass of milk. He went back to his room and grabbed the book he had been reading. Then, the scratching.

The noise he had about gotten used to. Sounded almost as if someone was trying to scratch through the wall. *It's time I took care of this,* he thought. He slowly crept out of the bedroom into the hallway. He flipped the switch for the flood light outside, which lit up the front porch closest to where the sounds were coming from. The scratching stopped momentarily, then started again. He walked over to the source. Then, it moved, now coming from the wall by the fireplace, which divided the rest of the house from his room.

"Darn squirrels." He slapped the wall right where he heard the noise, and a few moments later, the scurrying moved across the ceiling until it disappeared altogether. This battle had gone on nearly every night since he moved back in. He needed to do something about it but didn't quite know what to do.

Then it started up again; they just wouldn't quit. This time, the noise sounded like it was coming from the closet in his room. *Maybe I will catch them now,* he thought. Slowly opening the door and shining his light inside, he saw it. A crate. *Hmmm... never noticed that before,* he thought.

It had been well preserved, given its apparent age. It wasn't that large – had the owner had access to air travel, it would easily be used as a carry-on. Wanting to get it into better light, Colin carried it into the kitchen, where he sat it on the counter. He took a dish towel lying nearby and wiped it down, taking care not to cause any damage. The hinges were almost rusted through, and the hasp securing it wasn't in much better shape. He pulled a knife from the knife block on the counter and pried at the hasp. It broke free fairly easy, and he slowly lifted the lid. The hinges were frozen with rust, and even with being careful, there was a sudden snap as the two hinges broke, and the lid came free in his hands.

Maybe expecting something wild and exotic, Colin was disappointed to find only two items inside – both books of some sort. He picked up the first one, which he quickly discovered was an old Bible. He carefully cracked it open, as the binding was in pretty bad shape, having obviously been read a great deal. As he went to lay it down beside the box, he noticed something sticking out from the pages – it was a photo of a small boy sitting next to an older man in a rocker. Standing behind both of them was a young woman. He looked closely at the photo, trying to think of where he had seen her before.

He flipped to the front cover and saw the name of Sissy Childers written on the front page. So Sissy had to have been an ancestor, but it was only after he flipped to the center section, and in it was 4-5 pages of writing. At the top of the list were the names Jacob & Sissy Childers, along with additional entries over the next several pages of various family members. Each one showed a date of birth as well as a date of death. He noticed at least one that had died in the Civil War. Obviously, Colin had never cared much for history, especially that of his family, but he was starting to get interested, realizing what he had in his hand.

Whatever the other item was in the box, it was wrapped with a strip of leather that had been wound around the package; then, a narrow strip had been tied around it to secure the wrapping. Colin gingerly unrolled the leather case until he had exposed its contents.

The book was in pretty rough condition. The leather binding had broken down long before, and someone had used some of the same leather that had wrapped it to wrap around it. *Someone made a great deal of effort to make sure this was preserved,* Colin thought. Colin cut the leather cord that had secured the book, then opened the cover. He wondered who it might belong to. It didn't take long to realize he was looking at a story. It didn't look like a normal journal, as there were no individual notations as to the dates, only writing. He started reading the first few sentences.

Someone else, likely his grand-dad, had handled it before, as there were little slips of paper throughout It was some sort of journal. He thumbed through the book, with some of the pages being barely legible. He wondered where it all had come from - likely from the old cabin. Being careful not to damage the extremely fragile book, he walked over to the couch with the journal and sat down.

I was one of the early pioneers in these parts. I was born in North Carolina. 1810 or 11, I think. I grew up in a community of pioneer settlers at the edge of the Blue Ridge. Life was hard in those times — it was a day's journey to town, and we lived with about a dozen other families in the small valley we called home. There was plenty of game; the bottom lands were good that my dad grew his crops on. I had three brothers and a sister. I was the youngest by several years. Besides my mom and dad, most of the other settlers in the valley were related. My granddad came to the valley when he was a young boy with his father, who was provided land to help fight the French.

Colin laid the book down and thought. *This could get interesting. He* laid back on the sofa, his eyes getting heavy, but his mind churning over what he had just read. *At least I will have something else to dream about this morning,* he thought.

He had dwelt too long on the mysterious truck in front of the house, and now, as he dozed off, not only was it in his dream, but now there was a wagon with a young man riding right along behind him, waving at Colin. There was a hearse in the back of the wagon.

Colin woke up and then went back to his bed. It was likely nothing, but one could never be too sure. Add in the dreams returning, and there was a new level of paranoia. He almost dreaded going back to sleep because he knew what was coming. For some reason, 3:30 was the magical time. For weeks, this had been his sleep pattern. Strangely, it started right after the strange turn of events that had pretty much changed the direction of his entire life. Was he crazy?

Maybe so. He didn't know. On the one hand, as the days passed since the Chicago affair, the better he was feeling. But, on the other hand, the darkness had not disappeared, but was replaced with something different. He hid it well, and it was pretty easy with the new people he was meeting here. He had to be very cautious in a small community like this. Now, this strange journal. As much as he would like to read the whole thing, right now, he just didn't need to start a new chapter of craziness about this place, that wasn't already in place to begin with.

Things were quiet for a couple of nights, but then, on the third night, they started up again - this time, it seemed like something different. This time, he was determined to start to get rid of whatever it was. In going through the things in the house, he came across an old pistol, complete with a box of shells.

At least I can scare off whatever is doing this, Colin thought, or *If things get too crazy, maybe this will be my ticket to escape this whole stinking life...* he quickly chased that thought out of his head. He never, ever even considered that but where did that come from? Dressing quickly, he went outside and found a good spot where he could detect if something, or someone, was trying to get into the place. All he could see was the evil grin from the driver of that truck. He wasn't planning to actually kill anything; in fact, other than the makeshift tragedy practice the week before, he hadn't HELD a gun in years, much less fire one. Simply put, the situation was a recipe for disaster.

The moon hung over the trees that had shed a great deal of their leaves; although cool, it wasn't unpleasant as he took up his spot. As elusive as sleep was indoors, it was quickly upon him here; he had to fight to stay alert and awake. He ran through his mind all the possible things it could be. He had assumed it was a squirrel, but maybe it wasn't - too much noise just for a squirrel - Probably wasn't a human since there were not a lot of folks, especially homeless, that lived here. Maybe just a stray cat. He had never seen a raccoon other than in movies, but it could be that. Hopefully, it wasn't something bigger, like a bear.

He dozed off, then was awakened again. He heard it. The scratching. It was out HERE somewhere. He flipped on his flashlight, generally in the direction of the now metallic grating sound that had woken him for a week. He flashed his light by the window to his room, but nothing. The grating continued. He trained his light on the roof line, and for a moment, he saw nothing, but then a head popped up as if caught. *A squirrel. Nothing but a freakin' squirrel,* he thought. *I guess I do have too much city in me.* He chuckled to himself, then turned to walk in the house. "A freakin' squirrel. I let a freaking squirrel get me out of bed." Then, he heard it. It sounds far off, but yet close by. The music. It seemed like every morning, right before the squirrel woke him, the same music played in his dream. *This is what has been waking me up,* he thought. He felt his hair prickle up on his neck as a new terror hit him – was this more evidence he was going crazy? Was he dreaming? The music seemed to come from the other side of the woods. He was drawn to it, while at the same time, fear kept him away. He slowly sank back into the chair he had been sitting in earlier. It went on for a couple of minutes, then it was gone. The end of the music brought on a stillness that stayed for a few seconds until the early morning light prompted the birds to get started. He had to check it out.

He started. The leaves crunched under Colin's boots as he trudged down the old dirt road that went into the woods next to the house and towards the direction the strange music had come from earlier.

He had walked about a half mile when the trail opened into a large open area – the campground. Again, another faint memory came forth into his consciousness. He had been here several times as a child but had all but forgotten about it. There was a row of wood frame structures that sat around the edge of the clearing, which was now covered by many large trees. In the center of the clearing was a large wood pavilion that provided shades to what pretty much would be described as a church. Colin walked slowly, realizing likely where the music had come from – but at 4 o'clock in the morning? Couldn't someone wait until later to play? He walked over to the structure and arbor, as it was called, and gingerly sat down on one of the weathered pews.

He sat there for a few moments. The arbor was obviously very old and showing its age. He looked up at the roof, which was built of beans hewn from massive chestnut logs. He could see the underside of the tin roof, which helped to amplify any sound that was produced under the arbor and explained why he could hear it a half mile away. What puzzled him was that no one else seemed to know anything about it.

She walked quietly through the woods, carefully moving from one tree to the other. That was him, she was sure. She sat down against a tree so she had a good view of the place and placed a call.

Chapter 13

The gravel crunched under his care as Colin pulled into the unpaved parking lot next to the administration building. After realizing his BMW Roadster didn't quite fit as well in the local community, he traded it in for something more fitting. He couldn't quite bring himself to get a pickup truck, at least just yet, but settled on a two-year-old Range Rover. He also found it was better for exploring the property, and it helped him not to stick out so badly when he was driving around town.

With all the new growth and prosperity, it was only a matter of time before the county would begin to upgrade some of its public buildings. The new government center stood a couple of blocks off Main Street, within the site of the old historic courthouse, which was literally in the center of town. The new facility allowed for several county functions to be consolidated under one roof and gave a shot in the arm to the local community. Opening the front door, he exchanged pleasantries with the rather dowdy-looking deputy providing security and, after walking through the requisite metal detector. He proceeded up the marble steps that took him to the third floor as the natural design of the lobby and rotunda steered visitors toward taking the stairs. Soon, he found the office he was looking for – that of the county administration. He figured he should go big first and start at the top.

"Good Morning, sir. How can I help you today?" The office had a short counter, behind which a rather elderly lady stood guard over the offices behind her. The lobby was simply decorated, with a small sofa on one side and a tall, glass-fronted bookcase on the other. On the coffee table lay a couple of large books featuring the mountains and hills in which the county sat.

After about 10 minutes and growing impatient, Colin thought, *Is this normal everywhere?* He thought back to the time a few months earlier, which seemed like yesterday when he first arrived in town and met with Jack Smith. He heard the phone ring on the desk in the office.

"Ms. Simmons will see you now", as she pointed to the door next to the counter.

Colin pushed the door open, and there she stood. The lady from the diner. "You! Well, at least this time, when you opened a door, I didn't end up wearing your coffee..."

Usually, Colin was quick to respond; after all, he had met a few sassy women in his past, but something about her tied his tongue up, and he had a difficult time responding. On the one hand, she was serious, still looking pissed, but then she broke out in a smile that was tamped down with the professional need to be business-like. "You can come on back," she stated as she turned and led him back to her office.

"I... I... didn't realize you worked here," Colin said, trying to make small talk to cover the awkward silence.

"Where did you expect I worked?"

"Well, I didn't imagine you were..."

"The county manager? Yeah, you are not the first. Maybe I was a secretary for some chicken farmer? Yep, that is pretty much it, isn't it?" she said, as she looked at Colin with somewhat of a sassy smile.

That smile. And, the look. It made it hard to concentrate for a moment. Yeah, he had worked around many women in the business, and having even dated a few of them, he still had little time for anything but business. It had suddenly struck him how lonely he had been for at least some sort of human contact.

Linda sat there, looking at the computer monitor. "So, Mr. Childers, what can we do for you today? Mr. Childers?"

"Oh, sorry, I was caught up in my thoughts. Lot going on lately." He was stammering like a 14-year-old at his first dance.

"As you already know, I recently inherited the Childers property over near War Hill. William Childers was my granddad. Good property. Lakefront. And, I have started the process to develop it."

Linda looked unimpressed, but even being that way, she still caused something to stir in him that he hadn't felt in a while. Okay, so maybe it was the cup of coffee he had before arriving this morning.

Colin moved over to the small conference table she had set up next to the window and then spent the next 10 minutes going over the drawings with her.

"So, you plan to build a marina, put in a retail space, restaurant, and 40 estate-level homes. I have my doubts, but I don't make the decision. It will be up to the board to determine that. When can you be prepared to present to our board?"

"I have already been talking with the architect. Maybe the next couple of weeks?" Colin knew even this would be tight but workable.

"Fine – we have a work session next week, followed two weeks later with the formal meeting. I will pencil you in on the agenda. We will need to talk again before then."

Out of habit, Colin reached into his pocket to grab a business card, then realized his old cards were worthless. "You have a piece of paper so I can write down my contact info?"

"I've got a better idea. I'm starving – I think it is time for you to pay me back for that breakfast I bought you a couple of months ago when you first arrived. Plus. it will give me a chance to learn a little more about how you ended up here/ I mean, I do need to collect on my debt at some point." For the first time since they met, a grin broke out on Linda's face.

Things may just work out after all, around here, Colin thought as they walked the two blocks to the diner.

"So, how did you end up here? You really did inherit that place? The place has always had an air of mystery about it. Always heard of strange things happening over there."

Colin shared with her how his grandparents owned the place, how he had been the CEO of a software company in Chicago, and how he basically wanted to make a change and simplify his life. What he didn't bother to tell her was that he really had no choice, had been drug down here kicking and screaming, nor how his finding the "simple life" by leaving the company was not exactly his idea. But, no need to fret over the details at this point.

"So, what about you? Seems like if people are surprised you are here, then there must be a story there?" Colin sat, genuinely interested in what she had to say.

"I am actually a native. When I graduated, I went to school over in Dahlonega, met the love of my life there, married, and followed him off to the Army. Two years after marrying, he was deployed to the Gulf. A month after he left, he was involved in a head-on collision in Saudi. So, married and widowed at 23. Lost myself in my work and moved to Atlanta, where I worked in the finance office at Fulton County for 15 years. Then, out of the blue, the county had an opening for a county manager, and I was asked to apply. Next thing, I am hanging my name up outside the door. That was 10 years ago. I guess I could go somewhere else, but this is home."

"So, family? Parents still alive?" This is getting too deep in a hurry, Colin thought.

"Actually, my parents died when I was only 9 years old. I was raised by my aunt and uncle. My aunt died last year. My uncle is still alive. Have a couple of cousins I am close to that were pretty much siblings growing up, and of course, being in a small town, have several distant cousins here…"

"Hey Cuz! What's up?" The booming voice could be heard all over the place. Colin turned to see who was talking. It was Junior — the man with the winch. This really is a small town.

Linda broke out in a grin and slid over in her seat. Colin could feel the strain on the booth when the big man lowered his huge body into the seat.

"Colin, meet Junior – my cousin. Junior, Colin Childers."

"Oh, we've met," Colin said with a smirk on his face.

"Yep, we sure have. You still got that fancy sports car?" Junior helped himself to the bowl of homemade chips sitting on the table.

Linda looked puzzled, but by the time Junior got through telling the story of the truck, she and Colin were both about to bust a gut from laughing.

"So, no wonder you were in a bad mood that first morning," Linda said as she began to tell Junior the coffee story.

"Well, I just stopped by to get a burger before heading to the woods. Getting ready to sell some timber, plus I need to get ready for deer season. You hunt Colin?"

Colin could sense a credibility moment in front of him. "No, never have, but I do have a pesky squirrel out at the house I have been trying to get rid of."

"Well, maybe I need to take you some time, or at least take you out to my land. Have some great views of the mountains. Anyway, guess I better get going."

Linda and Colin watched as he walked away, stopping at ust about every table to say something to the other patrons.

"Looks like he's quite the character," Colin said.

"Yep, that he is. He was really there for me growing up. You really should get to know him. He is fun to be around. Plus, by this time tomorrow, half the county will know that you and I had lunch together." She paused for a moment on the last sentence. "I'm sorry. Did that sound as bad as I thought it did?"

"Nope. It didn't. One thing I have learned in the short time I have been here - news travels fast in a small town." Colin replied.

"Yep, I have to say our meeting at this time was definitely more pleasant than the last one," Linda commented as they walked the two blocks back to the county office.

"Yep, it was. Let's plan to do this again soon." Colin said.

"By all means," Linda replied over her shoulder as she left him standing on the front steps. "We will need to discuss those plans again before the meeting next week." She was suddenly all business again,

Those words reverberated in Colin's ears as he drove out of the parking lot. The weather was comfortable that day, so he rolled down the window and soon found himself humming a tune he knew from long ago. It seemed that, finally, the city was being washed out of his mind as the wind blowing in the window brought smells of summer through the windows. He felt better than he had in a long time. Maybe all of this was really meant to be, after all.

He was brought back to reality a moment later when he spotted the truck coming up behind him in his rearview mirror, obviously desiring to pass. Around a curve in the road was a long straightaway, so Colin slowed down slightly to let him by, but the driver didn't take the offer. Colin slowed more, but the driver stayed behind him. *Okay, I still have enough Chicago in me,* as he accelerated, hoping the driver was about to turn off, which didn't happen. So, he slowed down again

– real slow, almost stopping. He waved the truck around. It just sat there.

"Fella, not sure what you are trying to do," as he sat there, growing more fearful of what might happen next. He looked around for anything he might use for a weapon if attacked, but the only thing was an empty soda bottle, which wouldn't do much good. It seemed like an eternity had passed when suddenly the truck lurched forward, finally passing him.

Colin was certain it was the same black truck that had driven slowly by his house several times over the past few weeks. The windows were tinted so he couldn't the driver, but as soon as the truck got even with him, the driver gunned it, belching black smoke from the tailpipes, and a few seconds later disappeared around the curve ahead.

Colin pulled over on the shoulder and sat there for a moment, his hands shaking over the encounter. In Chicago, it was routine to spar with other drivers in traffic, but it was a natural part of surviving in city traffic. This was different. It all seemed sinister. He hadn't been here long enough to make any enemies, had he? He finished the drive cautiously, keeping an eye out for the truck, which could be lurking anywhere, waiting for him in the shadows. Five minutes later, he had arrived at the house and locked the doors safely behind him. *Apparently, not everyone is happy to see me here*, he thought.

Chapter 14

Grant & Associates sat high on a bluff looking out over the lake below. Stephen Grant was the primary partner in the architectural & engineering firm started by his uncle fifty years earlier. Steve, as he was known by most, had built the firm's office to take advantage of the niche they had carved out over the last three decades – to leave their distinctive signature on the lake through their design of custom homes and developments. Even with the availability of open, undeveloped lakefront property growing less and less every year, now many were beginning to buy older homes just for the property. For some, just a glimpse or view of the lake is enough to fetch a good price for the design of a custom-built home.

The receptionist showed Colin into the large conference room at the back of the office. Around the room were various photos and framed plats showing the various projects the firm had worked on, especially the last 10-20 years. Completing the atmosphere in the room was the large, curved wall of glass that completely covered one side of the room. Whatever view he had of the lake from the parking lot was nothing compared to the view from here. The windows gave a panoramic view of the lake, which was framed by the changing autumn foliage and the deep blue late October sky. *By now, Chicago would be expecting snow,* Colin thought.

"Like the view?" Colin turned to see a short, balding gentleman carrying a large cardboard tube under his arm. With him was Jack Smith. Colin was surprised to see that Jack took time himself to be here as well. "It's good to see you again", said Steve Grant, sticking out his hand.

He and Colin had met a few weeks prior after a strong reference from Jack. After a brief discussion and short tour of the property to get Colin's vision for development potential, the firm completed an initial engineering assessment to identify any issues or impediments that could slow down or stop the development, thus determining the feasibility of Colin's ideas. As for the discovery of the journal, Colin did not mention it because, frankly, he felt it wasn't relevant to the task at hand.

Steve pulled several plats out of the tube he had brought with him and handed Colin a copy of the report the firm had completed.

"I REALLY like this property. Although we were only doing an assessment of the property, I took the liberty of drawing up a preliminary plat to show its potential." Steve then laid out for Colin a large map similar to what he had seen for the first time a few months earlier.

Colin sat quietly. For some reason, his mind went back through all he had been through the past few months, with his dismissal and then move here. He also for the first time, felt almost nostalgic.

His trip down memory lane was suddenly interrupted. "Colin, what you are experiencing right now happens a lot when people see their family's homeplace and legacy property being developed. There is often a sense of excitement, but at the same time grief, over things that will be changing. This is usually minimized when the developer shows them how they stand to make once the development goes through. In your case, however, since you will be developing it yourself as the owner, you are going to see a tremendous increase in how much you will get from this property once it has been completely developed."

Colin replied. "Oh, it's nothing. What is puzzling to me is that I really don't have much personal history with this property. I have only owned it for a few months. But I do have some very faint memories, some of which I would rather not talk about right now, especially with someone I hardly know, so not sure why the sudden sense of nostalgia. What say we steer this thing back to what I am paying you to do? I didn't realize I was also paying you to be my counselor", Colin said.

Steve started. "Colin, my apologies - as you have probably learned, small talk is big talk in these parts."

How well I know, Colin thought.

"Let me begin by saying this is one of the more unique and challenging properties I have worked with. These will be obvious as we start. There were a couple of surprises we may have to deal with."

Colin looked at him with an obvious puzzled look on his face.

"First, let me show my ideas for how it could be developed, then we can go over what the challenges may be."

He continued. "The lay of the land provides us with the opportunity to have a grouping of estate lots on top of the hill, with smaller but equally exquisite home sites, all lake-front, ringing this upper layer.

Colin looked at the plat, nodding with approval, entranced with what he saw.

Steven continued. "We will also be taking advantage of this small cove, with cuts into the south edge of the property. This gives us an excellent place for a small marina, which will provide water access to the clubhouse and small water-front retail shops. In essence, this will create one of the more unique developments to ever be built on the lake."

"That's great you did this, putting down my ideas on paper, but since we are actually looking at how feasible these plans are, shouldn't we be looking at those first?" Colin talked like he had a full schedule to tend to. In reality, he had all the time in the world.

Steven looked briefly at Jack, who winked at him. Steve appeared to be flustered that his plans were rebuffed. "Okay, my apologies. I just got carried away with all the possibilities. Let's get going then."

Steven reached over, lifted a plate on the table, and pushed a couple of buttons. "My new toy."

The natural landscape that in some ways defined the room began to fade, then disappeared as the windows darkened. The lights in the room also dimmed, except for a small ribbon of light, which lit the surface of the table at which they sat. Finally, a screen dropped from the ceiling at one end of the table, along with a projector.

Steve began. "If you will look at the plat, you will notice several areas I have highlighted."

"First of all, I want to point out a particular location on the plat – one you may be familiar with." He pointed at a small, highlighted area, which took up about the size of two of the lake-front properties. Colin knew this area well. It was where the old chimneys stood he had spotted a week earlier. "It is not clear what this was, but it appears from our review to have a small settlement. Also, the small road that runs adjacent to this down to the water was likely the course of the old Hightower Road". He flashed up the first photo. "You can see the cut on both sides of the path, which shows the trail at some point was wider, and work had been done to make it more accessible."

"So we have an old road. What makes it so special? I mean, old roads are graded over every day in this country."

"I forget that you are not from around here", Steven said with a slight grin on his face. "Hightower was a Cherokee town west of here, sometimes called 'Etowah'. It was a trading center for the Cherokees that lived in this part of the state. The Hightower Trading Path connected Gainesville to Hightower and was the principal path across the river into the Cherokee nation that ran from Gainesville to the Cherokee village of Hightower, about 35 miles west of here. This was one of the main routes into and out of the Cherokee nation at the time. It was every bit as important as one of our modern interstate highways."

"So there were Indians on the property at one time?" Colin was suddenly curious.

"Ever hear of the Trail of Tears?" Steve asked.

"Yes, but what did that have to do with this?" Colin replied.

"In recent years, the federal government has increased its enforcement activities surrounding Native American art & artifacts. If we were to find anything on the property that we suspect is of native origin, we would have to halt development until it can be evaluated. Some projects have also been permanently halted due to these issues."

"But how does that affect this?" Colin was growing concerned.

"Lots. First of all, the river itself was the boundary between the United States and the Cherokee Nation at one time. Also, by the fact that you possibly had the main road into and out of the Cherokee nation running right through the place, there is a chance of some significant archeological finds once we begin the project. You just need to be aware of that."

"Great. I guess you are going to tell next there is 'gold in them thar hills!'?" Colin said sarcastically, mimicking a billboard he recently drove by.

"That brings me to the second issue." Steve unrolled another large sheet, of which the Childers property was highlighted. It was a much larger scale, which pretty much showed all the parcels in the southeast corner of the county.

"I wanted you to see how the properties developed over time in this part of the county. Thanks to an enterprising intern I brought on board last summer, I was able to plot the transition of the land lots from their beginnings when drawn in the 1830s."

He continued. "She used the property data to show how, beginning with the land lots, which is shown with the red grid, were literally chopped into hundreds of parcels as the land was divided, first among children and grandchildren, then divided even further after the lake was built, and the demand for weekend housing increased."

Colin interrupted. "I still don't follow you on how this is an issue."

"Notice that in the area, other than the largest parcel, which is your land, only two others have pretty much retained the dimensions of the original land-lot boundaries.

"What do you mean?" Asked Colin.

"This prompted some research on our part. It was strange that the property remained largely in its original form, that is, except for the east side, of which the government bought a part for the lake. So, we did some digging, and found out something strange."

Colin was really beginning to believe he was in some strange science-fiction flick.

Steve talked on. "To ensure that land was distributed fairly, a series of lotteries were held, in which the land was divided into lots that were awarded in a drawing. Very few people actually took possession of the land they were awarded; most either sold it to "consolidators" or just simply never claimed their prize. Because the land was already full of squatters, miners, and still had Cherokees living on it, many parcels were either given to the people living there by carving up their land."

Colin gazed at the map. It was very interesting to what he had been told, and why there was such interest in the Childers property.

There was literally no other parcel this big anywhere in this part of the county.

"What's this?" Colin pointed to another smaller parcel that appeared to be intact, adjacent to his.

"Oh, that's a church, cemetery, and an old camp meeting ground, which has pretty much retained its original shape over the last two centuries. You familiar with it?"

"My… family is buried in the cemetery." Colin started to go into the details about his father but decided not to. The guy probably didn't want to hear about it.

"So any other issues?"

Steve replied, "There are a couple of other things. Give me another moment here to finish explaining. As the land has remained in the Childers family since it was first acquired in the 1830s, the transfer process from generation to generation at times was rather slack. When Dawson County was formed in the 1850s, the baseline was pretty much established at that point. The deed that you hold mentioned nothing about another piece of property, which was filed in Lumpkin but was forgotten about. We found in the deed book this transaction, which was entered on June 11, 1838."

Colin looked over the photocopy of the entry. The handwriting was hard to read, but it clearly laid out the boundaries of a section of land that was transferred to someone else; the clause that jumped off the page was this: "None of the property, or portion thereof, shall be sold outside the Childers family without being offered first to Ben McDonald or his descendants."

"So, what does this mean?" Colin asked, rather puzzled. "So where is the actual deed? Who the hell is Ben McDonald?"

"That's the problem. We cannot locate the deed, nor have any idea who Ben McDonald is. It appears that the page on which the deed was found is missing. Without clearing this up, I am worried that the lots, when sold, may have a hard time getting financing."

Colin sat back in his chair. He was starting to become perturbed. He had inherited a parcel of land that, in some ways, could be considered worthless.

"So, how do we know what parts this covers?"

"That's just it. We don't know. The only way we know what the property looked like is to look at the deed for the property, with the section taken out."

Steve then unrolled a third parchment that again showed the Childers property. The only difference was this time, the amended boundaries clearly divided the property nearly in two, with the excluded portion rather cleverly highlighted by red hash marks.

"This is clearly how the land had remained intact all these years. There is no deed; the property is intact for now, but when we go to divide up the property, there is no telling what might happen. Since it has been so long, it should be fine, but if someone who claims to be descended from Ben MacDonald shows up, well, you never know what might happen."

Colin sat back in his chair. "You are just a ray of sunshine then, aren't you? So, there is an outside chance now someone could challenge the whole thing if I go to divide and sell the property? Someone connected to a family from almost 200 years ago? Or that we could find some old rocks that stop all human progress? What a country we live in. Geez, at this point, I think I will take my chances. By the way, who is the owner of the other large tract next to mine?"

"I've done some research on this one as well. The owner in the county tax system is shown as Blue Ridge Services, LLC. The principal is…Rufus Bryant. Somewhat of a local kingpin, don't know a lot about him, the family has been involved in a lot of activities over the years, some of which are actually legit."

Colin thought, turned to Jack. "Do I need to be concerned with Rufus Bryant?"

Chapter 15

For Luis, it fed his family – plus, it kept them alive. The bags under his eyes and the greying of the ever-thinning hair told the story of a man aging much faster than his 35 years should have shown. The stress of having to constantly look the other way and the consequences to his family if this was discovered were all too real. He had thought of sneaking away with the remainder of his family in the middle of the night, but THEY would still find him. So, sleeping during the day, he left for what his wife thought was a legitimate job cleaning and repairing boats at the local marina. It was cooler to work at night, he told her, in an obvious cover story. If she found out what he really did, then it could be the end for both of them.

The old houseboat chugged its way slowly across the lake. The other two men on board were in the same situation as Luis – but they were there merely for window dressing. They sat quietly at the stern, cast their lures into the darkness, trying to look interested. They would be the biggest ones surprised if they actually caught anything.

This was no ordinary houseboat. It was nearly 40 years old when the boss found it. It had been upgraded to appear as any normal houseboat traversing the lake, as there was nothing special about it – unless you knew what was in it.

The houseboat had been equipped with a small, cramped space behind the sleeping quarters in the front of the boat. It was big enough for 10 people without cargo and 5 with. Although the ferries only involving people were the most profitable, any time he was dealing with people, there were always potential complications. Cocaine didn't try to run.

The boat had left the small marina just outside Flowery Branch at about 11 PM, within an hour after the pickup truck with the small utility trailer had pulled up beside the dock. The security guard who normally worked this time of night was always in need of a little extra money and was pleased to take a break when he saw the truck approaching, especially when it involved a $100 bill being pressed into his hand.

It hadn't taken long to load the cargo. First, the large bricks of cocaine which filled up half of the space, then one by one, each of the girls was loaded, beginning with the biggest. They fit better that way. After loading, the boat left the marina quietly and moved its way slowly to the middle of the lake. It took about 90 minutes to travel the distance of the lake.

Their journey had started two days earlier when they had been separated from their families at the border by the coyotes. It was pretty simple – the choice was to let the girls go, or they would be left in the desert to die. Since most had no money, it was also a fitting business exchange for the perfectly fake ID cards they would receive in return. Two days later, and here they were.

Once the boat had crossed the lake and went under the last bridge, they cut the lights on the boat. Up in this part of the lake, neighbors were usually more suspicious of old houseboats lumbering through the dark, and the channel they had to navigate was much narrower, making it easy to identify if questioned.

Soon, after the exchange of a quick radio message, the boat took a left turn into a small cove. It was much more dangerous this time, as the lake was at its lowest point in years. In fact, it had not been this low since its impoundment over 50 years earlier.

5 minutes later, the boat had negotiated the small cove and was safely inside a large hangar-type dock that also was the lower level to a large, expansive house looking out over the water below.

The process was the same. Each child, usually a mixture of girls and boys – most were 16 or younger, with some as young as 10, was given a quick medical check, shots, and, most importantly, implanted with a small chip. Having finished this, each was sorted to the final destination – some would be going to the several estate homes located just a few miles away in the mountains, and some would travel as far as North Carolina, Tennessee, and even Virginia. At 7 the next morning, a small convoy of vans would pull out of the fenced yard next door with their special cargo. To the casual observer, it was nothing more than service vans rolling out for the day. For a few, especially the rich and powerful men, were willing to pay top dollar for quality – they knew what the vans were for - and that was what was being delivered.

Chapter 16

Rufus Bryant sat back in the big leather chair that was the center of his office. He leaned back, the chair creaking from the 300 pounds it was never meant to support. He looked around the room. There was a matching leather sofa against the wall. Above it hung a non-descript painting that had been hung years before and forgotten about. The paneled walls gave a cozy feel to the room, along with the beige carpet that probably needed to be replaced years ago. In the corner, next to a door leading to a small bathroom, was a well-stocked bar, which was always ready to entertain friends or colleagues that happened to stop by.

On his desk was a picture of him from his college football days at UGA. Beside that was another photo of him with his two grandsons – from ten years ago, the last time he saw them. On the wall behind him hung a picture of him with an elk he had killed years ago while hunting in Montana, right beside the rack hung on the wall. His desk was organized in chaos. One could barely see the desk for the papers, which formed one interlocked pile that only opened up to allow room for a computer monitor and keyboard. And, of course, the ashtray with a half-smoked cigar lying in it. When the cigar wasn't resting there, its second home was in Rufus' mouth.

His wife was the one who had the place decorated – right before she did what the first two had done took off and left him.

Rufus was a giant of a man – in more ways than one. He was physically imposing – his large stature was able to hide his weight well. Few people had crossed him and not regretted doing so.

But his physical stature was not all that was big about Rufus – he was one of the most powerful men in the county. His business ventures were wide and varied – and some of them legal.

This family business was now five generations old. Their family had been involved in some sort of business venture in this area since before the Civil War. Rufus' great-granddad had taken a small, run-down dry goods store and turned it into a thriving hardware & building materials distributorship that had supplied lumber and materials to houses throughout the region. Once the lake was built, Rufus's dad expanded the business to include real estate and property maintenance services for the multitude of weekend and summer places that dotted not only the shores of the lake but throughout the mountains to the north all the way to Asheville and Knoxville. The ventures paid off.

No one in the family was sure where it started, but somewhere in the recent past, the realization was made that more money could be made doing business in the shadows. At first, Rufus's granddad discovered that the abundance of corn in the area was much more valuable when converted to the liquid state and sold in quart and pint jars. The skill had been brought to these hills generations before. After many run-ins with the law, Jesse Bryant would do time in federal prison for his shenanigans. While there, he put forth a good front of reform, but in the end, he used the time to grow his network and craft a business model for the "other side of the enterprise."

By the time Rufus Bryant's dad, George Bryant, had taken the reins of the family business, they had had a whole network of moonshine operations, and as the need and demand for tax-free liquor died down, the still was replaced by other gigs involving the transport and sale of marijuana, cocaine, heroin, and even meth.

Over the past five years, another money-making venture had presented itself, to which Rufus was at first reluctant about getting involved – after all, his operation was mainly regional in scope, but this was something that far more sinister and was much more dangerous – human beings. Not just any humans but young girls. Rufus had at first said no, as even he had some scruples. Given his connections to the drug cartels, however, and their ability to make life difficult for him, he had no choice. Soon, he found himself fully connected to a nationwide network that, at its core, was pure evil and made moonshining look like a Sunday afternoon hobby.

Today, Rufus was not in a good mood. He looked over at the glass jar that was set on the small end table next to the sofa. To the casual observer, it looked simply like the remains of an ashtray or grill that had been cleaned out. He knew what it actually contained, which were some of the rarest metals known on earth, with the largest deposits known to exist on the North American continent sitting right under his feet. Well, sort of. He already had lined up several investors willing to take a shot at the extraction plan. He had already convinced several of the other neighbors in the area to sell the mineral rights on their property, but the last thing he needed was another Childers showing up. Thinking he would clearly sell the property to him, the whole game changed when he said no. This had happened before with the elder Childers, and soon he was no longer an issue.

Soon, his main investors from China would be paying visits and want to know what progress had been made. He had to move quickly to try and scare this newcomer into leaving town with his tail tucked between his legs.

Chapter 17

Colin sipped on a cup of coffee and ate his usual breakfast of a bagel with cream cheese. He wondered sometimes if anyone here even knew what one was but was pleasantly surprised to find some at the local grocer. He took a bit of the bagel, which tasted divine. It had been a long time. Back in Chicago, he either ate out or gave his housekeeper a list of things to buy. Thinking back to the incident a few days before still had him shaking his head. What was bugging someone so about his being here? As he often did, he found himself overthinking the situation. Other than the incident in the diner when he first arrived in town, he could think of nothing else that would cause him to be targeted for harassment. Although it took some getting used to, he had started speaking to people he saw around the community and engaging in small talk. He had just gobbled down the last morsel when his phone started to vibrate. It was a local number that looked familiar, but Colin couldn't quite place who it was.

"Good morning, this is Colin."

"Hey, Colin! Junior-Junior Simmons here. Hope you are doing well. Just wondering what you are up to today."

Colin paused for a moment. He had met Junior twice, and the last time had talked extensively about hunting. Maybe he wanted to take him deer hunting or something like that.

"Let me check my calendar", he said as he loudly shuffled the pages of the book he was reading. "Really nothing, to tell you the truth. I had a meeting with my board of directors this morning, but something came up, and they couldn't meet". He tried to inject some levity into the conversation.

Junior didn't catch it.

"Great! I was hoping you would come up to the farm today – want to show you around a little. Pick you up in about 30 minutes."

"Are you asking or telling?" Colin was put off a little by Junior's assertiveness.

"Well, I guess you don't hafta go, but what else are you gonna do today, anyway?"

His newfound friend was right. What was he going to do today?

"Okay, you've convinced me. How do you get to your place?"

"No worries, I'll pick you up. Thirty minutes. And also – dress for the outdoors. No ties or wing-tips."

A half-hour later, Colin could hear the growl of the diesel truck pull up in front of the house, and after a lesson from Junior on how to properly mount and dismount the front seat, which sat at least 4 feet off the ground. After driving through the country for what seemed to be an eternity, they pulled off onto a gravel drive that was marked by a couple of old rust mailboxes. About a mile back in the woods, suddenly, the road opened into a large clearing, with a large stately brick house sitting in the middle. Colin had a puzzled look on his face at the spaciousness of the place.

"What were you expecting? A van down by the river? Best way to get yourself shot is to advertise too much of what you got. Come on in, got a fresh cup of coffee brewing. I will get you a cup."

Colin followed Junior into the kitchen, where the smell of coffee drifted through the air. Beside it sat a plate full of – bagels surrounding a bowl of cream cheese.

"Hope you like them – didn't know whether you ate bagels or not."

Colin broke out in a smile and chuckled inwardly at the irony of the moment. Bagels. Who woulda have thought… Junior Simmons with bagels.

They soon found themselves sitting in two big rocking chairs on the covered patio that extended across the back of the house. The view was spectacular – a couple hundred yards away was a large pond, then beyond it, a lush green pasture seemed to stretch forever until it met the stark blue wall of mountains that gave the Blue Ridge its name.

"We will get going in a bit after everybody gets here. The missus had to run out for something should be right back. Also expect someone else to join us today." He made the last statement with a certain twinkle in his eye.

Colin started to press a little, but instead, they found themselves involved in the now-required small talk. Which he was starting to get comfortable with. He was no longer guarded sharing how he ended up here, including his former life. He was surprised to learn that Junior himself was actually Ralph Anderson Simmons, Jr, and in a similar story to Colin, had also ended up here, other than Junior had grown up here.

"So, looks like you did okay for yourself," Colin replied, looking around.

"Yep, it was just a matter of finally putting the past behind me. This place was also my grandparents' old farm, so I just kind of took up where they left off. After Linda's folks died when she was nine, she came to live here with us. I became somewhat of a big brother to her." Junior sat back, the chair creaking under his weight. "Yep, that young lady has been through a lot.."

"Sinceyou brought it up, care to share?" Colin was growing more curious.

Before Junior could answer, the golden retriever that had been lying at their feet suddenly perked up and began to wag her tail and bark loudly.

"Millie is my alarm – she can hear any car. Don't have to worry about intruders. They must be here."

He and Colin walked around the house to the driveway as the car pulled in. Although older, Junior's wife Tracy was still quite attractive and seemed quiet and reserved, but Colin quickly learned she was the perfect match for Junior's boisterous personality.

"Colin, Tracy. Tracy, Colin." The two shook hands. Colin hadn't noticed the other passenger, who slowly emerged from the car and appeared a little apprehensive.

"Junior, you DIDN'T tell me we had other guests today. Okay, Junior, this looks like one of your operations" It was Linda. From the look on her face, Colin could tell she was as surprised as he was. I guess now he would get a chance to ask her directly.

Tracy broke the awkward silence. "Pleased to meet you." Then, turning to Junior, she said, "You didn't tell Colin that Linda was also coming today?"

"I didn't want him to back out. I guess I can say the same for Linda, right?"

Colin looked over at Linda - they didn't have to say wa word to know each other's thoughts at the moment. It was pretty obvious what Junior and Tracy were up to, but for Colin, it didn't upset him too bad.

Tracy broke the long, awkward silence. "I got us some stuff for a picnic today – Junior I need you to help me get this stuff in the house?" Colin could tell that she was far stronger than first impressions could tell.

Colin looked back at Linda. She had made quite the transition. The last time he saw her, she was dressed smartly in a business suit, with her hair pulled up in a bun. Today, her hair was pulled back in a ponytail, wearing a pair of perfectly fitting jeans, boots, and a flannel shirt that did a poor job of concealing what appeared to be a very athletic yet curvaceous figure. Topping it all off was a baseball cap with the distinctive large A on the front.

"Had no idea you would be here," Colin said rather awkwardly. "What did you mean by 'this looks like one of your operations'"?

"Oh, Junior has always been looking out for his 'little sister'. It's
_"

"You two ready to go? We're burning daylight." Junior and Tracy
appeared again with a rather large basket of food. They walked over
to the barn, where two ATVs were sitting, ready to go. Tracy strapped
a basket on the back of one of the ATVs.

"Me and the missus will ride on this one. You two got the other
one."

Colin looked rather dumbfounded. He had never driven one
before, but now was not the time to show his lack of skill.

Normally full of confidence, Collin began to feel uneasy. Put him
in a boardroom, and he was right at home. Problem here was – he had
never been ON a four-wheeler, let alone drive one.

He tried to fake it. Nonchalantly, he threw one leg over and sat
down. This should be pretty easy, he thought. I will just go slow until
I Learn how to operate it.

Junior pulled away, with Tracy and the picnic basket precariously
perched on the back. Colin just sat there, still figuring out how to start
the darn thing. He dared not even look at Linda.

"Let me guess. You probably didn't need one of these in Chicago.
Get off, I'll drive."

Suddenly feeling like a 14-year-old on his first job, Colin climbed
off, and watched as Linda mounted the ATV like she owned it. She

reached up, turned the key, pushed a button on the handlebar, and it roared to life.

"Okay, think you can get on this thing? You will need to hang on."

Colin climbed on the back. He knew the obvious place he wanted to hang on but instead reached to grab ahold of the small gear rack behind him.

"That won't do it. You'll get thrown off. Here, give me your hands." Linda said as she reached behind her.

Colin felt like the 14-year-old again, except this time at his first dance.

"Put them here – I promise I won't bite, nor do I have cooties," Linda said with a big grin on her face.

Colin reached and put both hands on her hips. She reached and pulled his hand around her waist.

"See, we need to be one unit. That helps us to be more balanced." Colin caught the faint hint of citrus from the perfume she was wearing.

The first five minutes of the ride were terrifying, but Colin gradually relaxed. Apparently, Linda had done this many times before as they sped down the small gravel road, following behind Junior and Tracy. In a few weeks, these woods would be painted with a tapestry of gold, red, brown and green. It would be almost too much for the senses to bear. As for now, however, it was the peak of summer, and even with the heat, the breeze generated as they rode along felt great on their faces.

They slowed and followed Junior as he swerved off the road down an even smaller trail. "Hang on. This is where it gets fun!" Linda said as she followed him. They slowed a bit, as the road was not as well defined, and occasionally, a tree branch would slap them as they drove through the brush.

Before he could really prepare, they dove down a hill, Colin hanging on for dear life as they burst through the trees straight into a creek. The water splashed up and over them as the motorized horse they were on hit the creek bottom and scooted across. Then, back up the other side.

"You still back there? We will be there soon. Made this trip many times." Lind shouted over the noise of the engine.

They climbed up what appeared to be a huge hill or a small mountain, then skirted along what appeared to Colin to be a ridge of some sort.

Five minutes later, the trail opened up onto a large outcropping of rock…

"Welcome to Preacher's Mountain," Junior exclaimed as they dismounted. "Wasn't that ride worth it?"

Colin looked around. It was, without a doubt, the most beautiful view he had ever seen. The hilltop was void of any trees, just covered with an open meadow. What trees there were ringed the clearing, providing an arena for the hundreds of wildflowers blooming in the meadow. Colin walked over toward the overhang, where Tracy had been unpacking the picnic basket.

"Take a look at this." Junior had grabbed a pair of binoculars. He handed them to Colin while pointing at the ridgeline off in the distance. "Amicalola".

"So what is it?" Colin asked. Then, as he panned the ridgeline, he saw it. A long ribbon of water that appeared came off the top of the mountain, dropping to the valley floor below.

"We are fortunate - usually, in the summer, it is hard to see it for the leaves. You get a treat today. The conditions are perfect."

"Y'all hungry? Let's eat." Tracy, who hadn't said two words, had been busy spreading out the picnic she had so carefully prepared and packed.

Linda was right. This was not the first time they had done this. There was a small circle of stones sat in the middle of the rock outcrop, along with several Adirondack chairs. There was also a small wooden table, on which sat a couple of plates piled high with sandwiches and fried chicken. The most amazing thing was how this much food fit in that tiny picnic basket.

They were ravenous after the morning's adventure and talked little while eating. The sun had warmed the rock they were sitting on, and after finishing the meal, as they talked about everything from sports to the weather, Colin's eyes began to get heavy, and he dozed for a second until he heard Linda. "Don't move", she said.

Junior had already seen it. Apparently, they were not the only ones who loved the warm rock they were seated on.

Colin looked around, wondering what the alarm was all about. Then his eyes fastened on the nice fat copperhead that had come to partake in the picnic, parking itself next to Colin's chair.

He wanted to get up and run, but Junior motioned him to sit still. A few minutes later, he calmly got up and appeared with a small telescoping rod and a hook on one end. He reached down, scooped up the intruder and walked him to the edge of the woods.

"Whew. That was close." Colin said as he was able to breathe again.

"I agree. Junior, you did that like you owned it." Linda added, with a bit of shakiness in her voice.

"Oh, Bertha wouldn't bite. She's too lazy," Junior quipped as he spits a stream of tobacco juice. "She just wanted to be with us."

"Come on – We have some more riding to do." Junior had jumped up, helping Tracy repack the picnic basket.

Two hours passed quickly as they seemed to explore every corner of Junior's place. After stopping for another break, Linda turned to Colin with a big smile, "Okay, lets now see what you can do on this thing."

They had stopped in another clearing that was once a pasture. Colin was tentative at first but soon found himself pretty adept at guiding the mass of steel and rubber around the trail that ran around the field's perimeter. On his third lap around, he looked up to see Linda beside him on the other ATV.

"Wanna race? Catch me if you can!" She took off.

Colin twisted the throttle, trying to stay up with her, which was an impossibility, or so he thought…

He realized he was gaining on her, then passed her at the last second before screeching to a stop in a cloud of dust in front of Junior and Tracy.

"Bud, having never driven one before, looks like you a pretty fast learner!" Junior shouted as he winked at the ladies standing nearby. "Since it's starting to get dark, I guess we better head back. Plus, with deer season starting tomorrow, I need to get my rest so I can be out in the woods at the crack of dawn!"

The way back was much easier, as they soon found themselves back on the gravel road they started out on.

Tracy volunteered to drive them back to town, and they continued to chat all the way.

As they pulled into the parking lot at the county building, where Linda had left her car, She said, "Tracy, just let us both out here. I will get Colin back to his place."

They climbed into her car, and as they left the parking lot, an awkward silence sat until Linda broke by exclaiming, "Please understand that was not my idea today. Junior means well."

Colin quickly replied. "Nor mine as well. I take it this is not the first time Junior has done this?"

"Nope. It has happened three times before. Somehow, he is worried about me being alone for the rest of my life. I guess he has some idea to get us together…"

Colin had thought the same thing but dared not voice it. Instead, he replied, "I agree, Looks like he means well, and looks like we did have a good time today."

"Oh yeah. That we did. That we did."

They pulled up in front of the house and sat there for a few minutes. Linda finally spoke. "Hope you have a good night."

"You too. Safe travels. Talk to you later."

Colin sat down on the front porch for a moment as he watched her drive away. Something inside him stirred for the first time in many years, and he was reminded that somewhere deep inside, he was still a beating heart.

Even though he was tired from the day's activities, he had too much on his mind to try and sleep right now. *Maybe I will do a little reading,* he thought, as he opened up the journal again to the next marked place in the book…

Chapter 18

Colin arrived early for the meeting. Colin walked into the large room, which was in the old courthouse. The main courtroom, which had been the scene of many cases, both mundane and titillating, had taken place here. Now, with the new courthouse, this space had been remodeled specifically for the county's various boards to meet. There were a dozen rows of hard, refinished theater-style seats that matched the oak paneling covering the walls. Hanging on the walls around the room were framed photos of former commissioners, sheriffs, and other elected officials who had served the county. Up front was a raised platform, with a large, arced dais behind where the board sat. In front of the dais, at the exact center of the arc, was a large podium from where speakers could address and interact with the board.

Colin was early enough so that he was one of the first ones in the room. There were a couple of staff, busy preparing for the event which was to shortly take place. The excitement surrounding his project had overshadowed the disconcerting and seemingly random harassment with which he had been targeted. At a preliminary meeting two weeks earlier, Colin had presented the plans to the board, and they had voted unanimously to consider the proposal for approval at this evening's meeting. There were a couple of the board members that had that had raised concerns, but he had completed additional research, and was prepared this evening to answer any additional questions. He arrived 30 minutes early for the meeting, hoping maybe to catch a couple of the board members who had verbally voiced their support for the project and thank them.

Ten minutes after he sat down, Steve appeared and sat down next to him. Although Colin would pitch the general concept of the project this evening, Steve would be the one to provide the technical details, as well as share some preliminary sketches of the project.

As the meeting time approached, Colin felt he was standing out more, as he was way overdressed, as this was nowhere as formal as he envisioned it being. Also, there were several "regulars" who also arrived early and had nothing else better to do than to sit through the monthly meeting. A group of scouts was outside the chambers, rehearsing their procession and flag presentation that would mark the start of the meeting, which, in essence, defined the character of communities all across the nation.

"Glad to see you found yourself here," said Linda as she approached Colin. Once again, she was all business. Whatever informality that had developed between them over the last few weeks was once again replaced with a very stoic bearing. She gave him a copy of the board's agenda – "As you can see, you are down a ways in the agenda – there are a couple of things we have to deal with first. You will need to be patient. We will get to you."

That was the understatement of the century. Besides all the usual pomp & circumstance that goes with a meeting like this, it took nearly 20 minutes just to get to the business at hand. There was really only one issue the board had to deal with prior to getting to his item - tethered dogs. Somebody, obviously a newcomer, had complained about too many dogs being chained up outside and had taken it upon herself to change her new community's culture. Needless to say, this didn't go over well. It wasn't so much about the dogs being chained, as most of the folks in the community didn't follow this practice anyway. What was wrong with it was they didn't want or need the government telling them what they could or could not do with their animals.

By thei time the meeting started, the room was packed, with standing room only. Most of the folks you could tell were the locals, while a smaller group all clustered together toward one side of the room, and were mostly the "transplants" that had recently moved here, mainly from Atlanta, but some from Florida and any number of "Yankee" states which meant pretty much anything north of Georgia.

Colin didn't know where he belonged or quite how he got into this mess. Knowing this was going to take some time, he started to move outside to allow the discussion to take place but was concerned he would not get his seat back, so he stayed put.

He listened half-heartedly, but surprisingly, most of the attendees just sat quietly, nodding their heads and quietly whispering amongst themselves as a few spoke on both sides of the issue. After about 15 minutes, the chairman ended the discussion, and the vote was taken quickly, approving the proposal.

The chairman called for a 10-minute break to allow for a transition to the next topic and the raucous crowd to clear the room. Colin expected to see most of the people getting up to leave, which about a third of the crowd did, but when the meeting was called back into session, Colin noticed that the room pretty much remained. Had all these remained just to hear about his project?

Colin leaned over to Steve. "Do you think this crowd is here for us?" Whispered Colin.

"No doubt", Steve answered. "I've been in a lot of meetings like this..."

"We will now consider the next item, which is the proposed development in the War Hill community. I will recognize our county manager, Linda Simmons, as well as Mr. Colin Childers and the project's designer, Steve Grant."

For the next 5 minutes or so, Linda and Steve provided a full and comprehensive coverage of the project. Even though the presentation went well, Colin could sense the tension in the room, as it was now obvious that the crowd that remained was there for one purpose – to try and stop the project.

"Thank you, Linda, Mr. Grant. I will now open our public input portion of this discussion. Due to the late hour, I am asking that we set a 10-minute time limit for each side – those in favor and those opposed, to speak." Whispers erupted all over the audience, and someone yelled from the back, "Let us speak!"

"Mr. Chairman, I disagree!" The portly gentleman, who had been distracted all evening, suddenly came to life. "These good people came here tonight with the expectation of voicing their opinion. I don't feel we should take away their constitutional right to speak. I say let them all say something that wants to talk." Applause broke out throughout the audience.

"Commissioner Price. No one is losing their right to free speech. I just know that there are many signed up to speak, and given the late hour, I was merely suggesting…"

Another board member interrupted. "I don't see the harm in letting everyone talk.."

Sensing the tide was turning against him, the chairman relented with a half grin on his face. "You get your way. We'll let anyone that has something to say to say it."

Although the chair tried to alternate between those for and those opposed to the project, after about 3 speakers spoke in support of what Colin wanted to do, it was obvious that the rest of the crowd was there to voice their opposition. In addition to this, small signs, apparently from out of nowhere, began to appear. "Say NO!" was the simple message being displayed on the signs. Colin shook his head. This was not new to him – a "grassroots" movement – right. He was from Chicago, after all.

As each speaker got up to give his input, it appeared that speakers from the two sides pretty much echoed the same points over and over. And the body language of the commissioners was almost comical to watch. It appeared that one was checking something on his phone, another was paying rapt attention, hanging on every word that was said, and the others just seemed not to be too engaged in anything.

Then, just when Colin thought it would never end, it did. Suddenly, the balding portly man, who looked to be one heartbeat away from the grave, inquired, "Do we have anyone else here that would like to speak for or against the proposed ordinance?" A short silence followed, to which the chair quickly took advantage, rapping his gavel on the dais. An hour had passed since people had started talking.

"The question before us this evening pertains to the proposed ordinance. What is the board's pleasure?" About 50 black and red signs suddenly rose into the air across the crowded chambers.

"Mr. Chair," the commissioner that seemed to be the most engaged with hearing about the project, including asking several questions, spoke up. "IT is clear to me that there is a need for a project such as this. It will be good for the continued progress of our community, and the new homes and retail will add to our tax base. This part of the county has been largely isolated from the rest of the county, so it is fitting that they get to join the 21st century. I move. We approve the development."

As soon as he shut up, another chimed in – "I second the motion."

"Okay, we now have a motion and a second to approve the motion. Any discussion?" There began to be hushed murmurs throughout the room. Some understood that there needed to be a vote, others were confused, thinking it had already been approved. Soon, the hushed murmurs turned into outright conversations, and a couple of men in the back began to yell at the board - "Just Say NO!!!"

The whole room was descending into chaos. The chair was losing control of the entire meeting. The din went on for a couple of minutes until, finally the chair regained control.

"As you all can see, this is a very contentious issue. Again, do any of the commissioners have any comments or questions about the issue before we vote this evening?"

For the next five minutes, each of the board members gave a short silique on why he could or could not vote for the measure. Finally, when three of the commissioners had expressed themselves, The Chair, who Colin had now figured out was Jerry Dixon, turned to the last remaining commissioner, who had open this can of worms earlier by insisting all should speak, Gary Doster. Gary was well known as a folksy former pastor who could both create chaos and restore order to a room full of people. He thrived for scenes such as this. The locals loved him, for the most part. The newcomers couldn't stand him. When he started speaking, a creepy hush fell across the room.

"Mr. Chairman," he started with a firm yet soothing voice. "You know, I don't have a dog in this hunt..." A few chuckles erupted around the room. "I have looked at this plan, and I think there are a couple of things that need to be looked at. I appreciate Mr. Childers, who recently moved here from, I believe, Chee-cago, to take the time to develop this. He comes from a fine family that has been in this county for generations."

Again, murmurs floated up around the room. "But," he continued, "For this reason, Mr. Chair, I would like to see this tabled until our fine and capable county manager can bring us something we can vote on." A couple of the other board members appeared to nod in agreement.

Colin glanced over at Linda, who he could see display some hint of a sarcastic smile. He looked back at Doster just in time to see him nod and wink at someone on the other side of the room.

A couple of other commissioners joined Commissioner Doster in his assessment, and soon, the motion to approve the development was replaced with one to table it until the next meeting.

"All those for tabling the motion to the next meeting, say aye." A chorus of ayes burst forth. And those opposed say, Nay". One sole voice, plus that of the chair, was the only no-vote. Whatever plans Colin had to start the next week just flew out the window.

The man that Colin had spotted earlier was gone. Colin's anger began to well up inside him. "Mr. Chairman, may I ask..."

"Mr. Childers, we are not taking any more input from the audience. You may discuss this later with the staff."

By this time, the place was emptying out, and after a couple of minutes, the gavel banged, adjourning the meeting.

Colin immediately approached the large dais, but none of the commissioners seemed interested in talking to him at the moment. Instead, he strode over to the other side, where Linda was engaged in conversation with another gentleman, who Colin assumed to be an attorney.

Colin interrupted them. "What the hell just happened? You told me this would have no problem passing!" He was getting more animated, with all the frustration of the evening beginning to boil over. "What is it about this place? You can't tell me that this was not orchestrated. And just who was that man that got up and left…"

"Colin, let me deal with this other situation. I have a lot to say but won't right now…"

"You bet you have a lot you need to tell me. I look FORWARD to talking with you about this."

With that, Colin and Steve left the meeting.

"I guess you will need to call everyone and hold off on your plans," Steve mentioned quietly, his initial anger subdued somewhat.

"Yep, nothing we can do now but wait," replied Colin as he spotted two gentlemen at the corner of the building. Colin pulled Steve back behind one of the columns.

"Who is that man with the commissioner? I saw him in the meeting earlier. I noticed he got up and left before it ended."

"Oh, him – I believe that is the Rufus Bryant you asked me about at our meeting. I asked around. He is well known throughout the county, but not always for the right reasons. I owns the property next to yours. From what I have known and found out recently about him, about half the county owes him something. It wouldn't surprise me to find he is behind what happened tonight."

Apparently, the two gentlemen became aware that Colin was nearby and quickly got in their cars and drove away.

Rufus Bryant thought Colin. *I need to remember that name.*

The ride home helped to cool off a little as the cool evening air blew in the open window of his car. Pulling into the driveway and walking up to the front door, something caught his eye. Laying in front of the door was a shoebox with a note attached to it. The note had one crude message written on it:

YANKEE, GO HOME, OR YOU ARE NEXT.

Colin carefully cracked the lid on the box. There was a dead fish inside.

Chapter 19

"I'm not sure why we are even having this conversation!" Colin angrily flipped his phone shut, ending the call. Linda had called, trying to explain the dynamics from the night before. Colin knew what he had witnessed, as it was pretty much normal where he came from to see this kind of stuff happen. He certainly didn't think a community tucked away in this sleepy corner of Georgia could pull off something like this. His mistake was assuming they couldn't. Colin had become a master at watching his back. When you deal with the things he had to deal with in Chicago, you had to. He should have suspected something was up when the crowd hung around for his proposal. He should have anticipated but didn't. What was happening to him? First it was the dismissal, which he didn't see coming, then this. He was mad, but mainly at himself for letting his guard down. Whatever good vibes he was getting about living here was replaced anew with suspicion. He felt alone again – even whatever good thoughts he had about Linda had been replaced with sourness. He was ready to quit and let them have it all.

As had always been his weakness, his Achilles heel, he would tend to give up too quickly. Now what? He could just take the offer that had been presented to him last week, sell everything outright, and head back to Chicago. He was still employable – maybe. He had burned some bridges with the way he left Humantix, but there were other positions, other places for him. The doubts began to creep in again. Then again, there was Atlanta. After all, it was not far to the north side, where there were plenty of opportunities. Maybe I should look for a recruiter… but then again, with no network and no contacts in the area, an almost 50-year-old newcomer wouldn't stand a chance.

Any warm and fuzzy feelings about It?

The moon had now risen, and even though it wasn't full, there was enough light reflecting off the water to illuminate where he was walking. His eyes were also fully adjusted so he could see clearly as he walked. His thoughts wandered back to what had just transpired. The move back here had made it harder and harder to hold in the fact that his dad had been missing most of his life, and there was no one anywhere who could fill the chasm in the middle of his soul.

The shadows cast by the moon formed some spooky shapes. Pieces of driftwood lay along the bank, and occasionally, there were the remnants of a tree stump, long ago cut down to make room for the onslaught over a half-century before of the invading waters.

That's strange, Colin thought, as he spotted what looked like a crab half buried next to one of the stumps. He squatted down to have a closer look, thinking there were no crabs this far inland. He reached down gingerly, trying to uncover the newly discovered treasure. It didn't take long before he sat down in horror as he stared at the remains of a human hand.

The "hand" became the talk of the town over the next couple of weeks. Although something like this would have garnered little attention in Atlanta or Chicago, the local newspaper had picked up the story to include all the possible theories as to its origin. With the lake's almost 60 years of existence, there had been plenty of tales and legends that had developed. As with them, many opinions and theories were circulating – some claiming the hand belonged to the "Lady of the Lake," a ghostly story of a wreck early in the history of the lake, in which the young driver perished in the waters but was never found. The most likely theory was that it was from the many old family cemeteries or grave plots left behind by some earlier generation that were long forgotten and covered by the waters.

Colin had received a phone call this morning – after forensic analysis, it had been determined the hand was at least 150 years old – so it confirmed there was really nothing to it.

Once the news came out about the age of the hand, Rufus Bryant breathed a sigh of relief. For him, the discovery had not been a good one. Investigators and curiosity seekers prowling around the area and possibly discovering his operation had not only made him nervous but had also raised the anxiety of those who had put him in business and could just as easily shut him down – with him joining the other unknown bodies in the lake.

The discovery had accomplished a couple of other things as well. First, Colin's roller-coaster relationship with the area was back on again. As he had circulated the last couple of weeks, he had become somewhat of a celebrity around town, even for some of the ones who had spoken out against him at the board meeting the previous month. He had noticed now, on his weekly trip to the diner, that more people were warming up to the project. What it also told him was how much the opposition to his project had been manufactured – from what he had deduced, likely by Rufus Bryant. The more he had asked questions about the man around town, the more he was getting a negative impression of the man.

Finally, Linda and he were back on speaking terms. She had called a couple of days after the discovery of the hand had made the news, and later that day, had shown up unannounced with a pot full of chili and a 12-pack.

"Well – aren't you the romantic type? You appear to know the way to man's heart is through his stomach."

"Had to make amends some way." She said with a half grin.

Colin soon had a fire going in the fire pit on the patio, and for the next couple of hours, they laughed and shared stories from their past. As the fire began to die down, they both became silent, and the same thoughts began to enter their heads.

"Guess I better get going. Early day tomorrow." Linda said sort of awkwardly as she got up.

Colin agreed although he could think of nothing better that would happen tomorrow that should end their time together tonight.

Linda gathered up the stuff she had brought with her.

"Let me help get those things to the car." He picked up the slow cooker which still held the remains of the chili. "You are a pretty good cook—"

"Well, didn't expect that, did you?"

Colin thought, *uh-oh, blew it here.*

They walked in awkward silence to Linda's car. She opened the back door for him.

"Oh, almost forgot to tell you – my uncle would like to meet you. He has some interesting things to share that may tell you a little more about the place." She said, trying to prolong their conversation.

"That sounds good – just let me know when." Colin walked with her around the car.

"Thank you for a wonderful evening. She said, "I'm here if you need anything."

Colin smiled and held open his arms for a goodbye hug. He knew they wanted more but had to settle for this. They stood there for a long moment; then Colin slowly turned his head. As if on cue, Linda did the same, as their lips touched. Tentative at first, but then the kiss deepened.

"Whoo. Where did that come from? Gotta scoot!" Linda said as she broke off the embrace. "I'll let you know when we can visit my uncle."

Colin felt like a fourteen-year-old after his first dance. He smiled as she shut the door, then rolled down the window. She stuck out her hand and touched Colin's.

"It's complicated, you know?" And with that, she pulled away.

Colin slept like a baby, even with the chili dog barking most of the night.

Chapter 20

"Come on; I want you to come somewhere with me." Linda had called Colin. "How long since you have been to an old-fashioned camp meeting?"

"You know, I am really not the religious type," Colin explained as he tried to figure out a way to get out of this.

"It doesn't matter," Linda replied "It will be fun. Besides, this is the last day, and we get to eat afterwards."

Colin finally relented. "Okay, you win. I guess one night won't make me a fanatic."

There was another reason for Colin's reluctance – it had nothing to do with God. In fact, he wasn't AGAINST religion; it was more of an indifference. Although he and his mom had attended services briefly after his father's death, they gradually stopped. By the time he had finished school and went into the army, the role of the church in his life had long disappeared.

But another reason for not going – the past. The very thing he was going to wa the same event they had been at many years before – when he lost his dad. So many things were happening now that brought back the sad events of that day – would this be one more reminder of that?

Either way, Colin was torn. On one hand, the more he could blend into the community, the better. This included the burgeoning relationship that was building with Linda. On the other hand, he had to be extra careful – his therapist had cautioned him when he left

Chicago that there would be lots of triggers, and experiencing these memories before he was ready could be devastating.

Unlike the campground he had seen a few weeks ago, which was quiet and lonely, Today it was a beehive of activity.

"Our family used to own a tent here," Linda said, as Colin looked puzzled at her comments. "Oh, I don't mean literal 'tent,'" she said. "I guess that's what they called them in the early days, so that's what stuck."

Colin thought, *what do you call them, then, shacks?*

They really did look like shacks – They were crude structures thrown up for the truly American tradition of the camp meeting.

Colin followed Linda around as she stopped periodically to chat with some of the other folks there. Twenty minutes or so had passed when they found themselves sitting under the old arbor at the center. It had also come to life, as there were at last a hundred people crowded under the place. At the front, a makeshift band was playing some songs, and soon, the whole place was singing as the service got well underway. Finally, after about 20 minutes of singing, a young man stood up, and for the next thirty minutes or so, the audience was held in rapt attention as he talked. Colin was growing bored with it all until it seemed as if everything in the room had disappeared, and it was just him sitting there, with the young man talking directly at HIM. There was a clear message that he heard that shook him to his core. "God loves YOU – and there is not a thing you can do about it."

He had to get up. It was the strangest thing. Suddenly, everything was back to normal. He got up, squeezed by Linda, and soon found himself standing by one of the many oaks in the place, heart beating out of his chest. He stood that way for what seemed like a long time until he felt a touch on his shoulder. It was Linda.

"Hey – you okay? I thought maybe you had gotten sick."

"No, but you are going to think I am crazy, but.."

"Yes?"

"I think God just talked to me."

Chapter 21

The incident, for the moment, was soon forgotten. The service now ended, they walked with the others over to where the closing meal for the whole week would be served. For most of the week, families had, for the most part, eaten alone or only with one or two others. But this evening, the final service was done, and the endearing tradition that had been in place for over 100 years once again began – the final meal before they all departed.

The old marble-covered table that sat at the edge of the campground, near the adjacent church, was not covered with every imaginable dish. Several platters of chicken, BBQ, casseroles and potatoes of every kind were spread out before them.

Colin stood there for a moment. He wasn't sure if it was the incident earlier that had triggered it or the sudden rush of memories of a day long ago when he had stood at this very spot; he suddenly found himself frozen in place, really unable to do anything.

"I am beginning to get worried about you – let's eat." Linda took him by the hand and led him over to the table.

Whatever anxiety he was feeling was soon forgotten as they sat on the tailgate of Linda's SUV, munching quietly on a homemade biscuit.

"This is pretty good," Colin said as he began to feel full. "I'm glad you asked me to come."

"Sure thing – you said you wanted to feel more part of this place; well, this is the most central event we have every year, but since it brought back a lot of memories."

"It did, and not all good.." Colin would have continued, but they were suddenly aware of another presence joining them. Linda immediately felt uncomfortable.

"Hi – Colin stuck out a tentative hand. Linda's uneasiness was now becoming an angry look.

"Colin, been wanting to meet my new neighbor for awhile – Bryant – Rufus Bryant. Glad to finally meet you."

Colin, realizing who it was, broke out the immediate charm he had learned in the years of dealing with some of the biggest thugs in Chicago. "Well, Rufus Bryant. I've heard a lot about you. What can I do for you today?"

Both of them shared a lot of small talk over the next few minutes, each trying to outdo the other with charm. Before it could descend into something more, Linda cleared her throat and looked at Colin, giving him the "let's go" signal.

"What was THAT all about?" Colin asked Linda as they drove off. "Afraid I can't handle myself??"

Linda shot back, "That's not the issue. Rufus has a lot of power around here. I would rather just limit my contact with him as much as possible. If you have any further desire to get your development approved, I would suggest you do the same. A couple of our board members already seem beholden to him."

"Besides, he's not the one I wanted you to meet today. Well, didn't mind the part about God, but...

"Hi, Mom!" Out of nowhere, Linda was grabbed by a young boy, no more than 6 or 7. Walking up behind him were Junior and Tracy.

"Did he say – Mom?" Colin's expression surely showed his shock. "Okay, when were you planning to reveal this?"

"I've been trying to think of the right time, and I guess I thought this would be as good of a time as any. Luke – this is Mr. Childers. Mommy's new friend."

"Pleased to meet you, Mr. Childers." He stuck out his hand.

After hesitating for a moment, not knowing quite what to do, Colin responded, and Junior could have sworn he saw a tear in Colin's eye. Colin said, "Pleased to meet you, Luke."

Linda continued. "I adopted Luke three years ago. He was in foster care, and there was a shortage of adoptive families in the area. Junior and Tracy helped me out a lot with him. I wanted to wait and tell you when the time was right."

Colin appeared to be a little rattled. "Just understand, seeing him brings back so many memories… I mean… I was almost the same age when…You'll need to excuse me for a moment." Colin turned and walked away, over toward one of the big oaks.

Soon, he felt Junior's big hand on his shoulder, gently massaging it. "You okay?"

Colin nodded, then said, "Just a lot to take in. Lots of memories rekindled today, not all of them happy ones. You all will just have to bear with me."

Chapter 22

They were back at Junior's place. Tracy had fixed a big breakfast for them all. Luke had made buddies with Colin, and they were sitting on the patio, enjoying the warm sun and cool breezes this time of year brought. Colin was drawing Luke a picture.

"Thank y'all for coming back over this morning. Colin, after the encounter you and Linda had with Rufus Bryant last week, I feel like I need to get you a little more educated."

With a puzzled look on his face, Colin looked over at Linda. "Okay, I'm confused. You said Junior and you were cousins. I know everyone here appears to be related to each other, but..."

Linda laughed. "I am not a Bryant. My dad's sister married Rufus's dad. So, you don't need to worry yourself with that!"

Junior continued, "Rufus's and my grand-dad were brothers. Both of them got into a lot of trouble, and it ended badly for both of them. One of them ended up in prison for the rest of his life. My granddad, Lloyd Bryant, was killed in the shootout."

"Left without a father, the sheriff took a liking to him and took him under his wing. It turned his life around, as he was certain to go in the same direction as the rest of the Bryants. I am sitting here today in part because of what Sheriff Graham did for my dad. With his family all gone, I am the only one he has left."

Colin sat there silent for a moment, then replied, "That's great, Junior, but what does that have to do with why you asked us here today?"

Linda had mentioned him before, but with the aftermath of the meeting and finding the hand, there had not been any further discussion.

"Red and I were talking recently, and when I told him who you were, he was very excited and felt you needed to know some things. So, if you all are ready, we need to go see him."

Although he was not expecting it, Colin was ready to learn as much as he could.

After a short drive, they found themselves sitting in the living room of a small frame house, stuck back in the woods near town. Colin looked around; the room was filled with all the remembrances one would expect from a career in law enforcement. It was obvious that the former sheriff had been highly respected in a community where often the local sheriff had found himself with many enemies.

"I want to tell you how we got to this point." The big man pulled himself up in his recliner, which had clearly seen better days.

"There has been bad blood between the Childers and Bryant families that goes back for many years, maybe more than a hundred. Of course, this was also on top of the problems the Childers had within their own clan." He took a deep breath, then continued. "If you will humor me, I will tell you all I know."

Colin glanced over at Linda and Junior, who smiled and nodded. Apparently, they had heard his stories before, probably many times.

Red continued.

"First off, your family and mine go back a ways. A lot of what I am about to tell you about your folks came from my grandma, who was good friends with your great-grandma."

"The stories about the place have been told as long as I can remember. It is easy when you have your very own ghost town on your property. According to what I have heard, the Childers had a grist mill and lake that powered it. It all had fallen in, and the dam was removed by the time I came along. The whole family seemed to be cursed. Most of them moved away, with your great-grandparents remaining. The old man lived well into his 90s."

He took a deep breath, then continued. "Apparently, Jacob's son took on a second wife, much younger than him. Within a year after they married, he was killed in a logging accident. Having nowhere else to go and pregnant with their son, she stayed on and lived in the same house. Caused quite a scandal. Rumors were started about their relationship."

"As I remember, it was summertime, hot as hell. They were just building the lake. Many folks had already had already settled with the government to sell all or part of their land. Survey crews had been working for over a year, starting first down toward Buford, then working their way back upriver. We were part of the last group to get their land surveyed."

"One of the properties we had to survey was your Childers property. All the land that is now covered by water was bought by the government. Part of that land was where ole Tom Childers lived. We called him Tom-Tom." He paused for a moment, reaching and taking a sip of water from the ever-present glass on the table next to his chair.

"Tom-Tom was about as crazy as they come. I've been told he wasn't always that way, that he had been hurt in the storm in '36 and wasn't the same afterward. Most days, he would just wander around the community, talking about gold, Indians, and other crazy stuff that make for great tales. In fact, that's why people started calling him 'Tom-Tom.' He wanted so bad to be an Indian."

"Anyhow, I remember that day well. I was sent down by the sheriff to meet the survey crew and then escort them around to the various places to complete their work. We went over to the Childers place, and all seemed to go well. We stopped by, and I talked briefly to an older lady who assured us everything would be okay. We took her word for it, which was a mistake on our part."

"I will never forget what happened next." He paused, collecting himself. "I know if I had been there, I may have been able to stop it. Tom-Tom was apparently waiting for us, but he stepped from behind a tree and started shooting. I heard the gunfire, but it was too late. By the time I got there, one of the crew was dead, and another was nowhere to be seen. I thought he had run off, but when Tom-Tom took a pause, I tried to get him to put down the shotgun, but it all happened so quickly. Apparently, the other crew member, I think they called him Hank, was able to get to the pistol they kept in the truck for killing snakes and such and finished Tom off."

The old man paused briefly, then reached and pulled up his pants leg to show the scars on his leg from the long-ago wound. "I jumped into France in the war and served as sheriff in this county for 10 years… but nothing I saw then, or since then compared to this."

Moments passed while Red pondered what he had just shared with Colin. The only sound in the room was the slow tick-tock from the old clock sitting on the mantle, interrupted periodically by the soft, low rumble of thunder in the distance… Red then handed Colin a large envelope, which had been laying on his lap. "There was a lot said about the shooting. Newspaper people showed up for a few days, even from Atlanta and Greenville. The lady that lived in the old home place turned out to be Tom-Tom's aunt. She was so distraught over the incident that she was found dead a few days later; apparently, the stress was too much for her.

I made it my mission to find out what had led to this. All I found out is in that envelope I just handed to you."

"Oh, and one last thing

No one knows just why there is so much bad blood between the Childers and Bryants, but there is.

"The place sat empty for about 5 years, I guess. Think there might have been a family squabble or something, but I was happy to see your grandparents move in. It seemed like things would be patched up, but that all changed with a group of folks talked him into running for sheriff. They felt like new blood was needed. Rufus's dad, Larry, backed him initially, which bodes well for ending the "feud," if you want to call it that."

"Things were going well until your grand-dad apparently took a position on an issue that Bryant didn't appreciate. Maybe your granddad didn't know what he was getting into. After the lake was done filling up in about 1960, there was a great discussion about how the community could prosper from it being there. Some were still angry and upset that their valuable bottom land had gone away and wanted things to stay just as they were. There were others who were ready to move into a new era and welcome newcomers who would come and want to build around the lake. Of course, the Bryants and the Childers were sitting pretty – the land they occupied made of a large share of the shoreline, so they stood to make a lot of money. But, there was a very public withdrawal of support, and excuse my pun, but it was as if a dam had burst. Soon, William lost most of his support, and that ended his foray into local politics. Of course, he and I developed a good friendship after that, but he kinda kept to himself after that. Your granddad had little to do in the community. It was almost as if Bryant had something on him. That's where you come in. The Bryant family was trouble then and still are, as I am sure Junior can explain."

Colin watched as Red's last words trailed off, and the old man dozed off. "Probably enough for today," Junior said, "plus it looks like a storm is coming up, so let's go." Linda went over and kissed Red on the forehead; then they left quietly.

"Well, that was certainly interesting." Colin said as they drove back to Junior's, "This certainly explains a lot of what has been happening."

Linda replied. "Sheriff Red is quite a man. He has seen and done a lot in his life, but the incident seems to be the only thing he wants to talk about."

Colin said as they pulled up at Junior's, "I think we have some exploring to do."

Chapter 23

Colin pulled the door open to the cabin, this time almost breaking it off its hinges. Now armed with flashlights, they would be able to explore the cabin in more detail. In the adjacent room, which Colin had not even entered the first time, there was an old iron bed sitting there, with what appeared to be a mattress whose better days were past. Sitting in the corner was another table with a pitcher sitting on it and a mirror above it. On another wall was a framed print. It was clearly from sometime in the 1920s of an attractive black woman.

"Interesting. Wonder who she was." Linda said, stopping to stare at the photograph. "Seems kind of out of place here."

Colin walked over toward the bed. "Looks like someone got their money's worth out of this," he said as he sat down. "Wanna join me and give it a test ride?" Colin said, half joking, as he winked at her.

"Don't get too cute now." Linda shot back at him. "Besides, I... Hey, look over here - looks like some sort of hatch in the floor."

They took a couple of steps over to a spot that an old rug had partially covered. It was some sort of hatch.

"Grab that crowbar we brought with us. Let's see what we have here."

The hatch didn't exactly cooperate after not being touched in decades. Finally, after a few minutes of prying, they felt the hatch break free, and they slowly lifted it away, revealing a hole underneath. A cool breeze blew out of the newly discovered chasm as both of them stared down into the darkness.

"Looks to be either some sort of root cellar or maybe a safe space in case of attack. You want to take a look?"

"Not me," said Linda. "This is your place. "I will give you that honor."

Colin turned the flashlight to shine into the space. It appeared to be about 10 feet square and was about 6 feet deep. It was empty, but there was a broken-down shelf on one wall with several objects on it.

"I need to get in there – hold the light for me," Colin said as he slowly lowered himself over the edge. He misjudged. The space was a little deeper than six feet, and he landed with a thud, kicking up a small cloud of red dust as he landed.

The only light came from the open hatch, as well as small ribbons of light that penetrated the cracks in the floorboards, creating a roof for the small sanctuary.

Linda tossed the flashlight down to him. With the light, Colin could investigate further.

It was quite obvious this space had been used for various purposes. There were the remains of a couple of old fruit baskets that had slowly decayed with their contents over the years. On the other wall was a set of shelves, attached to the floor joists above, that contained a few glass jars of canned vegetables that had long ago seen their contents dried up.

"Not much down here – looks like more of a pantry than anything…"

By this time, Linda had retrieved an old ladder from behind the nearby barn and had lowered it into the space.

"Kind of cozy, in a creepy sort of way," she exclaimed as she looked around the space. "Surprised there is nothing alive down here."

One more time, Colin trained his light around the room, and then, he saw the small shaft. "Linda, I have found something else..."

He walked over to the opening. Shining his light down the hole, which was large enough for a grown man to fit but not large enough to stand up in. It looked almost like someone's early attempt at a water-slide.

Linda could see the shaft from where she stood. "What do you think is down there?"

"Not sure, but inquiring minds want to know. If I'm not back in 30 minutes, go get some help."

Chapter 24

Colin slowly crept downward through the shaft. It was big enough to stand up but not without crouching or bending. Colin soon found that it was easier to scoot along seated, sliding slowly along. The descent was steep enough that all he needed to do was keep himself from moving too fast. *God only knows if I will be able to climb back out of here,* he thought, as the shaft suddenly leveled out, and he found himself in a long tunnel; marks were still present from where someone had worked long and hard to build it. Periodically, the ceiling and walls were braced with timbers. The floor was muddy, and he could see watermarks on the wall where there at one time had been water at least six inches deep in the tunnel. One direction seemed to disappear into infinity. The tunnel terminated in the other direction, appearing to open into a rather large cavern. Now able to stand up, he walked slowly toward the opening. He was beginning to feel a little foolish. In his haste, he had not checked the batteries in the flashlight, which were beginning to grow dim. Not wanting to chance it and realizing that not having a light down here would not be good, he turned to make his way back up the shaft. His light reflected off something, then his hand began to shake, and although he tried to yell, nothing came out.

Had this been one of those old horror movies, this is when he would have spilled his popcorn. Lying in front of him lay two people, both having been dead for quite some time. Ragged clothes hung off them both, having about rotted away. They were both in some state of mummification – whatever the environment was in the cave had helped to preserve them both. One appeared to be a young woman, laid out as if in a coffin, her hands crossed perfectly over her chest. Someone had taken the time to prepare her for her final journey.

The other body was not so. From the tattered coat dangling off the body, Colin could tell it was once a man who had apparently died a more violent death, as there was a part of his skull caved in. He also noticed that one of his arms was lying separate from the body, with a hand missing. *Well, at least I found who the hand belongs to,* he chuckled silently. He froze there for a moment, strangely awed by the sight, taking it all in but at the same time letting his mind race as to what to do next. Before he thought too long, his light flickered and went out.

Panic set in. Here he was, no telling how far underground, in God only knows what kind of environment, with no light and two corpses. He would have to feel his way out of this one. He suddenly felt helpless and all alone. His heart was beating out of his chest. *Think you idiot, think,* he thought, as his eyes slowly tried to adjust to the darkness. After a few moments, he realized that it wasn't pitch black, as he noticed another smaller tunnel branching out of the room, almost on the opposite side. He shuffled slowly over to the tunnel. It was apparently another exit out of the cave. There was a small hole that was letting light through and a rather large, flat rock that took some effort to push out of the way and out of the cave he popped. He found himself standing next to the lake, no far from where he had found the hand.

Back in the cabin, Linda was getting worried. When Colin didn't return, she tried to decide who to call. Valuing her privacy, she hesitated to summon the local fire department, as it would lead to other questions she didn't want to answer at this point. So, she pulled her phone out to call Junior.

"Looking for me?" Colin said as he walked up behind Linda. She turned and let out a shriek, then began to cry and laugh at the same time. Standing before was someone who sounded like Colin but looked like some swamp creature. He stood there, covered in mud, with a dead flashlight in his hand.

"Where did you come from?" Linda asked as she didn't know whether to hug him or hand him a water hose. "Did you find anything?"

"There is a tunnel of some sort – maybe an old mine. Not exactly sure. But there are other things down there…"

"You look like you have seen a ghost. Is it haunted?" Linda asked.

"No, but I did find out who the hand belongs to. Come on, let me get cleaned up, and I will tell you." They walked slowly back to the house. After a few steps, he felt Linda's hand reach out and take his.

"I'm glad you're okay." She said as they walked along. "I've lost too much in my life."

"Me too," he said as they neared the house. Pulling his shoes off on the back porch, he went directly to the shower.

The needles of water felt great, as his muscles were already getting sore from the excursion. He also had a couple of scrapes he would need to tend to. He closed his eyes and thought of all they had been through today. It was bad enough dealing with this latest discovery that could derail everything, but also, he was beginning to realize how lonely he really was – and how Linda was awakening in him all kinds of emotions that he would never ever feel again. Actually, he kinda hoped it would progress like in the movies, and she would suddenly open the shower door, but that would not be the case. He finished up, then dressed and went back to the living room.

Later, as they both sat by the fire, Colin had grown very quiet.

Linda finally broke the silence. "What exactly did you see down there? Was there a dead body or something?"

Colin sat there for a moment. "Yes, actually. There was. Not one, but two."

Given her position, she had probably heard more than she needed to. Regardless, she needed to know. He spent the next few minutes detailing what he had found.

"We have to let someone know," Linda replied.

"We can't let this get out just yet; this could change things completely," Colin interrupted. "At this point in time, I don't need anything else delaying this thing."

They spent several more minutes discussing all the options, and finally, Colin agreed that they couldn't just forget what was there and discovering it later would lead to all kinds of issues. Never in a thousand years did he think it would be something this big. It wasn't just a bunch of arrowheads he found. Remembering what Steve Grant, his architect, had told him, something like this had the potential of stopping everything in its tracks. But, also not letting anyone know about it could set himself up for a huge legal liability in the future.

They both sat there silently, staring at the fire. Linda finally scooted over closer to him. The warmth of the fire, coupled with the wine they had been sipping on, was causing both of them to grow sleepy. She leaned over on him, and the world stopped for a time.

Colin jolted awake. He looked at his watch. It had been almost an hour. He gently untangled himself from Linda, who slinked down on the couch where they were sitting. He grabbed a blanket that was draped over the back of the sofa, covering her up. He then reached over, turned off the lamp, and padded softly back to his room.

Sleep didn't come easily. Tossing and turning, Colin's mind was racing. Although he had dozed off quickly, he awoke suddenly an hour later, with visions of dead bodies dancing in his head. In spite of trying not to, his mind kept going back to what all this meant and what his next steps should be. With sleep being elusive, he groaned as he flipped on the lamp. He wasn't 20 years old anymore, as every muscle ached from his excursion the day before.

He padded into the kitchen, moving quietly, mindful that Linda was asleep on the couch. He noticed the wine glasses had been rinsed; the wine put away from the evening before. He walked over quietly to the couch, looking for her, looking for her sleeping form, and the only thing he saw was the blanket folded neatly. The log in the fireplace had slowly died down, and everything else looked normal. He picked up the note she had left.

Didn't want to wake you. Straightened things up a bit. Enjoyed the day yesterday. Call me tomorrow – Linda.

He had halfway expected the evening to end differently, but at this point, that would only complicate things. Colin had made little time in his life for friendships and even less time for well, romance. Something was stirring in him that had not been there in a long, long time, and although he liked being around her, he had to be careful. Sure, he had dated over the years, and he smiled as he thought of how many times he had been "set up" on a blind date here and there. For

Colin, work was his god. For most of his adult life, this is all he had done. He had no time for relationships, so there had been few friends.

The next morning, Colin awakened to the light streaming through the curtains and, looking at his watch, realized he had surprisingly slept soundly after returning to bed. His back complained loudly as he sat up, so he took a few extra moments to let his muscles complain to each other. Sitting there, he couldn't help but let his mind drift not toward the discoveries he had made but toward something else – Linda.

No time for that right now, he thought, as he quickly turned his thoughts back to the discovery from the day before and how he would handle it. He looked at his watch. It was still too early to call anyone. For some strange reason, he still was not sure, but he picked up the old Bible and slowly started leafing through its pages pausing every now and then. He hadn't looked at a Bible in years, and not sure why he was suddenly drawn to it. Being careful not to tear them, he picked up the journal again, knowing there were still a lot of secrets to be discovered.

Fifteen minutes later, at about 8, he couldn't wait any longer. He quickly punched Jack's number.

"Morning. Can you get over here? It's rather urgent. There's been some discoveries. We need to talk." He really knew no one else to call. At this point, only he and Linda knew about the bodies, and now, only he knew about the book he held in his hand that hopefully could explain some of this mystery that surrounded the place.

"I can be there in an hour. May I ask what it is about?" Jack replied.

"Let me just say I have found some things right under my feet. Literally."

Colin proceeded to tell him about the discoveries made the day before, including the books he now had spread out across the table.

"You found WHAT? We do need to talk about this. I will be there in about an hour." Jack sounded concerned, almost fearful.

Colin laid the phone down and turned his attention back to the books that lay in front of him. Picking up the journal, he picked up where he left off. There wasn't much exciting, as it mostly talked about the travels Jacob made as a "wagoneer," what they grew on the small plot of land next to the store the family owned, and of his growing relationships with the Cherokee families nearby. It was also clear that Jacob had not been too pleased with what was going on involving the efforts to push out the Cherokees. HE wondered if the bodies he had just found may have had something to do with this.

Colin was startled by a knock at the back door, and he heard Jack's voice, "Anybody home?"

He had no time to put things away, so he guessed this wasn't some deep, dark secret, as the books, although important, would not bring the kind of reaction the bodies would.

"So this is what you have been doing with your time. Where are they? Do we need to call the authorities?" Jack was now appearing very agitated.

"Jack, settle down. These aren't fresh bodies. They have been dead for a long time. I found them in an old mine or cave of some sort, which, by the way, you never eluded to when we first met." Colin said as he tried to maintain a calm voice.

They soon found themselves back in the cabin, where Colin showed him the entry to the root cellar, then the opening that led to the tunnel.

"They are down there," Colin said as Jack started toward the small opening in the cellar. "It's very muddy; you probably don't want to attempt it right now."

Jack agreed, "I guess you are right. We need to think now of what to do about what we have found. Does anyone else know about this find?"

Colin hesitated for a moment. Revealing Linda at this point would lead to the need for further explanation. "A friend of mine was here with me when I made the discovery. She can be trusted."

"Let's hope so." Now, if you will excuse me, I do have other clients. Let me do some thinking about our next steps."

"Jack, do you think this will be the end of the development?"

"It's all according to how we handle it from here."

Ten minutes later, Jack was on the phone with someone else. "There is a problem."

"I thought you had him under control!" Came the voice on the other end of the line.

Rufus Bryant hung up the phone. He was furious, mainly at himself. First, his efforts to acquire the Childers' property had been thwarted again. Apparently, this outsider didn't know who he was messing with, and you just don't tell Rufus Bryant no. Then, whoever Colin Childers was decided he needed to develop the place. This would have been disastrous. Having a couple hundred homes sitting right next door would not have been good for business. Then, to top it all off, he had been snooping around in his business and was getting too close to the fire.

In the short term, the discovery would do what he desired – shut down any further talk of development. However, the longer he thought about it, he realized that things would actually get worse. Even though this would likely end the development, it would also shut down what his long-range plan was – to gain control of the what was under their feet. He knew his partners would not be very happy about these setbacks. He had to move fast to get Colin Childers out of the picture before he had a chance to develop the place and found out too much.

It was time to crank up the pressure. He picked up the phone.

Chapter 25

"I am not sure how this new issue is going to affect things with the development," Jack warned, sitting back in his chair. Colin and Jack were all sitting around the table at Colin's. "Then again, you never know what you may find. That's why it was a good move to hire an expert to take a look at things."

The small talk continued for a few more minutes when there was a knock at the door. Colin stood up. "This must be our guest."

Ten minutes later, they were unloading the equipment from the back of Junior's truck. There were helmets, 100 feet of rope for each of them, carbide headlamps, and since they didn't know what water would be there, rain suits for all of them to wear.

Dr. Koch was a small man, who was a college professor over in Dahlonega at the college. He also was renowned throughout the region as an archeologist who specialized in native/early American settlements. After the intros, Dr. Koch spent the better part of the day in and out of the mine. Every time he came back out, he scribble notes in a notebook.

Later that afternoon, they sat on the patio, as Dr Koch shared what he had found.

"This looks very similar to a tunnel over on the Etowah that was built during the gold rush. It was at a bend in the river and allowed for the diversion of most, if not all, of the water through the tunnel, which allowed for better access to the original river bottom. The men that came here would do anything to get to the gold they felt would make them rich."

He continued. "Although similar, it was not done at the same time. This tunnel looks to be much older. Here, let me show you."

He pulled up a series of photos on the laptop he had set up that showed various features of the underground structure. "There are lots of prehistoric mysteries around these mountains. This cave was likely originally cut by some unknown people hundreds of years before the Cherokees came to this part of the country. Some have even speculated that the Mayans migrated here, and even built a temple up in the mountains. Whatever it was, this place gave us our own research lab right here in our backyard. That is, of course, if you are open to us to continue our exploration."

Colin didn't give any acknowledgement, knowing the impact this latest discovery had on any dreams he had about developing the place. He looked over at Jack, who was furiously taking notes, as well as having a rather puzzled look on his face. He finally asked, "Dr Koch, how far does this tunnel go? I mean, if it was a water sluice, wouldn't it go all the way through?"

"Yes, you are correct; however, I found a rather strange feature in the mine itself. Often, these old mine structures eventually collapse, which blocks access to the full mine. This mine is blocked, almost at the property line. It looks to be rather recent; there is a solid wall made out of concrete blocks. It appears the mine may still be in use on the other side of that wall. That is probably the most puzzling thing of all about the mine."

It had really come as no surprise to Colin that the secret was not a secret very long. In the two weeks that had passed since their discovery, it seemed like every news outlet in the region had descended on his little corner of the world. He had even been contacted by a couple of film producers, all eager to tell his story.

Colin was fuming, and his moods were swinging from angry to depressed. He had felt betrayed. After all, he had only shared the news with three people – Dr. Koch, Linda, and Jack Smith. He wasn't sure who to blame – he thought he trusted them all to maintain confidentiality. Dr. Koch had too much to lose professionally for such and ethical lapse such as this, but at this point, he wasn't sure which one, or all of them, had let the news slip. He had not talked to any of them. Frankly, he didn't want to.

Regardless of what had happened, he had to continue moving forward. He had hoped to bring his architect, Steve Grant, into the circle of confidence but ended up scheduling an emergency meeting with him once the news leaked out. Surprisingly, Steve approached the situation calmly, without displaying the "I told you so" mentality Colin expected. He and Colin had discussed the options.

The best they could hope for at this point was to alter their plans to accommodate the discoveries that had been made. The bodies were one thing, but worse was the possibility of the whole hill being honeycombed with other tunnels and shafts, all waiting to collapse once homes had been built on them. This was a nightmare scenario., It was risky, but at this point, the main thing was to get approval from the board at their next meeting the next week. Colin agreed, but reluctantly.

Just as he was leaving Steve's office, his phone began ringing. It was Linda. He shut off his car, deciding Jack could wait a few more minutes.

He wasn't in the mood to talk with her right now, but since she called, he might as well confront her. He was not happy that she was the one who likely let it slip; deep down, he was hoping for the best.

"Linda, what the hell is going on? I really don't want to have this conversation." Colin tried to hold it together. "You still don't quite understand what I am trying to do here."

"Maybe I don't, but I can tell you that one thing I can do, and that is to keep a secret. You actually think I told the news media and invited this onslaught?" Linda was getting just as animated. "Who else did YOU tell?"

"I am headed to see him right now – Jack Smith. He is the only other way this could have gotten out." Colin replied. "I was hoping to have the conversation with him before I called you. Sorry for jumping the gun a moment ago… but you need to realize how big this project will be and how important it is for me to get a win. I tell you what – how about dinner tomorrow? Let's go somewhere nice and get out of this town for the evening."

"Sounds like a plan to me – anytime after six will work." Linda was relieved they had quickly put this to rest. "Also, sorry I was so short with you."

"No problem. Will pick you up at about 6:30."

Colin put the phone down. He had something to look forward to.

As he reached the outskirts of town, he looked up in his rear-view mirror to see the flashing blue lights of a patrol car closing on him.

Great, as if something else could go wrong today. He turned on his blinker to pull over, but instead of stopping behind him, the car sped around him, heading to another emergency. Colin breathed a sigh of relief. Then, two more appeared, and passed as well.

As he got closer to Jack's office, he noticed a myriad of flashing lights, and he realized the building Jack's office was in had caught fire. Walking up to the building, the fire was just about extinguished, with several people gathered in one area over in the parking lot. It was then he realized that it was Jack Smith's office that was on fire.

"What happened?" he said to everyone and no one in the group at once. Anybody seen Jack Smith? That is his office!"

A man in the group spoke up. "Not sure, just glad we all got out. Good thing that building is concrete, or we all would have been killed. Just feel bad… Did I hear you say you knew the guy Jack Smith?"

"Yes. Is he okay?" Colin was beginning to feel sick to his stomach.

"If he is okay, it would be a miracle. The blast shook the whole building."

By this time, the fire had been extinguished, leaving behind what looked like a warzone. There was glass scattered all over the sidewalk, and two cars parked in front of the building were definitely going to need a paint job. By now, a couple of agents with ATF emblazoned across their backs were starting to gingerly make their way to the black cavern that was Jack's offices two hours before.

By this time, with everyone in the building accounted for, most of the gathered group began to disperse. In a halfway state of shock, Colin thought immediately of Linda. He quickly punched in her number. She immediately picked up. "Are you okay? I just saw the news report on TV about an explosion in Gainesville. The news crews camped here, and all took off that way. Are you okay? I was worried as I knew you were headed that way after we talked."

Colin tried to speak clearly but was still shocked by what he had seen. "Linda, the explosion was in Jack's office, where I was headed. I just barely missed being in it. In fact, had we not had our conversation, I would likely have been here when it happened."

"Do I need to come over?" Linda asked.

"Not necessary. I am a big boy. It appears that I have ended up kicking a hornet's nest." Just need to start watching my back. It's obvious somebody is out to get me."

Linda was quiet for a moment, then said, "I'm just glad you are okay. Could think of losing someone else."

"Sir, Officer Miller, ATF. I understand you may have known the victim. We would like to ask you a few questions."

Chapter 26

Colin slowly opened the door to the barn. He had a hammer in his hand, hoping to confront who or what was out there. With the increased suspicious activity going on, he had to be extra careful. After the well-orchestrated "accidental" meeting with Rufus Bryant at the camp meeting, it seemed like everyday something new was happening – whether the strange black truck that kept driving by slowly in front of the house or the weekly delivery of the dead fish, neatly wrapped in newspaper, laying on his front steps. He had hoped to catch who was doing it and teach them a lesson. He was just about certain Bryant was behind it all. Just why he would resort to these tactics was puzzling to him.

The weather had turned cool and damp. As he slowly played the light around the small storage room, he could sense someone was there. He walked slowly from the front room into the adjoining room. He paused. Someone was definitely in there.

"Anybody here? Show yourself if you are." He paused for a few moments. Then he saw her. Her clothes were ragged, her hair in a tangled mess, and smudges of dirt on her face. Two large brown eyes stared back at him. She couldn't have been more than 13 or 14. She was shaking and terrified. He reached out his hand.

"Hi there. It will be okay; you are safe here. Come, let me get you to a warm place." She took his hand. She had on little more than rags for clothes. It looked as if she hadn't bathed in weeks, and the old dress she had on was riddled with holes. Wrapping his coat around her; they walked the short distance back to the house. He soon learned that she spoke no English. He called the only person he knew to call: Linda.

Twenty minutes later, Linda and he were sitting in the dining room, trying their best to communicate with her. She had gotten cleaned up, they had fixed some soup for her, and she was sitting quietly at the table. Her hands were no longer shaking as she held on to the warm mug in front of her. She hadn't slowed down eating until she was on her third mug. She had also devoured a grilled cheese sandwich they had made for her.

"In what little Spanish I know, I can only pick up bits and pieces. Apparently, she was with her family but was separated weeks ago right after crossing the border."

"We need to report this now," Colin said, watching the young girl eat. "Makes me wonder how she got this far from the border. Everything just looks suspicious."

A few minutes later, there was a knock at the door.

Linda looked at Colin, "Did you call someone?"

"No, I thought you did," she replied.

"Take her to the bedroom – now." Colin suspected that whoever she was involved with had likely tracked her here. Linda quickly took the young girl and hurried out of the room.

Walking quietly over to the door, Colin saw three men – one was a deputy in uniform, but the other two were in black suits.

Colin opened the door.

"Sir, Special Agent Ferguson from the FBI child exploitation task force, as well as Special Agent Walker from the GBI. Can we speak to you for a moment?

Not waiting for Colin to step back and invite them in, they brusquely entered the room.

"What are you doing? What can I help you with?"

Mr Childers, we had a report of some possible criminal activity involving this address. Mind if we ask you a few questions?"

"Yes, of course," Colin answered.

"We have been tracking some human trafficking in the area over the past couple of years. Apparently, they are using the lake itself as part of the transportation route to the area. How long have you lived here, Mr. Childers?"

"Oh, about nine months now," he replied.

"Have you ever seen anything suspicious in the last few months?" The agent was setting this up nicely.

Colin started to answer, but before he could, a commotion broke out from the back of the house. Apparently, Linda was having issues with the girl.

"We actually were just about to call you." Colin started. "I have just found a young girl hiding out back in the barn. I'm just curious: how did you know to come here tonight?"

By this time, Linda had overheard the conversation and appeared with the young girl, holding her by the hand.

Colin started to explain what had happened earlier when he happened to glance at the girl, then he saw it – the girl had dropped her hand by her side, and her hand was folded into a modified fist, with her thumb covered up with her fingers.

Immediately, the GBI agent began to speak with her in fluent Spanish. She nodded her head quickly to both questions they asked. They quickly escorted her away, and Agent Ferguson nodded at the deputy, who spoke first.

"Colin Childers, you are under arrest."

"For what, may I ask?" His voice was almost cracking.

"Trafficking of a minor. If you would please turn around and put your hands behind your back."

Colin was incredulous, "How could this be? I only met this girl an hour ago. She would have probably died had I not found her when I did."

The agent snapped the cuffs on Colin's wrists. "You need to come with us."

"But I can explain – I had nothing to do with this! I am being framed! This is not what she is saying!"

Linda looked in shock at what had just happened. Before Colin could even say anything, she slipped out the door and was gone.

Chapter 27

Due to the gravity of the allegations made against him, Colin had no choice but to spend the night behind bars. Since he had not been arraigned yet, he was put into some sort of holding cell after a brief interview with the magistrate, who made sure he understood the charges against him and the fact that no bail was being granted until his arraignment the next morning.

It was bad enough that he was facing federal kidnapping and trafficking charges, but after he had been detained and taken away, additional officers descended on the house with a search warrant, where they quickly uncovered three thumb drives full of pornographic images of young girls ranging in age from 10-16. This would likely result in additional charges being brought. And to top it all off, evidence found in Jack Smtih's home had made him a person of interest in his death/ In short, all the walls had tumbled in on him at one time.

He had not talked to Linda yet and was not sure what to think. He never had a need for a defense attorney, and now that Jack was dead, he had no one he could consult with to give him the assistance he needed. The only person he could think to call was his old friend Matt. He picked up after the third ring, and within an hour, He had been contacted by a local attorney who had been referred to him by a mutual acquittance in Chicago. He would be there by 8 the next morning.

That night was one of the longest of Colin's life, even with the many sleepless ones he had endured before. He spent most of the night pacing the floor, with his mind generating two questions for everyone he answered for himself. There was no question that he was being framed. He was confident everything would be worked out the next morning when his attorney would talk with the DA to explain what had transpired. Was there a connection? He had been a victim the last few weeks of some kind of scare campaign, and then there was Jack Smith's tragic end, along with the chance to meet up with Rufus Bryant and his discovery of the girl in the barn the night before. He knew deep down in his soul that Rufus Bryant was behind all this, but he was a slippery eel, and it would be very difficult to get anything on him.

He finally laid down on the thin mattress that was provided for his sleep. The dream returned that night, but with a twist – Rufus Bryant was the one shoveling in the dirt.

The next morning, the attorney showed up. Colin expected some older, more seasoned attorney would be the order of the day, but instead, standing in front of him was a tall, slender kid who looked like he had just finished law school. Whatever his youthful experience had projected, he was surprised by the width and breadth of knowledge he displayed, as well as how much he already knew of the case. This was driven home further when, instead of a large bail being set, Colin was allowed to go free with two stipulations – he had to surrender his passport, which wasn't a huge issue since he had no plans to flee the country. The other requirement was the ankle bracelet that would be put around his ankle. With it, he could be anywhere within a mile of his residence, but the authorities would be notified if he traveled any further away than that.

If there was hope that the worst was past since he had regained his freedom, it wasn't. As soon as he got his phone back, the first call he made was to Linda. The phone rang several times before he hung it up. It would be the next morning before she would return his call.

"Colin, this is Linda. I hesitated about making this call but did have some business to discuss." She sounded very cold.

"Are you okay?" Colin asked her, hoping everything was good still between the two of them. "Will you let me explain?"

"Well, other than feeling played for a fool by someone I thought was authentic, I'm just fine." She made sure she emphasized the "fine."

"But Linda, let me explain…" Colin replied.

"There will be time for that one day, but right now, my call is not personal. I just finished an emergency meeting with the board of commissioners; they have pulled the plug on your project."

These words cut to the quick. "They were looking for an excuse. I will fight them in court over this."

"Colin, remember what Red told you about taking on these guys? There is one other thing that happened at that meeting." Linda paused for a moment, then continued, attempting to control her emotions.

"I was fired. It seems to have something to do with the company I have been keeping recently."

Colin replied. "It looks like you now know how I feel." He regretted the words as soon as they left his mouth.

"Have a good day, hope you find your way," she said, and the line went dead.

Colin sat there for a long moment, collecting his thoughts. He was not sure which was growing larger in his chest – the hole or the lump.

Chapter 28

The house was a wreck. Having all your stuff combed through by cops will do that. Colin walked through the house. He was glad he had gotten rid of so much stuff, so it wasn't as bad as it could have been. He slowly started picking up and putting stuff back where It belonged.

Thankfully, they had not disturbed the old documents he had found in the cabin other than to move them around a bit. It almost seems like they knew exactly where they would look.

The room. He went back to the hallway. The door was open. They had been in there. *I can't do this,* he thought as he reached to pull the door shut. Then, he noticed the closet door was open. He stood there for a moment, not wanting to go in, out of fear, out of facing whatever. So he shut the door. Again. *Maybe tomorrow. I will have plenty of time tomorrow,* he thought. He walked back into the other room. The journals lay spread out on the table in front of him, practically yelling for attention.

Maybe I just need to get my mind off everything going on, he thought, then wondered if maybe all this might just be connected. He picked up the book and opened the cover.

Interesting, Colin thought as he sat back. He hadn't even thought about any history, not just his since he was in school. It just wasn't an interest. Obviously, he was related in some way to this Jacob Childers, afterall, they did share the same surname.

He sat back, with his mind churning. This guy was pretty courageous. And he had also lost his father and made the best of it.

He sighed deeply. *How hard can this be,* he thought, as he rose to take the hardest 50 steps he had ever taken.

He pushed the door open slowly and took the first step into the room. He stopped, almost backing out, but didn't this time.

The room smelled and looked exactly like one would expect with no one being in it for the last four decades. There was a single bed made up with a simple bedspread. In addition was a nightstand with a lamp, and a small dresser. He walked over, gingerly opening the closet door, which had been left open when the house was searched. Several old shirts hung in the closet. Colin picked up one, holding it to his face, inhaling deeply. He was hoping that there was something there to remind him of HIM, but nothing. *I was scared of this?*

He opened the drawers in the chest, one by one. Some of his dad's clothes were still there. He went to the closet and found the same. *Was he dreaming? I mean, this is like a time capsule...*

He noticed something else in the closet - stuck behind the clothes hanging, there was a small, two-drawer file cabinet. It looked like it had been placed there later. It was rather heavy, as it felt full of stuff. Seeing how it would be difficult to move, he would have to get it open first. Pulling on the drawer, he realized it was locked. Then, remembered. The note. The key. The one that he had angrily tossed in the trash a few months ago. "You will need this." He could kick himself.

Returning 10 minutes later with a drill, he quickly dispatched the lock, and as he started to pull the drawer open.

There were several old files in the cabinet. Looking through them briefly, it appeared they were mostly personal papers, Then, He found it in the bottom drawer – a shoe box. He gingerly lifted it out of the drawer, then went over to sit down on the bed. His heart was about to beat out of his chest as he cracked open the box. He opened the lid, not knowing what he would find. There were several items – first was a small Bible, which he looked at with curiosity, flipping through it, then laying it down. Before he could pick up the next item, his phone started ringing. It was his attorney. Colin dropped the things he was holding and walked into the other room as if staying in there would violate some sort of sacred code.

"Colin, Ross Jenkins here –"

"Yes, Ross, get to the point. I know who you are." Colin was anxious to get some good news.

"There have been some new developments in the case. Apparently, as part of the investigation, an apparent suicide note from Jack Smith was received this morning by the DA – in it, he basically confessed to being part of a child porn ring."

"Wow – what does that mean for me?" Colin sounded hopeful they were getting to the bottom of this.

"Unfortunately, he identified you as his chief cohort and mastermind behind the whole idea."

"So, you know he's lying, or this thing is fake, right?" Colin said, with an air of apprehension in his voice.

"Sorry to say no. They are treating it as the real thing." Ross replied.

"This also means you are now facing the additional charges - over a dozen, in fact. This could put you in prison for the rest of your life. Colin, I am going to level with you. It may be time for you to start thinking about a plea. Maybe the judge will go light on you."

Colin screamed at the attorney on the other end of the call, "I am innocent! I didn't do anything wrong! I was just trying to help someone in need! Can anyone see that I have been set up?"

He disconnected the call. Everything that had been eating at him for years began to surface. He felt like he was being sucked into a whirlpool. Six months ago, his whole life was in order; now, it was in shambles. He was at the top of his game, running a multi-million dollar enterprise. Now, here he was, a thousand miles away in this backwater community, accused of God knows what, having lost the one relationship that had made this whole thing worth it. It was all too much, too much to handle. Now, this. Mysterious goings on. A culture totally foreign to him, yet one that had drawn him in. It was as if he had never left. The man he had worked so hard to build up – was being destroyed right before his very eyes…

The hell with all of it, he thought. *I know what I need to do.*

He pulled on his clothes, grabbed the pistol out of the nightstand drawer, and walked out of the house. *Too messy to do it here,* he thought. He walked quickly down the dirt path to the lake, then found the small john boat that he had bought a month ago. He had intended to take up fishing since there was so much water around but he never thought that the first time he used it would also be the last. It would make a good boat for someone, he thought as he pushed off. Tomorrow, or the day after that, or on whatever day it was found, it didn't matter. He wouldn't be here.

The water was cold around his ankles as he slowly waded in and got into the boat. His mood was getting darker. But, soon, the end would come, and there would be no more pain, no more anxiety, no more need to cover and push the past away. He paddled for about five minutes out to the deepest part of the channel. The lump in his chest was growing stronger, and he began to sob. He was now crying openly and standing up in the small boat; he turned so the blast would knock him into the water. He put the gun under his chin and – pulled the trigger. He expected that to be it.

He heard nothing but an audible click. He realized nothing had happened. He tried again. *Click* He sighed deeply as the lump in his chest began to spill out in great sobs. The misfire of the gun apparently had awakened him from whatever state he had been in. He started to just roll over the side into the water, take a deep breath, and end it all there. Something stopped him.

He looked at the horizon – a half-moon was beginning to rise, with its light casting a ribbon along the water that seemed to come right at him... he looked up at the stars, their lights blinking in the dark tapestry overhead. From somewhere in the past, the thought ran through his head from out of nowhere it seemed: *When I look at your heavens, the work of your fingers, the moon and the stars, which you have set in place...* Colin paused. *Where did that come from?*

"Who ARE you!" He cried, shaking his fist in the air, not knowing who or what he was crying to. He yelled. "Why did you do this to me???" Everything was coming loose at once. The terrified 10-year-old that had been buried for the past 35 years was coming out and would not be denied any longer.

Then he heard it. The whisper. The soft, tender voice. *Believe. Trust me.* Whether it was audible or not, Colin *felt it* deep in his soul. The weight was crushing on his chest as if a sack of rocks was sitting there. His sobs became anger – at something or someone, but he wasn't sure at what or who. He finally yelled out, shaking his fist in the air, trying to reach heaven. "Damn you God! I can't trust you!!!" He wailed loud enough that he was sure to wake everyone within a mile of the place.

He sobbed. The soft, tender voice came back again.

"Believe in me."

"Trust me."

"I will heal your heart."

Those last words stopped Colin cold. *"I want your heart."* He was suddenly taken back to that point, so many years earlier, when he had been held close by his dad, the day he left, when he had uttered those same exact words to him – *"I want your heart."*

Now spent, Colin began to respond in yells to the heavens: "I'm scared! How do I do this? I am broken. HELP ME GOD!"

He couldn't believe he had just uttered those words. In all these years, he had never asked anyone for anything to help him. He was half seated again, sobbing, and said it again… "God, please, please help me…" his voice trailing off in a whisper, the last bit of his breath spent.

"God, what do I need to do?"

There were no claps of thunder, no earthquake, no angels singing. Those would not be adequate to explain what happened next. It was as if a gigantic arm had swooped down, grabbed that bag of rocks that was sitting on his chest, and flung them as far as they could be thrown.

There was a lightness to his soul. There was a peace that flooded him, one he had never felt before. Was he exhausted? Maybe that was it. But something was different that had not been there just moments before. Definitely. Where moments before he felt all alone, at the end of his rope, now he was different. He felt a connection to everything. A peace descended on him. He had no energy left, even to row back to shore. He slept safely in the boat.

He was not sure how much time had passed, but he was shocked awake by a splash of water in his face. It was on him before he knew it. It came lumbering out of the darkness. Neither one of them could see the other one. The houseboat passed by within a few feet, barely missing him.

The wake almost caused the small boat to capsize. He was soon left in its wake, as he saw it cruise on and just as it veered left for the small cove that was home to Rufus Bryant. He saw a solitary light come on; then the boat slipped into its berth.

Realizing the moon could come out again at any second, Colin started paddling toward the shore as fast as he could. Getting out of the boat, being careful not to make any sound that would give him away, he crouched behind some bushes and began snapping photos. He saw something that shocked him to the core. They were unloading - *human beings.* He counted 5-10 young girls, all appearing to be tethered together, who were now standing on the dock, trying to stay warm in the chilly night air. One of the men from the boat grabbed the lead girl by the arm and proceeded to move the whole group to a small concrete block building near the dock.

Then, as if on cue, the ring of his phone pierced the darkness. He had forgotten to turn the ringer off.

He had no time to look now. He had to get out of here. He scampered back further into the woods, hearing yelling behind him as flashlight beams flashed in the trees above him. He didn't have time to get back to the house. Besides, that would be the first place they would look. They would probably be there, waiting for him. He headed to the only place they did not know about.

The cave. Not being sure he could find it from this direction, he uttered a short prayer as he slowed. Looking valiantly as he walked quickly along the lake shore, he came to the small opening he had crawled out of a couple of weeks prior. He wiggled his way into the small space and crawled through the tunnel until he popped out in the small chamber that had become a tomb. He sat there in the darkness, catching his breath. *At least I will be safe here for a few minutes anyway,* he thought.

In the quiet darkness, his mind began to churn. It finally all started to fall into place. The reaction of the people at the meeting. The veiled threats that had been made against him. The strange people stalking him. The great interest Rufus Bryant had in the land. And there was the Jack Smith issue. He had been growing suspicious of Jack, especially the way he died and left the note with the fabricated story. Finally, there was the girl and the thumb drives. The strange conversation with Rufus. It had all been there to cover Bryant's criminal activities.

There was also the other thing that happened out there. He couldn't explain it, but with all the chaos of the last few minutes, the strange peace was still there, unmoving. It wasn't going anywhere.

Maybe he needed to talk to someone, well, more spiritual than he had been. He had heard of people who said they heard from God, but is that what happened? He was somehow changed, but not in creating a new habit or anything, through his own efforts. It was like a peace that seemed to grow stronger. His issues were still there, and yes, there were challenges ahead, but somehow, he had something he had put much stock in before – hope.

As he lay there in the darkness, tears began to trickle down his cheeks, and this time, sobs of joy began to reverberate in the small space. What would have been tears of rage or frustration before became tears of joy and release. He finally fell asleep, leaning up against the red clay wall of the small cavern. Colin Childer's healing had begun.

Chapter 29

He awoke with a start. Although the dream had been there, it was strangely peaceful as he lay there for a moment. He wasn't sure how long he had been asleep. He looked at his watch – 9 hours. *Wow, I should have been sleeping down here all along,* he thought.

He stood up, full of aches from lying on the cold, damp floor of the cave. He carefully climbed up the old airshaft, then, a moment later, popped out into the cabin above. He was extra cautious about approaching the house, not being sure of who might be there. As he got closer, he could see it was safe to go inside.

A half-hour later, he had cleaned up. His first call was to his attorney to let him know what had transpired. Not getting him, he left a message. He also realized, in all the excitement, that he had never seen who it was that called him the night before. He looked at his call log and saw that it was Linda. She had called him three times.

"Colin? Is that you? Are you okay? I was worried about you. Where have you been? I thought you were supposed to be at home. I came by last evening and couldn't find you." She sounded almost frantic as she spoke.

"I'm okay. I just took a walk. I discovered some things." Colin replied without elaborating too much.

He explained to her about the night before and what he had witnessed next door.

There was a pause. "I also wanted to tell you that I am sorry for my reaction to everything. It was just after I had let my guard down; it was like getting slapped in the face."

"Trust me, Linda, I was so focused on myself that I couldn't care less about your career vs. my going to jail."

She then replied, "Can we hit the reset button?"

"You bet. And I think I talked to God last night."

"You're kidding, right?"

"Nope – I think I may need to talk to someone – not a shrink, but someone, like a priest, or preacher, or something." Colin didn't quite know how to proceed.

"Anyway, if you want, you can bring a pizza over. I'm starved."

"Will do", she said.

"Oh, and one other thing, Linda – I love you." He had never uttered these words in many years, to anyone.

There was a short but awkward pause, and then Colin heard the words he hadn't heard a lot in his life – "I love you, too."

Chapter 30

In spite of all he had seen, Colin was still stuck in the house with an electronic bracelet around his ankle. He had secretly hoped it would malfunction after getting wet the night before, but obviously, with some of the characters that were required to wear it, they had to be pretty tough. Then he chuckled to himself that with the charges he was facing, he guessed he fit into the same crowd.

He could have sat around, feeling sorry for himself, but he suddenly had no desire to do so. Besides the strange new peace he was feeling, he suddenly found himself flipping through the old Bible that he found in the trunk. The pages were extremely fragile, and after a few minutes of flipping through them, he realized he was subconsciously delaying finishing something he had started doing two days before – going through the things he found in his dad's room. The fear of what he might find was not as strong as it had been before, but it was still there, hopefully not tormenting him.

The items were still laying on the bed, next to the empty shoebox, just like he had left them earlier.

He sat on the bed. He picked up the first of the four items. It was a small New Testament. He had seen one before – in fact, he had found one in his stuff when he was packing up to leave Chicago. This one was his dad's. He held it in his hands, slowly flipping it over, almost as if he was trying to absorb his dad's thoughts and memories as his own. He held it up to his nose, drawing in a deep breath. In spite of the mustiness of laying there for 40 years, he thought he could smell the faint smell of the cologne his dad used to wear. He flipped it open and was surprised when it opened to a verse that had been underlined – in the Psalms. There was also a single gray spot and a smudge like a thumbprint on the page – dried blood. As he gazed at it, Colin began to feel a swelling in his chest as he realized this was his dad's.

He sat there for many moments, almost hyperventilating, as he thought of the significance of what he was looking at. Reverently, Colin carefully laid it aside and picked up the next item. He knew what it was the moment he picked it up. He opened the hinged box slowly. The light reflected off the perfect violet colored medal, with the golden bust of George Washington in the middle. The Purple Heart. Not just anyone's Purple Heart, but that of his own father, his dad's. It lay peacefully in its felt-lined box, as it had done for the last four decades. No one had shown him, and he had never asked about it. But here it was, in front of him for the first time. Tears welled in his eyes as he held it, gently staring at its reverberating message.

I'm not sure I can continue, Colin thought, as he took a deep breath and reached for the next item. It was a photo. It was obvious from the uniforms and the background of the photo that it was from Vietnam. There were two men in the photo. He thought it was his dad, but as it had been so long, he wasn't sure. And, of course, he didn't have a clue about the other person in the photograph. He looked at it longingly, as if willing for many moments that his dad would actually come to life and speak to him, but it wasn't going to happen. Colin sat there for many minutes, looking at the photo, holding the purple heart in his hand, even pinning it on his own chest at one point.

After a few minutes, he carefully began to place the sacred items back in the box. Then, he noticed something else – he had overlooked it laying on the bottom of the box – he reached and picked it up. It was sealed up, and when he saw his name written on the outside of the envelope, he was puzzled. Thinking it was someone's bad idea of a joke, he looked at it while carefully opening it. There was a letter in it. It was dated January 15, 1971.

Dear Son,

Obviously, if you are reading this letter, I did not make it home. I left this so that someone would give it to you. I just wanted to let you know, besides the letters and cards I have sent you and your Mom almost daily since I arrived here, I have continuously had you on my mind.

I wanted to let you know how much I love you, and even though I won't be around to see you grow up, I am confident you will be fine. You just make sure you take good care of your mom and your grandparents. You are a special kid, and don't let anyone tell you differently. As you grow older, please don't ever forget me. If you end up with another father, that is fine, and if you eventually have a little brother or sister, tell them about me as well.

God bless you, my son!

Love,

Dad.

Tears were splashing on the paper as Colin read and re-read the letter. Although almost 4 decades had passed, for Colin, a cleansing was taking place. All of the pent-up anger, all the sadness, all the tension began to pour out of him as he sat in that room. It was as if his dad were right there sitting beside him on the bed. He took a deep breath and sighed. He lay back on the bed, briefly shutting his eyes and taking a deep breath, then another, and the peace overwhelmed him. He slept like a baby.

Chapter 31

His attorney had awakened Colin the next morning – he was going to have to stop sleeping in places like this, as his body told on him as he sat up.

Colin shared with him in detail what he had witnessed. They agreed it was significant to the case.

"I will be there in about an hour to pick you up. Before I could call you back, the lead prosecutor called me. Apparently, there has been some sort of development in the case."

Two hours later, they were sitting across the table from a short, balding man who was the lead prosecutor on the case.

"Well, Mr. Childers. We have some news to share. It appears that once we started investigating the case to include the identity of the girl, it turned out she was not quite who she led us to believe she was. She is a bit older, like 22 years old, and she has been apprehended three times by immigration. Turns out she is a member of MS-13. The only problem is she won't tell us who hired her to set you up."

Colin looked at his attorney, then back at the prosecutor. "I think I can help you out in that department."

He took the next few minutes to explain the incident on the water from a few 4 nights earlier, then handed him a small flash drive, where he had downloaded the photographs.

"Well, that certainly will help, but there is also the matter of the child porn that we found on the flash drives. It turns out that by doing the forensics, the images on the flash drive were put there by Jack

Smith. We found a note in his house that he and you were involved in this whole thing yourself. It looks like this was a very sloppy attempt to frame you. That is why you were a person of interest in his tragic death."

"So what does that mean for my client?" Roy spoke up for the first time in quite a while.

"I will be turning over the new information to the investigation team, who may want to talk to your client again. As for the trafficking charges, I am dropping them immediately. But, the child porn charges will remain until we can do some further investigation. As for now, you will likely still have to wear the bracelet until a judge rules otherwise."

Colin let out a long sigh of relief. Knowing that he was also innocent of the other charges, he would just have to wait this out. Besides, there was another mystery that needed to be solved.

Chapter 32

"So I did some research. Turns out Jacob Childers is my 3rd Great-grandfather. I found an old notebook where it looks like my granddad started doing some research on the family's history." Colin was sitting in front of the fire with Linda, where they had just devoured take-out Chinese. A week had passed since the meeting with the attorney, and nothing new had surfaced. They snuggled closer, watching the flames crackle in the fireplace.

"Do you think this is the end of it?" Linda asked Colin, not really thinking he knew the answer.

"All I know is I have been cleared - not sure who was behind all this, but now I need to decide what I am going to do next. After all, I still want to develop this place, but I may need to wait a year or two and try again then. In the interim, it looks like I have some research that needs to be done on this place. Remember, we still have a dead body under our feet."

Their conversation was interrupted by the sudden tell-tale sound of an approaching helicopter, or better yet, two or three.

Colin went out on the porch to see where it was, as it sounded as if it would be landing in the field next to the house. There were three of them flying at tree-top level. Instead of landing where he thought it would, it continued, disappearing over the trees. It was clearly headed toward the Bryant place. There was also a strange glow in the sky from that direction. The sounds of the chopper grew fainter but were replaced with the sounds of sirens, all coming from different directions.

Linda was the first to speak. "Looks like something is happening over there."

"Yep. Do you think we should go see what is happening?" Colin replied.

"No way – you don't need to get involved in whatever is happening. We will find out soon enough. I probably need to get going."

It didn't take long to find out, as Linda called the next morning, awakening him out of his slumber.

"Well, it looks like ole Rufus met his match," She said. "The sheriff called me this morning. A joint task force showed up yesterday morning. Rufus and two of his sons have been arrested. Looks like a whole slew of charges against them, which will be announced at a press conference later today. They also recovered a treasure trove of documents that will pretty much seal their fate.

"That's great – but why the commotion last night? And, does this do anything to clear me?" Colin replied.

"Okay, okay, one question at a time. Apparently, in searching the place yesterday evening, they triggered some sort of booby-trap. The place was completely engulfed by the time the fire department could respond. Today, it is nothing more than a pile of burning embers."

"Wow. Have you talked to Junior? I mean, he is related and all…" Colin suddenly had something he hadn't possessed before – empathy. For the first time, he was actually concerned more about the others in his life."

"Gotta go – see you later today?" Linda asked.

"Why sure. We do have some things to talk about. Now, time to do some more reading…." Colin replied.

Colin spent most of the rest of the day carefully perusing the journal, anxious to discover more. He would doze a little, then read some more. This cycle repeated itself several times, only interrupted by his phone ringing. It was his attorney. The words he heard were like sweet honey to his lips.

"Colin, Ross Jenkins here. Got some good news for you. Just received a call from the federal prosecutor – they are dropping the remaining charges against you. You are a free man." Ross said.

Colin could feel tears of joy stinging his eyes as he let the news sink in. *There is justice in this world, after all,* he thought.

"Yeah, it turns out that besides the trafficking operations and drug distribution network that Bryant was running under the cover of his service company, he was also trying to work a deal with a Chinese company on exploiting something else that he discovered right under his feet – cobalt. From testing he had done in the old mine, it was not gold that was the most valuable, but the cobalt and copper deposits. He was trying hard to acquire your property in order to get to them."

That explained a whole lot. Colin couldn't wait to get off the phone to call Linda.

"It's over," Colin told her with a cracking voice.

"Yes, that is finished. What's next?" She asked.

"Well, there are a couple of things we need to take care of. For starters, I plan to find out what happened to Ben McDonald and his family. It is like I don't really care anymore about the development.

Deep down, I just feel like if I can ever find out what happened to Ben McDonald, a lot of questions will be answered." He paused.

"And the other thing?"

"Wanna get married?" He opened the small box and put the ring on her finger.

Chapter 33

Dawson County – Present Day

Colin and Luke sat quietly for a moment, watching a hawk catch a thermal as the sun started peeping above the trees.

Luke was the first to speak. "Wow – that's interesting. I didn't realize all that happened that brought me here and how you met Mom."

"Well, with everything happening, like with Mr. Anderson coming to visit and a lot of stuff you have seen. There has been a lot of stuff going on around here the last few years."

"But you mentioned Jacob and Tom – what about them?"

You had to have found out something about those things, right? Do those things have anything to do with why you went to Northeast Oklahoma and why Mr. Anderson is here? I mean, that's a long way from Georgia."

Colin smiled, then took a sip of coffee. "Sorry, got a little excited telling my story. I guess I should tell you about Jacob Childers, our ancestor, and his good friend, Ben.

Jacob has a rather interesting story himself…

Chapter 34

The Pioneer

South Carolina

1819

My granddaddy used to tell us stories about the Indians that lived on the land when they first arrived. They made friends with them, but things got hard, and one day, they got up and left. Granddad also would tell us stories about when he was just a boy like us; many men came and camped in the valley after their return from fighting the Brits near Charlotte.

Things were really going well in our little valley. By the time I was about 8, all of my siblings had left home, heading to Kentucky or Tennessee. For all except my older sister Melanie, we never heard from them again. Not sure if they died or just where they moved to; there was no way to get a letter back to us.

Everything in our family revolved around the farm and the church. Peace had settled into our part of the world. That is until the flu invaded our peaceful place. The flu epidemic struck in the early spring of 1820. Since there was very little contact with the outside world, people thought it came back with someone after going to town for court. How it got there didn't matter, as the effect was horrible. Many people died that spring – almost half the community was wiped out. Church was cancelled. People were scared to even visit with each other. We got suspicious. Things changed forever in our corner of the world.

The dreaded bug also touched our family. I held the hand of my sister as she faded away. The same thing happened to my mother. For whatever reason, Dad or I never contracted it. He and I suddenly faced life by ourselves, and because everybody was caring for their own dead and dying, there was no one other than us two to look out for each other.

Daddy took to drinking. I guess he felt the best way to deal with the pain and loss of losing my momma was to drink himself into a stupor. He stayed like this most of the time. I worked as hard as I could to keep things up on our small patch of a farm, but it was not easy.

One day, when coming in from gathering berries up on the mountain next to our place, I found Daddy in a heap on the floor, dead. He must have passed out and hit his head, as there was lots of blood. Whatever happened, I got very scared. I knew that now I was an orphan, I would be taken away or even questioned about my daddy's death and my role in it. I had to get out of there. Being a young boy of 12, I didn't know what to do. I had to leave before someone discovered the body. Hastily stuffing a few apples and potatoes into a my sack I used to gather berries, I quickly left the only place I knew as home, never to return.

I travelled for three days, initially not knowing where I was going. I considered going to Kentucky and try to find my brothers if they were still alive, or I could head back east toward Bethania or the Yadkin – there I know an uncle lived, but what would happen if they suspected me? I had to get out of there.

I soon found myself on a well-worn path that looked as though it had been there for years. Probably an old Indian trail, I thought. I began walking. From all signs, I was headed south. For three days, I walked until the small amount of food began to run out on me. Being hungrier than I had ever been before, I happened upon a small clearing with a cabin...

Jacob Childers

He was jolted awake by the clap of thunder. It had showered most of the day yesterday, and he was darned lucky to have found the small outcropping of rock to huddle under and get out of the weather. He had not seen another human being for the past two days since leaving Rutherford Town.

Where was he headed? Jacob had no clue. All he knew was that where he was going was away from THERE.

Walking kind of clears your mind, and after these four days since leaving home, Jacob had never felt freer than he was right now. This was in spite of the fact that other than the two unfortunate squirrels he had snared the night before, he had pretty much subsisted on the three hard rolls and the couple of apples he had stashed away in the small sack he had slung across his shoulder, as well as the berries and other wild plants he foraged along the way. Just out of town, he had managed to sneak a few more apples off a tree growing in a farmer's yard before being chased away by a rather mean-looking mutt.

The last year had gone by like a whirlwind. Long gone were the days of his early childhood. He used to enjoy hearing the tales of his granddad, who, along with others, had provided care and aid to the bedraggled group of men who had assembled over the mountains and were returning after having taught a lesson to ole Ferguson and Tarleton. His Grandpa would always get really excited when he told of how the men had "whipped the Brits asses" and were returning the hills and hollers from whence they came.

But that was all behind him now. So he journeyed on.

For another day, Jacob walked. Often, the boy would pop out again, and he would take to time stop and skip a rock in a stream, or to take a quick swim. The night's sleep wasn't so fearful, as the storms that swept through the night before had given way to clear blue skies and light breezes. The rain had also seemed to wake up everything, because it seemed as though all of creation had burst forth in hundred colors of spring.

By mid-afternoon on the second day, Jacob arrived in a small community. There was a small carriage house, a tavern, a general store, and several small cabins flanking the dirt paths that intersected in the community. It had been four days since he left home, and although he had eaten and foraged what he could along the way, there was only so much foraging a boy of 8 could do. To put it frankly, Jacob was famished, and then he saw it, or better yet, smelled it.

The simmering pot sat atop a fire near the edge of the woods that was his current refuge. Beyond the pot was a rather large house. As he watched, a rather matronly looking negro woman came out of the house, and after dropping what looked like a rather large size rabbit into the water, began to add other things to the stew. Jacob wanted to charge out of the woods, ask for something to eat, but dared not. He had no money. Most of the settlers at home never had any money anyway, as what they couldn't raise or grow was foraged for, and everything else was bartered. He could do this, but what was he going to barter? The burlap sack he carried over his shoulder? Then, as he was considering his options, he heard the voice of a man inside the tavern calling for the woman.

Wiping her hands on the large apron she wore around her waist, she turned around and WALKED away from the table, disappearing through the back door of the tavern.

This was all the opening Jacob needed. Taking a circuitous route through the woods, he crouched lowly in the brush, keeping his eyes on the door while also staking out the feast that sat before him. Forgetting to show discretion, hunger took over. There was a rather sizeable mound of potatoes, carrots, and onions, and several rabbits that had been skinned and dressed, awaiting their turn in the boiling caldron sitting a few feet away. Jacob first picked up a potato, stuck it in his mouth, and, between bites, started cramming a rabbit and some more of the newfound nourishment into his gunny sack.

"HEY YOU!!! What do you think you are doing???" Came a voice out of nowhere. The matronly black woman, who had disappeared into the tavern several minutes ago, had been replaced by a rather stocky built man, who looked at least 6 feet tall, who was now running at full speed across the small clearing that separated the tavern from the cooking area.

"You get away from there! Go on, git! Shouted the man. Jacob grabbed one last handful, and off he went. The race was on. He took off down a small trail that descended into the wood line, with what was apparently the proprietor hot on his heels. The trail he was running on was really no challenge for Jacob, and the further they ran, the greater the distance got between Jacob and his would-be captor. That gap grew, that is, until a nice-sized root from a nearby chestnut tree got involved in the chase. Not seeing it, Jacob's toe hooked perfectly under it, and down he went, flipping head over heels down a bank. He landed with a thud, and the last thing he saw before his world went black was the blood running out of the gash on the side of his head.

Jacob awakened suddenly and found that the bed of ivy he had found himself laying in earlier had been replaced by what had to be the softest straw mattress he had ever laid on. Of course, anything would beat the places he had slept the last three days. He started to get up, when trying, he felt the pounding in his head from the nasty fall he had taken earlier. Plus, someone had taken the liberty of TYING his left leg to the foot of the iron bed he was laying in. He had to get out of here, but unless he was able to untie the rope that held him fast, there was little chance of that. After a few minutes, Jacob was able to contort and manipulate his body to at least *reach* the knot and begin to regain his freedom.

About the time he had really begun to make progress on the knot, he heard footsteps and muffled conversations outside his door, followed by the slow creak of the door as a young woman entered the room. He quickly laid back on the bed, feigning sleep. She was carrying a towel and bowl with some water in it.

"There, there…" she said softly as if she knew what he was up to. "No reason to do that." She swiftly moved over to the bed and, reaching down, untied the knot herself. "Sorry to scare you, but we didn't want you to leave without you got a good, uh, well enough to travel. This was the only way we could keep you here."

Jacob was truly puzzled. "What is this place?" He asked.

"You are at Morris's Tavern. My name is Mary. My husband, Augustin and I live here."

"You know you were trying to steal from us, right young man?"
Her tone turned darker as the man who had chased him earlier
appeared in the doorway.

"Son, you took quite a spill out there. I thought for certain you
were gone. So, tell me, why did you feel it was your right to take what
wasn't yours? I am waiting for your answer." He seemed to grow
bigger every moment that passed.

"I'm, I'm sorry," Jacob stammered. His eyes suddenly stung from
the tears he desperately tried to hold in. "I was just hungry". He no
longer felt like the mighty woodsman but was again a little boy of 12
who had been away from family for far too long.

"Where did you come from? Does your family live around here?"
Gus queried as Mary stepped out of the room."

"My name is Jacob. I have been traveling for 3 days, come from
up in the mountains." Jacob continued – "My family is dead – the
flu." Jacob hoped he didn't press the issue too much, as that was not
exactly the whole truth.

Soon, Mary appeared once again, and this time, she had a large
bowl of steaming hot stew that soon had Jacob forgetting all his
troubles, at least for the moment. He quickly gobbled down the bowl,
along with the tall glass of cider that she had prepared. Soon after
finishing off the bowl, Jacob fell asleep and slept the soundest he had
slept in over a week. He wasn't sure if this would be his new home,
but for the time being, he was willing to give it a try.

Chapter 35

It took about two weeks before I was able to get up and about. Besides my head, I also hurt my leg pretty bad, although I didn't break anything. The owners were glad to have me there – they only had small children, so I was able to help out around the place. I remember the house being a large log structure – Mr. Morris had surveyed the area many years ago for the state, and they gave him the land to start a tavern. So, he built the place and returned with his family to live. Soon, business was brisk, as they were taking in travelers heading either to Georgia or from the coast over the mountains to Tennessee...

Jacob Childers

The sounds of an ungodly commotion awakened Jacob. He sprang out of his bed, which was set up in the back corner of the house. Since it was his job every morning to go out and tend to the small menagerie of animals Gus maintained at the small farm and tavern, it was best for his room if you could call it that, to be located near the back door.

Jacob was running across the yard, having quickly pulled on his boots and still pulling up his suspenders. Gus was not far behind, with his old trusty gun poised to shoot at whatever they came across. "Darn coyote," Jacob yelled to him as he sprinted full speed over the 100 feet or so of the barn and chicken coop. He tried to make himself as big as he could as he yelled at the top of his lungs at the four-legged intruder.

Gus, out of breath, soon caught up, and Jacob in a flashback to his old days fighting redcoats, took a shot at some direction toward the commotion.

They were not sure whether it was Jacob's yelling or the shooting, but whatever was there was gone by the time they got there.

"It must have been that coyote again. I heard him yelping earlier," Jacob announced, quite sure of himself.

"I put you in the barn for a reason…" Gooch stared rather menacingly at Jacob. "You keep this up, and you'll never repay for that meat you ruined."

"I… I'm sorry." Jacob muttered, fighting back the tears that were welling up in his eyes. A mere lad, how could he be expected to stop these wild animals on his own?? Besides, how long were they going to hold this over his head, anyway?

"Sure," Gooch said as he flipped over the dead rooster sprawled out in front of him with the toe of his boot. "I suspect that the coyote tangling with this guy is what convinced him to leave, the way it looks. I would like to say my old musket ball would scare him away, but I think this thing has seen its better days", the old man said.

"See the trail of blood?" The combination of their eyes adjusting to the early morning light and the dusting of snow that had fallen overnight revealed a small dotted trail heading out toward the wood line.

"With that amount of blood, I don't think he will be long for this world. Jacob, you take care of the animals here – I am going to follow this trail to see what I can find." With that, he disappeared into the early morning fog.

An hour later, Jacob had finished putting out hay for the three cows and two goats that provided milk and meat for the small tavern the Morris family operated. One of them, Maggie, was the family dairy cow, and after getting the food out, he found himself underneath her, getting the daily portion of milk for the household. As he was leaving the barn to head back to the house, Gus came around the corner of the barn, carrying his gun in one hand and, in the other, the carcass of the coyote that had feasted on their farm the last week.

For Jacob, the last two months had been, well, kind of strange. Sometimes, Gus and his wife Mary were like parents to him, letting him spend time with them and finding out more about him. At other times, however, he felt like another of the handful of slaves that the couple owned. For the past several weeks, as winter approached, it seemed as though the older couple became more tense.

One thing for sure – traffic was increasing, and it seemed as if most nights, two or three guests were staying at the tavern, most coming from Charleston, Savannah, and Augusta, heading to their new dream over the mountains to Tennessee and to Kentucky. Many of them were returning from driving livestock through the gorges and valleys to get them to market. As they were called, these drivers usually slept outside under the stars. Most of the other travelers did not take kindly to the bouquet of aromas that swirled around them.

This fall, however, a different sort of traveler arrived at the tavern. Not too far away, a second road was recently improved that provided a connection to Pendleton from Charlotte. From the direction of Charlotte, whole families, with everything they owned, started coming in, sometimes 1-2 a night. Because of the new travelers that now filled up the inn most every night, Jacob was pressed into service in the kitchen, helping to clean dishes and tend to other chores as needed to make the guests comfortable.

This went on for several weeks, when one day, out of the woods rode what seemed to be a small caravan of people. There were two HUGE wagons, different from the small flatbed mule carts or pack mules most of the local people used.

Jacob soon found out these strangers were different from the traders and drovers that typically stopped. Many of these were families, some with small children. Jacob often had difficulty communicating with them; some spoke little English. He soon discovered that there were Germans, Swiss, and some Dutch. All of them had one thing on their mind – getting to Georgia as soon as possible.

"How is your soul, lad? Are you doing good?" Asked the man who always sat in the same place in the Tavern. That was always this first question. He wasn't here often but appeared every few weeks, gaunt, tired, and filthy. Gus and Mary always made sure he was treated well, and if it was open, he was given the best room in the place to rest. Jacob also found out that he never had to pay anything to stay there. Jacob soon learned that he was a preacher – not just any preacher, but one of what they called at they called "MethodistsHis name was Benjamin McDonald, or Ben, as everyone called him. He was "riding the circuit," as they called it, in the area, and had found this as a good place to stay for a day or two. Sometimes, he was jovial with the other patrons, often beating them in a contest of arm wrestling, checkers, or some other game of skill. Other times, he sat there quietly, with the glint of tears in his eyes.

"So, the usual tonight?" Ben asked Jacob one evening. Often, when he was there, Ben would take the time to talk with him, and because of these times, Jacob was really warming up to the young minister, who didn't seem to be much older than himself. One night, when Ben seemed most distant and troubled, Jacob came out and asked him what was wrong.

"Oh Jacob, it's nothing really. It's just part of what I do – It looks like I will be moving on tomorrow. My work here in the Carolinas is done. I am being summoned back to Philadelphia to receive my new instructions from the bishop. I will be leaving behind some good friends I have made here that I may not ever see again."

"That's just not fair!" Jacob said, "Why can't you stay? Can I go with you?"

"There are many reasons, some of which I can't talk about right now," Ben said as he stared off into the dark of the night. And, no, there is no way for you to go. You are needed here, plus the church would never allow it. But God's got a plan, and we just have to do what we can to be a part of it."

With that, Ben hugged the young man, both of them fighting back tears. The next morning when Jacob arose, Ben was gone.

Jacob sat for a long time, just thinking. He certainly wanted a part of what Ben was doing. He didn't know yet whether he really believed in this God Ben spoke about, who loved him. The only God he knew about was the stern taskmaster portrayed by the stern pastors he had met back in the valley before he left, who had little use for him and his drunken dad. Maybe, he thought, as he drifted off to sleep later that night, that maybe, just maybe, the God he heard about from Ben was real, and maybe he had a plan for him, too.

Chapter 36

"My granddad brought these with him from Pennsylvania. They are made for rough trips." The young boy ran his hand over the wheels. "See how much wider they are - they are less likely to get stuck."

"I guess that's why you need such large horses then." Jacob couldn't help but admire the girth of the two huge horses that had pulled the wagon into the clearing two days before.

"James, my name… James Barrier. Most folks call me Jimmy." Jimmy stuck out his hand to Jacob.

"Pleased to meet you," Jacob responded. "So, are you all heading down to Georgia, too?"

"Yep. My dad's uncle is a trader. He sent my dad a letter to come help him. We are headed to Georgia."

"Georgia? Where's that?"

"I don't know exactly, but Dad said we just need to keep following the sun, and it will get us there. A lot of people are headed that way."

"Yea – Pa says we are stopping here for a couple of weeks to rest up. The rest of the journey won't be as easy. My Pa was there before and came back to get us. He told us of all the stories of the Indians, and gold, and all kinds of stuff. You ought to come with us. Maybe your dad will let you come with us!"

Jacob lowered his head. "He's not my dad. My dad died. I ran away. I just kinda just live here."

"Wow – then you can come with us? Let me talk to my Dad!" said Jimmy.

"JIMMY! You out here?" yelled his mom as she walked slowly toward them.

"Gotta go! See ya later!"

That night, after the chores were done and things had quieted down. Jacob lay on his bed, pondering the conversation he had earlier. He liked it here, kinda. There was plenty to eat, for sure, but he, most of the time, was treated only slightly better than the hired help. He still wanted adventure, and hearing the stories of the traders that came through here, he was enchanted with the idea of moving on and taking part in the adventures he was hearing about. Going north back home was not an option. He was scared that people would recognize him there and there would be too many questions. But – from all he was hearing, Georgia was the place to go. As he drifted off to sleep, dreams of what could await him filled his head.

For the next several weeks, Jacob and Jimmy became like brothers as winter set in. They would help each other with their chores, then find time to explore the woods around the farm, trapping, gathering chestnuts, and generally being boys.

As the days began to get longer, Jacob knew the time was coming when the Barriers would be preparing for the next leg of their journey. Jacob had also gotten to know Mr. & Mrs. Barrier, and they often hinted about what it would be like if he were their son. Jacob was flattered by the affection shown by them.

Late one evening, Jacob overheard the two men talking.

"I think we will be moving on in the next few days," Henry told the innkeeper, but I need to talk to you about the young boy – Jacob."

"What about him? Has he caused you problems?"

"No, no; quite the opposite. He has been helpful, and he and my boy Jimmy have become good friends. I want to see about him going with us."

"Hold on now – I don't know if that will work. I need him here, and he still owes me for stealing from me."

"Yeah. I heard about that. So you think after a year of working, he has paid you back for that? Huh?"

The innkeeper was starting to get agitated. "Are you trying to take my help away?"

"No, I am just saying that it looks like with your other help, you might be able to spare him. How much is he worth to you? I could really use him where we are going."

"What do you have in mind?"

Chapter 37

Pendleton, South Carolina, was a bustling town of several hundred people. Thanks to the treaty that was signed, all the Cherokee were gone, moving to better lands in Georgia and Tennessee. People from all over were converging on the frontier crossroads, and just like the other "new" towns in the region, the new settlers pretty much moved into established villages that were left behind. There was little else besides the few buildings that housed a tavern, blacksmith shops, and stables. A church was under construction. For many, this place was nothing more than a stopover, as the weary traveler headed to the new lands west of here needed a place to rest. Tomorrow, they would leave for Georgia.

But tonight, they would rest. They enjoyed a dinner in the Tavern, and because the inn was pretty full, and Henry wanted to make sure no one tampered with their stuff, Jacob and Jimmy rolled out their bedrolls under the wagon in the stable. The two of them lay there for a few minutes, talking about their day and the adventures they imagined facing in the days ahead. Soon, Jimmy became quiet, and he could hear the soft snores coming from his new friend. Not sleepy, Jacob laid there thinking. He had spent the day getting to know the people who, for now, were the only family he knew. He had already noticed the difference – even though he had stayed with the Morris's for several months, he never progressed much further than being a hired hand. His pay had been a place to stay, and that was about it. It seemed at times Gus, as people called him, was warming to Jacob, but Mary maintained her distance from the young lad, and Jacob never felt close to her. They had, however, made things comfortable. He also allowed his thoughts to drift further back – as he heard the coyotes yelping in the distance, he was taken back to an earlier time – to his time with his own dad, which seemed so far in the distant past. He had changed a lot in the year since he had snuck away, and for the first time since he left home, he felt like he had found his place – at least for the moment. As his eyelids slowly got heavier, soon, the memories would turn to dreams, and Jacob was asleep.

They had been there four days. Jacob wondered why they were just sitting there. Wasn't the goal to get to Georgia? The days became an endless chore of tending to the horses, straightening their stuff, and getting more provisions for the journey ahead.

The dawn's light was peeping through the spokes of the large wagon wheels when they awoke the next morning. There was also a minor commotion going on outside. Jacob rolled over, and as he wiped the sleep out of his eyes, he could see one of them was Mr. Barrier.

He was dressed like any number of the mountain men he had seen both back and home and at the inn. His clothes hung on him like rags, and he had on a pair of homemade moccasins. His long, graying hair was pulled back in a ponytail, and the long, flowing beard was nestled on his chin like a beaver pelt. Henry called him Grey Fox. Every once in a while, he would turn and spit a long brown stream into the dirt by his foot.

"So your uncle is not doing too well. I hope we make it in time. I had to delay the start of my journey by a day due to a big storm that blew through. Tore up some stuff pretty well, but we got it secured, okay. Looks like it will be smooth sailing for our trip the next few days."

"I was gettin' worried about you," Tom replied. "Was beginning to think you wouldn't make it, and we would have to make it on our own."

"No, as I said, there was nothing I could have done. But I am here now, so let's get some rest tonight because we have a tough few days ahead of us. So where's my cousin?"

By this time, Margaret had bounded down the steps and embraced her cousin in a long hug. "It's been so long! You've hardly changed at all. Well, maybe a little…"

Over the next several hours, they would spend time catching up. Zeke was what they called Ezekiel Bryant, Margaret's brother. Jacob learned a lot just by listening to the adults talk. Jimmy and Sissy sat beside Jacob and seemed just as enthralled as he was, hearing Grey Fox tell the stories of the places he had seen. They learned that he had been as far as the great river out west and had met lots of Indians and explorers on his journeys. He was a trader and brought back loads of pelts from beavers, foxes, and raccoons. He also learned about his newfound family.

Henry Barrier, Jake was soon to find out, was German. His grandfather had found his way to Carolina from Pennsylvania many years before. His parents were both dead; he had developed a close relationship with his uncle, whom he had not seen in about 5 years. In North Carolina, The Barriers and Bryants both lived near each other. Being neighbors, it was only natural for Henry and Margaret to eventually marry. Zeke was Margaret's younger brother Ezekiel was somewhat of a rebel, an adventurer. For some personal reason, many think it was because of a young lady who happened to be the pastor's daughter, Ezekiel had to leave home in a hurry. For two years, no one heard anything from him until late one evening in early April he came wandering back home. Margaret was about the only one happy to see him, and so for a season, he worked as a hired hand on the Barrier homestead. Also living there was Henry's brother Hans, and his wife Malinda.

Hans was the first to move on. He was restless, and when he got ready to leave to try to find his fortune in the newly opened areas in Georgia, Ezekiel was eager to join him. It was felt best that Malinda stayed behind in North Carolina until Hans and Zeke, as he was now called, could get the trading business established. As fate would have it, however, Not long after Hans left, Malinda died after being bit by a rattlesnake. When Hans sent for her six months later, Henry had to deliver the sad news to carry back to Georgia.

Now, after 5 years, the whole family was days away from being reunited. After his dad died, Henry sold the farm to a new family just arriving from Virginia, and here they were.

So, where would they be heading in Georgia? He learned that Hans had established his homestead near a place called Mule Camp Springs. They would be near where two rivers joined, where there was also a ford several other trails forked off, heading south and west. Hans had established quite a trading business with the Cherokee that lived in the area. Others had apparently heard of the area as well because it seemed like everyone they met, and all the buzz at the stops they made near Tugaloo and the new town of Carnesville the next two day was about the new areas that had opened for settlement. It didn't matter that most of them didn't own any of the land, but they knew they would have a place among the steady stream of wagons, horsemen, and those on foot seemed to appear and disappear as the road west lay the frontier they had been looking for since their grandparents and great-grandparents left the plantations of Ulster a century earlier.

They traveled along the old trading path, which the natives left as one of their few legacies. The road was slowly being improved, mainly by those travelers that took the time to clear a wider path, but progress was slow and frequently interrupted by a mudhole or other obstacle that would block their progress, but only for a time until it was cleared, and the journey would begin again.

Many of the travelers to Georgia had split off, heading to places like Athens, Washington, and the new state capital at Milledgeville. For these, the open plains beckoned with their promise of cheap land and, in many cases, grants that had been given to the veterans of the recent war with the Brits. As for Jacob and his newly found friends, they would be turning more toward the distant mountains. This was where the Cherokee were and where they would find the trading post.

The going from Carnesville to Mule Camp Springs was extra bad, as few had traveled this path. Whatever shape the roads were in before were pristine compared to what they found now. Although the road stayed pretty much on a natural ridgeline from this point, at points, it would narrow to the point that there were fears the wagons would get stuck and be unable to continue. The journey would take most of two days as the group wound its way slowly down the trail.

Chapter 38

I had to grow up fast. I guess when you leave home at such an early age like I did, then work for over a year as little more than a hired hand, you learn the ways of the world pretty quickly. Not to mention getting the chance to travel, to see things outside my little corner of the world.

We finally got to the springs three days later. The trail was rough, and the last few miles were across some pretty big hills until we finally reached the crest of the long, gentle ridgeline. They didn't bother me too much because they were much smaller than the mountains I had left in Carolina.

The small settlement was where several old trading paths met. At the center of the settlement was a rather abundant spring that was the magnet that had brought mainly traders there. There were a few cabins clustered around the spring in the middle of the settlement, and I remember the new courthouse was nothing more than a larger cabin sitting on top of a small knoll a few hundred feet away. Although we had called it Mule Camp Springs, now that it was an official town, it had now been renamed Gainesville.

We traveled a way down the path that took us closer to the river, and hence the Cherokees - Hightower, they called it. It sat on the high ground between the two rivers. We found the place to be in bad shape. Although Hans had tried to keep up, it was more than he could do – I had learned since being with the Barriers that this was the biggest reason they came here. We immediately began to work to help Hans, but within a few weeks after arriving, we found him dead one morning. We buried him alongside his Indian wife, Bluebird, on top of the hill in the meadow they loved so dearly.

With his death, Henry inherited the small general store, livery stable, and tavern that had so much potential with the new settlers and travelers passing that way. The place became a beehive of activity as the number of settlers poured into the area. Mainly, the people came from Carolina Virginia, but also from as far away as Pennsylvania and New Jersey. They all were farmers – looking for land they could settle on and raise a family. Many also befriended the local Cherokees, some of which had settled along the western fork of the river – Atsunsta Ti Yi, "place of lights." The settlers dubbed it the Chestatee. And it was the boundary the government had set up for what was called "The Nation."

A lot happened over the next few years. The new road the government had built from Augusta to the west began to flourish. New lands opened up in Tennessee and Alabama. It seemed no sooner had someone arrived in town they were off again, heading to promises of better land beyond the mountains. Soon, folks from South Carolina learned Pendleton learned that the road to Hightower from Gainesville would cut a full day's journey off the trip, so the traffic increased once again.

All these settlers were good for business, and because we had secured a trading permit with the Indians early on, we delivered many things to New Echota and beyond. It also meant we often brought cargo back, including providing transportation to Gainesville, which now housed a federal courthouse and provided much of the administration for the Nation. Times were good; even though they largely got along, the tension was increasing every day and every month; the settlers and the Cherokees had to live this close together.

On the west, there was a dotting of a small farm here and there, and even some adventurous souls had crossed into the Cherokee nation and settled there, but for the most part, these were mixed families. This had been going on for at least three generations and had caused resentment among many of the "full-bloods," who felt the old ways were being lost in the race to be like the new nation that was now their new protector.

They had tried to stop it, but all they could do was delay. For the most part, they were families that did not hurt anybody; they just wanted a quiet place to farm and raise their families. There were the others – those that, for whatever reason, were running – from the law, from an awkward family situation, from peace to chaos. This land provided it all. Even though the river was the boundary, most of the Indians were settled in villages that were further west – near the tall mountains that separated the rest of Georgia from Tennessee. I knew about these mountains as part of my regular trips.

I had one of the teams, and although at times Henry found me to be easily distracted, he trusted me more than Zeke, who was responsible for the other team. He went north, toward the settlements along what they called the Unicoi Road. I took the west route. Henry put a lot of trust in me to haul the goods to Hightower, where the wagon got unhitched and another wagon loaded up with whatever was being sold back in Gainesville. When the wagon wasn't full, I would find myself carrying extra passengers, usually Indians, who needed to make the trip...

Jacob Childers

Chapter 39

The sun was shining clear on this magical time between the heat of August and the cool mornings of October. The leaves in the trees overhead had just begun to get a hint of color, the corn fields that had been planted in the spring were now a golden brown in the late summer heat. Soon, the melodious call will be heard echoing through these hills as the quest will be on to find the hog that was turned out to graze in the spring. Although a bank of foreboding clouds hung back over the mountains, Jacob thought nothing of it. The weather was so good he was ahead of schedule. Besides, he had other reasons that only a young man in love could understand for wanting to hurry home.

Jacob found a clearing near the river, where he decided it would be a good place to stop and clean up before seeing Sissy. He also needed some time to work up the courage to talk with Henry. He pulled the wagon over into a small clearing that only he knew about, hopped down off the wagon, and grabbed the special bar of soap he had tucked in his jacket before leaving home. Stripping down to his skivvies, he waded into the river. The water was bitingly cold, even for a late summer day, but that was okay. For a few moments, Jacob let his thoughts drift back to the small branch that ran through their little valley back home. He remembered how he used to play up and down the creek as a young boy, without a care in the world…five years had passed, and now 20, Jacob had to start thinking about doing something he never dreamed possible - settling down and starting a family. During his travel, he had seen plenty of young Cherokee girls, but they did not completely strike his fancy.

For Jacob, he knew who it would be. She just didn't know it yet. The thing about being gone for long periods, as he did in being a wagoneer, was that things changed. Boy, did they change. To Jacob, Sissy had always been Jimmy's little pesky sister. She was five years younger than Jacob, and he never paid her much mind until two months ago. Suddenly, the little brat of a girl, that was always getting in the way had suddenly blossomed. For the first time, Jacob was drawn to her soft curves and, most of all, what had become a sharp, biting wit as the exchanges between them started taking on a different meaning. That was the major reason he decided it was time to bathe here. He wanted to look his best when she saw him next. Plus, he was prepared to ask her father for her hand.

While Jacob was wondering, pondering these things, he didn't notice the water, which had suddenly become higher and fiercer. The small pool he was swimming in was cut off by the rising water. He had paid scant attention to those clouds banked up over the mountains earlier but realized that soon he would drown if he did not do something. The torrent kept coming and swept him 50 yards or so downstream. He grabbed ahold of a branch that was hanging out over the water and pulled himself over the branch. Of course, he had to share it with a rather perturbed black snake, which decided he would rather get wet than be this close to a human, as it plopped into the rising waters. *I didn't think I smelled that bad,* thought Jacob.

After what seemed to be an eternity, the water seemed to reach its peak, but there was really no way off the branch he was on. Jacob hung there for what seemed like ages. He was tired, and sitting in the crotch of the big branch hanging over the river, it became quite comfortable, and he found himself slowly drifting off to sleep.

He was startled to his senses by the sound of giggles. The water was starting to recede, having almost returned to its pre-storm level. What replaced it was smelly mud, which replaced the water and made it impossible to get over to shore without getting dirty again. Having removed his skivvies when he entered the river, he had nothing on but a smile. He had no idea where his clothes went, but likely downriver. He spun his head around as he heard the giggle again. On the bank, not 10 feet away, was a young girl. She had coal-black hair which had been braided. She wore a simple brown colored cotton dress, and her feet were bare. Her skin was an olive brown, which gave her away as being a Cherokee. The only thing that did not fit were her eyes. Their grey-blue color seemed to jump out of her face, piercing anything she looked at. Jacob tried to cover himself but soon found that was impossible while sitting on a tree limb 10 feet above the river bank. He felt like one of the heifers he used to see put on display at the cow pens every fall.

"Little Fawn! What are you doing? Haven't I told you not to...". A man, somewhat older than Jacob, stepped out of the shadows. He took the girl by the arm and started to walk away.

"Look, Papa!" she exclaimed as she pointed at Jacob, trying rather unsuccessfully to make himself invisible.

"Oh my," said the man as he shielded his young daughter from any more of the impromptu show. "I will be right back".

10 minutes later, the man returned with two blankets – one he laid down on the mud to provide a path to get to the bank, and the other Jacob quickly wrapped around himself. A cool breeze was now blowing down the river, and with no clothes to keep him warm, Jacob

was starting to get chilled. It was obvious that he needed to get warm in a hurry.

"Come on, we'll get something in you." He stuck out his hand – "McDonald's the name. And you look familiar. Who are you?"

"Jacob, Jacob Childers," he replied humbly, as it is hard to be proud when talking to a stranger when you have no clothes on. "I was just stopping to bathe off before getting back home but got caught…"

"Jacob? From the tavern?" A big grin broke out on the older man's face. "Don't remember me, do you?"

Maybe it was the way he looked at Jacob or whatever clue he provided, but Jacob's eyes lit up. "Ben! Ben McDonald! But what are you doing here? I thought you went back to Philadelphia?"

"I did. Stayed there a few months, trying to figure out what the good Lord wanted me to do next, so I ended up here." Ben then looked at the young man standing in front of him with concern. "You are lucky you were not drowned. You really must watch those clouds. This river can be dangerous when the rain falls over the mountains. Let's get you dried out, then we can talk more.

Soon, Jacob found himself following Ben into a small clearing. Besides what looked to be a small, open-sided structure in the middle of the clearing, there were also 4 cabins arranged in a circle around the center shelter. They walked over to the biggest of the shelters, apparently Ben's home. It looked in some ways like the cabins that dotted the fields and byways on the other side – the river where the settlers lived. But it was clear that this place was different.

He had forgotten how famished he was. It had been almost 24 hours since he ate anything. Ben's wife, Tayanita, stood over the pot of soup. She wore a simple dress, with her coal-black hair pulled up into a bun on top of her head. She softly hummed a tune as she cooked. She simply nodded when Jacob spoke to her. Ben spoke to her in a strange-sounding tongue – she apparently knew very little English.

Jacob sat close to the fire, and within a few minutes, he was getting back to his old self. Ben was nearby, playing some sort of game with his children. He could see the love that existed between the young father and his children. He realized how much he missed this part of his childhood. He longed for the time when he would be able to have his own family – that was about to happen soon, as he let his thoughts drift toward Maggie, who would be greeting him when his journey was done.

Jacob wolfed down the soup that had been provided, but wanting to be polite; he refused a second helping; besides, Ben's wife and daughters hadn't eaten yet. Not sure if it was the soup, or getting warm and dry by the fire, but soon Ben's eyes began to get heavy. He roused briefly as Ben came back into the clearing, sitting atop Jacob's wagon he left by the river earlier.

"The river is still pretty high; why don't you just stay here tonight? It could be pretty dangerous crossing at this hour".

Ben was right. Even though he longed to get back home to see Maggie and talk with Henry, Jacob had worn himself out pretty well. "I will take you up on your offer."

Dinner was over, the kids and Tayanita, or Youmg Beaver as Jacob had learned her name, meant having eaten. Once the mess was cleaned up, Ben sat down with Jacob, each man sitting by the fire, with pipes in hand, while the last embers died down, and the small cabin became quiet with only the sounds of soft snoring breaking the silence.

The two men sat there for a time until Jacob broke the silence with a question that had been on his mind since they reunited earlier in the day – "So, how did you end up here?"

Ben took a long draw on his pipe, leaned back in his chair, and began to talk.

"When you saw me a few times back in the tavern, I was about to head back to Philadelphia to meet with my church leaders. I had been a riding a circuit about 10 years, throughout the mountains of Carolina and the Cherokee, stopping a day here or there and looking for people ready to worship. I had followed in my father's footsteps, as he was a fur trader and a part-time preacher himself – he had actually been an early student of Asbury himself. He was well known and sought out among the people. I naturally followed in his footsteps, but it wore on me, and I had to go to the church leaders to tell them I was done. Too much time in the saddle from a very early age. So, they sent me here to start this mission station and settle down in one place."

"That's how I ended up here," Ben continued. "The Church sent me here to do a new work in these parts. What you see here is just the beginning. We have already asked the Lord to bless this place and plan to do lots of other stuff as well – even a school for the children who live in the area. Little did I realize that the first person the Lord would provide would be Tayanita. I met her within weeks of coming here, and soon we were married."

But enough about me, how did you end up in these parts?"

At first, Jacob was guarded, but Ben seemed genuine, so Jacob started from the beginning. At times, tears welled up in his eyes, especially in talking of his growing-up years, but it was as if a dam had broken as Jacob shared how he came to know the barriers and almost became part of the family overnight. Ben sat quietly as Jacob told his story until he mentioned the name of Ezekiel Bryant. He started to say something, but the look in his eyes displayed his concern for Jacob.

"Do you know Zeke? He was also a trader." Jacob asked.

"We have met a couple of times. How much do you know about him?" Ben leaned forward in his chair.

"Not a lot – I think Henry's wife is his cousin. He served as a guide for us coming out of Carolina. He was very helpful and now uses the store as his base. Why do you ask?"

"Oh, not enough for you to worry about right now. Just be careful around him, that is all. Watch your back." Ben then quickly changed the subject. "You know trouble is brewing, right?" Ben said as he reared back in his chair.

Although one would have to be out of it to not know the tensions that were building, Jacob was unsure how much to share with Ben. Although they had taken up right where they left off years before, Ben was still guarded when it came to the "Indian problem," as it was now being called. You just couldn't be sure where people stood. If not careful, you could find yourself in a heap of trouble. Especially doing the traveling he was doing.

"It's becoming harder and harder to live here. We have seen more and more harassment. Some of our folks are already talking about leaving – they feel that we can live in peace if we just move west, get some distance, and make a new life out there. They don't control things right now, so I don't ever see that idea going anywhere." He leaned back in his chair, taking a deep puff on his pipe. "I happen to fall with those folks that are running things – we just need to stay put. First, I don't trust the US to get us safely out of here, and second, ole John Ross has ole Hickory's ear. I am sure they can work something out. What do you think?"

The young Jacob hadn't really given it much thought. All the chatter he was hearing was from the settlers – they didn't care how it happened; they just wanted the Indians gone. As for Jacob, he knew their livelihood depended a lot on the trade that had opened up with the nation. "I agree!" He chose his words carefully. Even though he was only 16, he knew that the wrong words in a situation like this could destroy their business, and soon they would have nothing.

As the evening continued and the fire died away, both men, having shared many stories, turned in for the night. Regardless of what the future held and how the Cherokee felt about leaving, it mattered very little. Although he had been diverted from his original plans to be back home tonight to see Sissy, he somehow felt this was a good night, one in which he had made new friends. But still, he couldn't help but wonder what the future held for them and the other others who lived close by. As he was drifting off to sleep, somewhere in the distance, he heard the whippoorwill singing.

Chapter 40

The next morning, the sun woke Jacob just as it was peeping through the trees surrounding the small hamlet where he had spent the night. There was something special about the place, he thought, as he climbed on the wagon. It was not far, but he did have to get across the river, which was no longer the angry, churning caldron it was the day before. Minutes later, he successfully negotiated the granite shelf that acted like an underwater bridge. For the next hour, as he rode down the dirt path that had now become a road, his mind couldn't help but wander to his task. He had business to discuss with Mr. Barrier.

"Where in the world have you been?" shouted Barrier, running out to meet him at the wagon. You were supposed to be back days ago! What were you doing? Don't you know I needed you here?"

Jacob stared at the ground in front of him. Here I go again, he thought. It seems like I can do nothing that will please this guy. "I'm sorry, it's just that the river was high from the storm, and as such, I couldn't... I almost drowned..."

Henry could see the sincerity in the young man. He had become more than just an extra hand but almost a son to himself. Jacob got along well with everyone he met and never saw a stranger.

"We were worried more than anything." Barringer then explained – "Something is going on, I just can't quite figure out. It seems this place is getting more crowded by the day."

Sissy was standing at the door, looking out at Jacob with a grin on her face. He couldn't help but blush a little as he unhitched the mules, Sam and Oscar, and walked them around the barn. After he had them put up for the evening, he was startled when Sissy snuck up behind him, goosing him in the ribs. Before she could defend herself, he had thrown his arms around her, lifting her off the ground and tied to plant a kiss. This girl, who was just a runt of a little sister three years ago, had blossomed into the loveliest thing Jacob had ever seen.

He had made up his mind while he was gone that when he got back, he would be asking for her dad for her hand in marriage. With his late return, however, and her dad's mood, he knew that he needed to hold off a couple of hours to let things cool off a bit.

It was not a typical supper. What was normally a jovial affair, in which everyone caught up on the news, and the atmosphere almost tavern-like, everyone was quiet tonight. Everybody in the room except for Jacob and Cissy thought it was because of Jacob and Henry's crosswords earlier in the day. That was not the case. Theo was the first to break the silence. "Hey, this is not a funeral. What if we get a little music going? He turned and grabbed the banjo, and leaned up in the corner. "What do ya'll want to hear?"

He was met with an awkward silence before he just launched out on some nameless tune. Regardless, it seemed to lighten the mood somewhat, and after a few minutes, Henry stood up. "I think I will go out and check on our on the fence out back. Anyone care to join me?"

"Mom, I will stay here and help you clean up," Cissy said, giving Jacob a little wink.

By this time, Theo had already disappeared, having headed outside to the cool air of the porch. Jacob knew this was his chance.

Bounding out the back door, he could see Henry leaning up against the fence behind the house, which was built in vain to keep the ever-present deer out of the corn. He appeared to be gazing off into the distance with something on his mind.

Jacob was the first to speak. "Mr Barrier (he always used his formal name when things got tense and serious), I am sorry about what happened earlier today. I guess I let the frustrations get the best of me…I've had a lot on my mind lately."

"That's okay. I got a little hot, too. I guess I was just a little worried. Trying to run a farm, while at the same time working this business, it can get to you. Plus, things are about to get bad, I get the feeling."

"What do you mean?" Jacob had some inkling, especially after the conversation he had with Ben McDonald the day before.

"These folks are good people," Barringer continued, "But I just don't see where it can be worked out for everyone to live in peace with each other. I even met a young man yesterday who was passing through – a minister, one of them Methodist. He said he was going to work with the Cherokees across the river."

Jacob then proceeded to tell him about Ben and the McDonalds living just on the other side of the river.

"From what is going around, the Cherokees are just as torn up as the settlers; they don't know what to do."

The conversation lagged for a few minutes as Jacob tried to find the right time to change the subject. Every time he started to say something, he stopped short. His heart was beating out of his chest, partly out of fear. What if he said no? What would he do then, steal Cissy away in the middle of the night, or just pack his stuff, leave, and start over somewhere else?

"It's getting dark; we better think about going back in. So, what are you waiting on – when are you planning to ask me if you can marry my daughter?"

Jacob almost passed out. "So you knew all along I was about to ask you… to marry…?"

"Anybody with a heartbeat can see it. I've seen how you two look at each other."

"So, what do you think? Can I?" Jacob asked quietly.

"I don't know, you seem to be a little scatterbrained sometimes, and I am not sure if you are ready, but you know what, Margaret and I weren't as old as you when we got together."

The big German then turned, looked Jacob in the eye, and with what Jacob thought were tears welling up, he stuck out his hand. "Welcome, son. We haven't spoken much about what happened to you before you joined us many years ago, but I have watched you grow and mature, and I will be proud to have you marry my daughter. Just understand that I can put up with a lot of stuff, but if you ever do anything to hurt her, you will have to deal with me."

Jacob felt the sting of tears welling up in his eyes, but both men began laughing, especially when they heard the low giggle and realized Cissy and her mom were both peering around the corner, having heard their every word. Within minutes, Henry appeared with a jug in his hand. "Made this wine several years ago for a special occasion. I guess this qualifies. With the pop of a cork, the celebration began.

Chapter 41

So, that is how Sissy and I came to be married. She was such a beautiful bride. I never imagined in a million years that she would transform from the bratty little girl, following me and Jimmy around everywhere we went, to the beautiful angel that I would make my wife.

We settled down and built a place on her dad's land. We really had nothing. I continued going back and forth, trading with the Cherokees. Sissy stayed at home, and when she was tending to our small plate with potatoes, she helped her dad and mom with the trading post. Our first child, Hiram, was born a year later, and then it became even tougher to leave home. On my trips, I did get a chance to know Ben and his family better. Sometimes, he would even come with me on my two-day trip to the small villages of the Cherokee – places like New Echota, Pine Log, and then up to Ross's Landing. We often found a place to stay the night outside, or if the weather was bad, we would indulge in a tavern. The second day, we would backtrack, ending up at the small settlement that Ben had named Crossville.

Ben's children were growing up. Soon, his son would go through the rituals to become a man in their customs, and before long, his daughter, Little Fawn, would be ready for womanhood and all that came with it.

The group of families that had formed Ben's little settlement were all in some ways wanderers – all of them had lived east of here, some even in Carolina. Many were mixed marriages. Some were even people who, for some reason, were running from something. Either way, I was soon to find out that the "nation," as it had come to be called, was really divided. The opinions were many, but some of them were intent on staying put at all costs, while others were eager to move west to the lands of Arkansas, to start over, away from the waves of settlers that were now moving closer and closer, threatening to choke them out.

Jacob Childers

"Come on – I want to show you something I found." Jacob had stopped off by the mission, as had become his habit. It was often easier to do this and continue his journey the next day, rather than chance crossing the river at dark, tired and hungry from a long journey.

Jacob followed Ben down a narrow trail that descended to the place where a small creek emptied into the river. Jacob was wondering why Ben had a lantern with him, as the midsummer days were long, and it was at least an hour until sunset. He soon found out, as Ben walked over and moved some branches aside, exposed a small opening in the bank amid two boulders sticking out of the bank.

"Is this the cave you have been telling me about?" Jacob asked as he bent down beside Ben.

"It certainly looks that way," Ben said, "but I think it was much more. I believe it was some sort of old mine or a storehouse of some sort. Come on, let's have a look."

The two men wiggled through the opening and found themselves in a small tunnel that appeared to be dug out long ago. The bottom was sandy, with some water here and there. It was obvious that, at times, water flowed along the floor.

They crawled for what seemed like forever; at least, that's what it felt like when the tunnel emptied out into a large, dome-shaped room. It appeared to be some sort of junction, as at least three openings along the wall looked like small vaults. The tunnel then went straight out the other side.

Jacob looked around in awe. Soot blackened the ceiling from countless fires that had been burned in the room. There were also strange pictures drawn, which told some story, but there was no way to figure out who had painted them or why.

"This place is amazing." Jacob stared intently around the room. "How did this get here?"

"I am thinking it must be some of the same people that left other signs in the area. This goes back many, many years before our people arrived. There are at least three other vaults just like this. Come, let me show you."

Over the next hour, they saw two more storehouse areas like this. Then, one final tunnel, and they popped out into the gathered darkness. Apparently, the tunnel cut off a section of the river.

"My best guess is that this acted as some sort of sluice," Ben noted. Water could be diverted through the tunnel, which would deposit gold on the bottom as it went through. Or, they could divert the river this way and get gold out of the bottom of the river when the water was low. Later on, it was discovered that the water helped maintain a cool temperature, so crops and other food could be stored there. One of the rooms even had a shaft that went to the surface.

Jacob was amazed by what he had seen. He had never seen anything like it. A ready-made warehouse. He began to think about how it could be used to store produce, thereby extending its life. When he shared this idea with Ben, Ben thought for a moment, then said, "Not such a good idea."

Jacob looked puzzled.

"We need to keep this place quiet. Right now, no one needs to know it even exists. It will be a miracle its not discovered. Besides – we may need this place at some point in the future. You never know what old John Ross and Andy Jackson are going to get us into."

With that, both men took a detour down to the river and did their best to wash the red Georgia clay off their clothes before returning to Ben's for the evening. As he drifted off to sleep, Jacob couldn't help but think of his bride and new baby waiting for him on the other side of the river.

Chapter 42

The next morning, Jacob slowly guided the horse and wagon across the shoals, almost home. Several times, Ben had jumped on the wagon with him and made the trip to Hightower. He had not gone with him this time. He stopped by and saw the new arbor they were building for the community. Over the last three years, Ben and the others had worked together to build a school and now what they called an arbor to worship in. In his travels, Jacob had heard about them being built in a lot of places. A lot of people were flocking to meetings and then responding to the call to repent and turn to the Lord. It only seemed natural that Ben would be involved with this movement.

Even though the pressure was getting greater on the nation to cede their lands to the state of Georgia, much of the controversy had seemed to pass by this little village tucked away on the banks of the Chestatee. The villages in this part of the nation were few and far between. For some, it made little sense not to cede this part of the nation to the United States, but the river made the most logical boundary, he supposed.

Jacob noticed a small commotion on the other bank as he drew closer. Several men were talking rather excitedly with each other as they squatted in the water. Jacob chuckled to himself. *Heck of a time to take a bath in such a public place,* he thought. Jacob recognized a couple of them from town, so he stopped to see what all the commotion was about.

"What's going on here, you all okay?" he asked, peering around them to see why they would be in the river. It was much too early for a bath; plus, who would bathe with all their clothes on in the middle of the day??

"You ain't heard?" said one of the men that Jacob knew to be a laborer named Bill, "Just heard the news this morning! Thar's Gold all over these hills! We all gonna be rich!"

Yes, I remember that day well. I had returned from one of my trips and first heard the news from those fellas that were down by the ford at the river. I left them there, thinking it was really the liquor talking that they had been passing around. But I was soon to find out that wasn't the case at all.

There was a group of men gathered around the steps of the store when I got there, all talking excitedly. Henry was a voracious reader and had the paper delivered all the way from the state capital in Milledgeville. After reading, he would tack them to a wall on the side of the store so anyone could read the news, that is, if they could read to begin with. I watched as, one by one, each man would go back and read the paper, then turn away, shaking their head in disbelief. I walked over to the paper on the wall to see the news – and saw what they were so excited about…

Jacob

GOLD.—A gentleman of the first respectability in Habersham county writes us thus under the date of 22d July: "Two gold mines have just been discovered in this county, and preparations are making to bring these hidden treasures of the earth to use." So it appears that what we long anticipated has come to pass at last, namely, that the gold region of North and South Carolina would be found to extend into Georgia.

Jacob thought, why such a huge issue now? From the friends he had made among the Cherokees, gold was pretty well known in these parts. Even the cave Ben had shown him the night by the river that someone had dug many years before. For many decades, all the tribes in these parts had collected the yellow nuggets from the streams and rivers running out of the hills. It was no surprise to anyone around the Cherokee that gold could be found if you really went looking for it, and sometimes, without even looking for it.

Later that night, as they sat outside under the spreading oak next to Henry's house, Jacob remarked something just didn't seem right about all of this. It seemed too coincidental that about the time of all this talk of sending the Cherokees west, gold was suddenly discovered. Henry had already shared his insights on what was about to happen – he had been a young boy when the gold fever hit the Carolinas.

"This will bring a different breed of people seeking their fortune. We best get ready for it."

Soon, the whole area would be overrun with new people seeking their fortune in the creeks and rivers of north Georgia.

"This is not going to help things one bit." Suddenly, Henry looked very tired. He had worked hard to get the place back on its feet and was now a trusted member of the community, even though it was a good three miles back to town where everything happened.

Jacob lived in both worlds and heard it from all sides. Everyone seemed to have an idea of what the future should be –whether they were Cherokee or not. When at home, there was great debate over how to deal with "them." Some felt like they could live in peace with each other, so they should be allowed to stay. Others were convinced that it was better for them to leave so they could rightfully claim the lands the federal government had promised them. When he traveled to New Echota, he heard it quite differently. From what he picked up on in conversations he overheard, the same debate was raging among the Cherokees as well. One group felt it best to go ahead and pack up and move to lands promised in Arkansas and west of there. These were the folks that were part of the Ridge group, with many missionaries and outside folks on their side. The only problem was that Chief Ross didn't see it this way at all – and he had the power as the chief to command the loyalty of the old-timers – many of whom were closer to full-blooded. He advocated that this land belonged to the Cherokee nation, and they weren't going anywhere. So, in the midst of all this turmoil, Jacob had learned to be very cautious about who he spoke with and who to keep his mouth shut around. All it would take was one idle comment, and their whole business would die in a matter of weeks. Yes, everyone was excited that day on the steps of that old general store, but deep down, as he stared at the setting sun on their small community, isolated as they were, that things were not going to be the same again -- And not necessarily in a good way, either.

The article seemed to trigger it. It started as a trickle, then became a flood. Many showed up with little more than the shirts on their backs, having left their crops in the fields and their families at home to go on their personal quest. Within a matter of weeks, it seemed as though every foot of every stream had someone panning or digging in the muddy bottom to dig up the gold.

None can adequately explain why men act this way, but they do.

It was as if the world had changed overnight. All the controversy and discussion about how to peaceably co-exist just ended. There was gold, and there was no stopping the march of progress. Over the weeks that followed, more and more people streamed in. There was no room for them. The two hotels in Gainesville were full. Men just started squatting on whatever land they weren't run off. Some even dared to drift across the river into the nation.

As for the store, business was booming. Soon, what had been a general merchandise store for the community and hub of a trading business became in high demand for things prospecting miners would need. When the store ran low on picks and shovels, fights broke out among the miners to get their hands on what remained. Henry just shook his head as these things brought back so many memories for him. Day and night, people came and went. It seemed like the whole world had descended on the hills and hollows of north Georgia.

After about a month, the first load of provisions arrived to restock the store. Jacob was surprised by the previous comments Henry had made about the gold rush. The farm implements, hardware and personal items normally arriving had been replaced with more shovels, picks, gold panning supplies, and other things needed to satisfy the ever-growing group of outsiders that had arrived. What had once been a community store was fast becoming nothing more than a gold-digger's supply warehouse.

"What are all these things? Ben pointed at the wagon load that had just arrived – "I thought you didn't like all this gold stuff?"

"Son, I don't –" Henry began, "But if we are going to survive, we need to meet the needs of our customers. Besides – As I have already learned, the real money to be made is not digging for gold, but selling them boys what they need to dig – trust me on this."

"Well, what about the other people – those across the river? They are our friends. We can't just abandon them!"

"We will be able to continue to serve them as well – once this thing dies down, we can settle back in. But in the meantime, these folks will need to eat – and that's where I need you to be able to help create ways for our friends to make money as well – from the food they grow. You have the relationship with these people – make it happen."

Chapter 43

It had been a little more than a year since the gold rush had exploded. Our small corner of the world had suddenly become smaller. It seemed as if the whole world had descended on us. There were so many people, and in my trips back and forth to New Echota,, I passed many who were ignoring the authorities and setting up homesteads among the Indians. Most meant well, but it was inevitable there was going to be tension...

Jacob

Jacob negotiated the wagon across the river's shallows between their place and Gainesville. Today was not just court day – always a good day for heading into town with a load of produce, freshly gathered from farmers throughout the valley, but today was a little more special, as it was December 24th - Christmas Eve. Tomorrow, families and neighbors would gather to celebrate and enjoy what was, for many, the biggest feast of the year. Jacob had been planning for this day for the last few weeks and had plenty of squash and sweet potatoes to sell today at the market set up next to the courthouse. Although most that would be there that day would have their own crops, many would come needing to buy food – and which Jacob would accommodate.

For some reason, there was a bigger crowd than usual today. Perhaps it was due to the time of year, but maybe something else. Jacob was thankful for the large harvest this fall, as it would be needed. More and more prosperity had reached the area as gold fever had gripped this part of the state. They had successfully traded the produce the Cherokees had grown on their fertile farmland to the west for the smidgen of gold the miners had stuffed in their pockets.

Times were good for the moment, but things were starting to grow more tense, even on a festive day like today. There seemed to be an added level of tension. Jacob could sense something was happening.

He found that his usual spot on the town square next to the courthouse was taken, so he had to park the wagon further away than he wanted. Even with the new location, he could still get a lot of traffic from people passing by.

But today, as Jacob was soon to find out, the crowd was more than just the miners. The crowd was buzzing about the news from Washington and Milledgeville.

"Yup, ole Governor Gilmer is going to show them Feds and them Indians a thing or two," Jacob overheard two men talking.

Jacob knew that the last time he was in town, they had convicted the Indian of murder. He hadn't kept up with him after that.

Jacob tried to play dumb with the two men. He knew exactly what the stakes were. "So, what is happening - when you mention about Gov. Gilmer?"

"You mean you ain't heard? Why, the Supreme Court itself told the state, they couldn't hang him but danged if the Governor done passed a law to counter 'em."

Jacob walked along with them as they made their way across the square, in the direction of the gallows that had been set up on the other side of the town, near the springs he and the Barriers had camped at not too many years earlier when arriving.

The crowd pressed forward, each hoping to catch the eye of the spectacle unfolding in front of them. The executioner stood tall and proud up on the platform, and a hush fell over the crowd when the wagon rode into view with its lone passenger. George Tassel had killed a man over at Talking Rock and, last month, had been convicted here in the courts. What Jacob was not aware of was that his case had went all the way to the Supreme Court, where they had ruled he was protected and couldn't be tried there. The Governor had disagreed, so here we were, about to see justice administered.

They escorted the man, who was about as dignified as any man would be that was about to meet his maker, up the steps onto the make-shift platform. The executioner then asked the Indian something and allowed him to step forward. He paused for a moment, then raised his hands bound in front, toward the heavens, in a gesture of peace to his god. Then, the men that had escorted him up to the platform took him each by the arm and led him over to the rope that hung down from the old oak that formed a twisted canopy over the whole show.

They paused for a moment as the executioner slipped a burlap bag over his head. A murmur broke out in the crowd as a handful of Cherokee that were there with him began to cry and chant softly.

"The state of Georgia, the County of Hall, given responsibility to administer justice in the NW territories known to some as the 'Cherokee Nation' has convicted George "Corn" Tassel for murder in the death of Sanders 'Talking Rock' Ford, and has been sentenced to die by hanging. By the power vested in me by the state of Georgia, I hereby carry out this sentence". And with that, the executioner turned and tripped the lever that opened the trap door under Tassel's feet. There was an audible thud and twang of the rope as the young Indian dropped through the hole in the floor and struggled for several minutes until his body went lifeless. A doctor waiting nearby walked over and, after checking for his heartbeat, nodded his head at the executioner. He was gone.

Most of the people that day didn't have a clue about what had just been set in motion, as this whole trial had served as nothing more than a way to increase the tension that could get much higher. Although he was just a lowly laborer to most folks, as Jacob would soon learn, he would begin to totally change their world.

News of the execution of George Tassel reverberated throughout the region as things became even more tense. Overnight, there was more scrutiny on anyone doing any business with the Cherokees, including Jacob. It seemed like the whole world was taking sides on the issue of the removal. Most of the new settlers only cared about one thing – finding a piece of land to settle down on and raise a family. There were many efforts to stop people from crossing the river and settling with and amongst the Cherokees, but few heeded the warnings. The sad thing about it, the worst was yet to come.

Chapter 44

Milledgeville, Georgia – 1832

So, despite the tensions that had elevated due to the execution, our small business continued to thrive. Henry had actually created something that would make us a lot of money. He had the stuff the miners needed, and they had the means; well, at least some of them did pay for it. But, it was a rough and tumble existence for us all. The gold fever brought out the worst in people. Fights were frequent. Many of the newcomers had no desire to join the community but just to find their bit of creek bank to dig and pan in. Not all did well, leading to foragers trying to survive when there was no way to pay for anything. After a few months, the initial wave of miners had played itself out, those with much more money – many of them planters or wealthy gentlemen from the Carolinas, opened up mining operations in the area. The labor was intense – so whatever slaves or Indians they couldn't put to work in the mines, they hired those who thought they could make it on their own.

Then there was the lottery. I remember first hearing of it in the Spring of that year. Sissy and I had been married for about 3 years. After Mr. Barringer died six months earlier, the business now belonged to Sissy and myself. Then, I heard about the lottery, and we ended up making one of the biggest decisions of our lives..."

Jacob

The town of Milledgeville had been the state capital of Georgia for the past 25 or so years, but looking at the activity, you would never know it was such a new place. It was a better location, as it also was guardian to the upper Oconee River, and from here, cotton and other goods grown throughout middle Georgia could easily be shipped to the coast, thereby avoiding the higher taxes and fees demanded in Augusta and Savannah.

The small town was a bustling place, with lawyers, merchants and ne'er do wells all plying their trades around the new state capital building. The governor's mansion, almost complete, sat just a few blocks away. Times were good. The state was booming. Boundless opportunities lay in front of any young man willing to take a risk.

Since taking over the family business, Jacob has done very well. After the business had become his, he walked the fine line between providing for the influx of the miners that had flooded the area 3 years ago. He had also maintained his existing trade into the Cherokee lands, with the ever-increasing danger it brought. Things had not been good, as the two sides, along with the other settlers that had been arriving almost daily, were at each other's throats most of the time.

Jacob was here for one purpose – land. In two days, the state of Georgia would hold another land lottery, this time to carve up the remaining lands that were also claimed by the Cherokee. Tensions were high – technically, the state did not own these lands yet but was hell-bent on establishing ownership in hopes that thousands of settlers moving into the area would force the hand of the federal government to remove them as they had promised.

As he had many times before, Jacob lay under the stars that night, staring at the heavens in front of him. As sleep began to slowly shut him down, he thought back to what had transpired to bring him to this place. The gold rush had changed the terrain forever. New types of people were showing up. With them also came more tension with the Cherokees. People were getting restless, wanting them gone. Many of them were looking at the President to do something – lots of people felt he would do the right thing, whatever that was. Jacob recalled the day the news came out back at home. The Indians would need to go west, leaving their lands behind in the process. It didn't matter that they had been there for hundreds of years. It was now time to move aside so those looking for fresh land to till, more gold to mine could do so. After all, weren't the new folks with the light skin destined in some way to receive this land? Weren't they more deserving? At least, that is the story you heard from just about anyone he talked to that evening and the next day as he walked around town, talking to the others who had come for a chance to become rich or at least find out who would be the lucky ones to draw a lot. However, the lots would go to deserving farmers and settlers whose interest was in just getting a place and a part of the American dream. Unfortunately, there weren't many of those here. Most of the men who showed up were already well versed in the process, having undergone several of these before. They were the speculators, the swindlers, the unscrupulous who, within hours of the lottery being done, would know who received every lot and would spend the next few weeks working out deals that would result in many people giving away something for nothing. Then, on top of that, rather than work with the smattering of Cherokee families that occupied much of the area, they would slowly drive the natives off their land. Jacob hoped to avoid that scenario for Ben.

Jacob woke early the next morning, having slept next to a big oak tree on the edge of town. Milledgeville was a bustling town. Not only was it the state capitol, but it also was the center of commerce for this part of the state. Warehouses sat along the river, waiting to store goods that had been grown, awaiting shipment to faraway places. The streets around the capital were especially busy, as the lottery was drawing a crowd. Peddlers had set up around the old converted warehouse, which was needed to house the lottery that was to be held today.

The process would be long and tedious, and there was no guarantee his name would even be drawn out of the large wooden drum that had been adapted to act as the next great shaper of destiny. In fact, several friends had thought it foolish for Jacob to even travel down for this, when he would be notified if he were selected. In addition, not only did he have to get a lot, but he also had to draw THE lot he wanted. This was narrowed down by the fact that the lottery had already occurred that carved up the new lands Georgia was claiming – this one was just for the lots near the gold fields, that he had his eye on. Still, the chances of being successful were almost non-existent.

Although all its doors were wide open, the converted cotton warehouse was already getting stuffy and filling up quickly with people. Jacob found himself in a spot near the front of the room. The rotating drum sat up on a platform in front of the room, and on the walls were four large maps – each one of them showed a portion of the area being divided. On each map, a large grid was drawn, with a number. Each of these districts was further divided into 160-acre lots. In some districts, they were divided even further. These were called "gold lots" and would be distributed on day two of the festivities. Each of the districts had been assessed by an army of surveyors, who had spread out across the northwest part of the state, marking roads, buildings, and the location of the natives that already lived there. These district information sheets were organized by region and district.

This couldn't be happening; whatever hope he had in the lottery giving him what he needed was dashed as the final name was called, and he was not one of the lucky ones. He knew the whole process was a long shot, and he knew that getting THAT land would be almost a miracle, so the best he had hoped for was at least an ONE parcel, perhaps closer to the gold fields that he could at least use as a bargaining chip, but it was not to be. Ben had reassured Jacob that all would be well – he encouraged Jacob to put it in God's hands, and all would be well. *What a waste of time,* Jacob thought to himself as he slowly navigated the dark Georgia night on Bess, his favorite mule. Growing tired, he knew that in another hour or so, he should come to the small tavern he passed on the way down. His thoughts naturally drifted back to many 20 years earlier – things had changed a lot for a man almost 30 years old. He thought about that first journey as a scared young man, almost starving before that fateful day when he ended up with a place to call home, then being mostly sold to the Barringer family, then coming to Georgia.

He found himself almost dozing off as he was riding and stopped for a moment to collect himself and thought of resting for a moment, but then caught a glimpse of light through the trees, and realized he was where he would stop for the night. *A good meal and sleep will do me some good,* he thought.

As he ate the hearty meal of pork and potatoes that night, Jacob also realized the other reason he was not happy about the land – not only did he not get the property where Ben and the others lived, nor any other lot, but it was WHO got it. Of course, at the lottery, he recognized several others who had traveled the long distance to get to be part of the spectacle but did not expect to see Ezekiel Bryant there. *The conniver,* Jacob thought. There had already been bad blood since he walked out on the business, which somehow Ezekiel wanted more of an interest in but was shut out. He had also gotten involved with a group of investors that had opened one of the largest mining operations in the region. It was interesting that he should take such an interest in the business, when he had left it before, then now lacked for nothing. Jacob suspected something was amiss, when suddenly and quietly it happened. Ezekiel got the lot. Not only that one, but before the night was over, he had gotten four more, all adjoining the original one. That was the biggest reason Jacob had left suddenly, before the event was over, with tears of rage welling in his eyes. He wasn't in the mood to have a confrontation here. He wasn't sure who Zeke had paid off, but he had somehow worked some magic to get the outcome he desired.

He tossed and turned as he stilled stewed over what he had witnessed the day before. Would Ben and his family have to move? Would Ezekiel want to exact rent out of them, basically forcing them into a twisted sort of slavery, or would he cause other trouble for them and the others, just as he had been doing through the local bands of "Pony Clubs" that was rumored he was the driving force for their existence? Jacob kept mulling over all the possibilities, each one getting more and more incredulous. Finally, after a while, an almost audible voice slammed into Jacob's thoughts. "I've got this. Stop worrying." It was so strong that Jacob sat straight up in bed, looking for the source. His heart thumped loudly in his chest when he realized there was no one else in the room. He then felt an unspeakable peace settle over his soul, just as the fog had slowly descended over the valley that night.

He sank back into the bed, finally succumbing to the sleep he was so desperate for.

Chapter 45

Gainesville

Jacob arrived back home two days later, cold, wet, and discouraged. Sissy, who was now within weeks of delivering their first child, hugged him with the comfort and love that only a wife could give. Hungry and dirty from the long journey, Jacob said very little about his journey, but Sissy could sense that he was distraught and things had not gone as well as he would have liked. She had prepared a pot of stew, and after cleaning up and eating, they sat by the fire. She did not want to drag it out of him, so they sat silently for the longest time before he began to tell her of the almost carnival atmosphere he saw in the state capital.

"I failed." Jacob was staring out the open window at the moon, casting shadows on the landscape outside. I don't frankly know what the next step is to be. Bryant now owns the property, no doubt the mission will either have to pay a big sum of money for rent or owe their very souls to that scalawag..." Jacob's voice trailed off as he tried to keep the anger and frustration from welling up within him.

Sissy walked over and put her hands on his shoulders, slowly rubbing his shoulders as she shared what had been eating at her for the whole time Jacob had been gone. "I have been praying. I have a plan."

"Okay, let's hear it." Jacob turned around to face her. "I know I have run out of ideas."

"Let's buy the land from Zeke. I am sure he has a price. He has always been greedy for more."

"With what? Our good looks?" Jacob said rather sarcastically.

"No – I remember mother & father talking about how Zeke originally felt the business should be his to begin with. If you recall, that's why he left here a few years ago. I think we should trade him the store and this land for the land." She said the words. There it was out.

"Okay, so we are going to get rid of the business your father started, built into something that we could be proud of, that puts food on our table, just to sell it a few years later? How will we live? Where would we go?" Jacob was standing up, pacing back and forth.

"You know how much the business has changed these past few years since the miners arrived. Before, we had a very thriving trade with our friends in the nation, but as more have started moving in, it is easier for them to trade at other places. Now, all we have are the miners. I think it is time to move on to what else the Father has in store for us". She paused for what seemed like an eternity, looking straight at Jacob.

"I am not sure; I wish my faith was like yours." Jacob rose out of his chair, stretching, then sat back down. "I need to think and pray about this." He reached over and put his hand on Sissy's belly. "It won't be long now." As if on cue, he felt a small thump against his hand, as if his unborn child was reassuring him, as well. He looked up at Sissy and, with that look in his eye, got up and led her into the next room. Soon, all the cares of the trip would fade away for the moment.

And somewhere in the night, a soft voice penetrated Jacob's consciousness with the same tender words as a few nights before - "Remember, I've got this."

The plan was pretty simple. With the new day, their minds were sharper, and they could discuss better.

"I have been thinking of this for some time," she said. "Daddy would not have had it any other way. We must help Ben."

Chapter 46

The young man had arrived a short while ago, and in his usual manner, Ben had offered the same hospitality that he had offered every stranger who stopped by his place. After a few minutes of small talk, the young man nervously handed him a letter. It was simple and straightforward. It was a notice that the land he lived on was now owned by someone whose name had sent a mixture of anger and fear reverberating throughout the lower villages – Ezekiel Bryant. It was no secret he wanted nothing to do with the Cherokees or anyone who supported them. Ben was furious.

"Did Ezekiel Bryant send you?" Ben asked him, quelling his rising anger, "What did you say your name was?"

The boy, who didn't appear to be over 12 at the most, fidgeted nervously. "John. Jonathan Bryant.."

"So you are his son, eh?"

"Yes, Sir."

Ben went inside his place, returned in a few minutes with an envelope, and handed it to the boy. "You've done your job; now I need to do mine. Give this to your dad and tell him I would like to meet with him tomorrow morning. Cannady's Tavern in Auraria."

Thankful that he was still alive after the encounter, The boy disappeared into the waning sunlight to meet his dad a few hundred yards away. He had passed his first test.

The exchange had been filled with tension. The seasoned circuit riding preacher, who had seen his share of misery, discomfort, and danger, now sat feet away from the man who had been responsible in many ways for the reign of terror that had been unleashed on the small farms and settlements that belonged and dotted the Etowah and Chestatee valleys. Ben was resolute. Being firm was not a problem. Controlling his temper would be.

"Mr. Bryant, you know that I have worked very hard, and the Lord has blessed us greatly as we have worked with the Cherokee people. I became one of them myself when I married one of theirs. All I am asking for is a little patience and mercy in being able to continue my work". Ben said humbly.

"You must understand that there are forces much bigger than this at work – the people I work for – the people that really have the money, want you and your people to leave. You must understand that the state of Georgia has claimed your lands, and now I have been the lucky person to receive a gift from that claim. I now own the place where you live. But, being a man of compassion, I have determined to provide you with more favorable terms to be able to stay."

Zeke slid a piece of paper across the table to Ben. "Since you don't have the funds to pay me immediately, then I will allow you to stay – with these conditions."

Ben read through the terms provided to him. The more he read, the more the anger and frustration of the last few days began to boil inside him.

Zeke continued, "These terms provide you with the option of paying me monthly – due on the full moon. Of course, if you choose to pay me annually, I will give you a break and discount the terms by 10%."

Ben was almost shaking with the rage building in him. Zeke then pointed out the next part. "In addition to this, I will allow you to keep for yourself half of what you cultivate on the property. The rest belongs to me as the owner."

Ben reached the tipping point, "You arrogant bastard. Who do you think you are? I know what you are up to. Your reputation is known far and wide among our people. May God smite you for this; you can burn in Hell!" He wadded up the paper and threw it at the rather shocked Bryant, who smirked at Ben.

"So I take it you reject my new terms. You don't understand. If you don't sign, then the full amount of rent is due immediately. If you don't have the means to pay me, then I will have you removed from my property. I am sure the new sheriff would be more than happy to have you be his first eviction. I also have friends that are ready to help him."

Squelching the desire to dive across the table and choke him, Ben instead rose, and stormed out of the tavern.

Chapter 47

When I found out about Ben's dilemma, I went to see Zeke. I hadn't spoken with him much since the day he left, out to seek his fortunes in the gold field. As I mentioned before, he had become quite the man of stature since he took over managing Senator Witt's mining interests in the area...was quite a switch for the old fur trader. As everyone knew him, Zeke could drive a hard bargain, as Ben had found out. Although he had become a powerful man, I was certain he did not know of the relationship that Ben and I shared.

When we first started talking, Zeke thought I was there to assume the debt of Ben, and pay his stead. In fact, I listened to what Zeke had to say, including his going on and on about how it was destined for the Indians to give up their land, so they all had to leave. I could not believe this was the same man who was a friend of the Cherokee for so long. Money surely had corrupted him...

Jacob

"So, what do you think of my generous offer?" Zeke reared back in his chair, then turned and spat in the spittoon that sat next to the table they were seated at.

"I've got a better idea," Jacob said, glaring back at him. "I have no interest in paying Ben's rent. I propose something much more permanent."

"I would like to buy the property outright from you."

Zeke sat there for what seemed an eternity, then a smile appeared, followed by a deep laugh. "You want to do what? What do you plan to pay for this land with, my friend? Have you a secret cache of gold we don't know about? Henry must have been pretty good to you."

Jacob now played his last card. "I'm prepared to offer you our store, the whole business straight up, in exchange for the property."

Jacob knew that there was one thing that Zeke craved more than controlling Ben McDonald, and that was getting control of the store. He had long been jealous of Sissy and Jacob because he felt he was the one who should have inherited it from Henry.

Zeke chuckled to himself. He knew his bosses would be upset at first about possibly giving away gold land, but the real money was not in the gold, but in taking advantage of the hoards that had shown up, thinking they were going to strike it rich. Besides, if he traded now, he could always get the land back later. He sat there for a few moments, staring down Jacob. It was obvious the young lad was serious about this. He sat up straight and stuck out his hand.

"You've got a deal."

Two days later, it was made official, and within the next week, Jacob started moving his young family to their new land. Ben was there to meet his old friend as he crossed the river. Even though a short trip down the road, they had entered a new world, one which would change their life forever.

Chapter 48

September 1837

Crossville Mission Station, as it was to become, was bound to grow. It had all the ingredients needed to prosper. It sat on a river that was navigable, at least for the locals. To the east, the bustling hub of Gainesville was only 10 miles away. To the west was the center of the Cherokee Nation at New Echota and Pine Log. The main turnpike from Augusta to Nashville could be intersected a few miles south, and the gold fields of Dahlonega and Auraria sat just a few miles north."

Add to this the mission school and station started and operated by Ben, plus the favorable treatment I gave to the other Cherokees in the area, and it was no wonder that what was just a couple of cabins soon found itself doubling, then tripling in size by the time the real troubles began.

Over the next five years, Ben and I opened a ferry on the Chestatee right where the old Ford had crossed. During this time was when I also dammed up the small creek before it flowed into the river, and buit the mill. Both of these things provided the money needed to fund the small mission school and church Ben had dreamed of having. The dreams Ben shared with me when we had reunited ten years earlier were now coming true. A separate cabin had been built to house the school. There were 20 students from all across the nation, and school was the last remaining mission school since the one at Spring Place had been shut down by the new owners of the property took over.

The population of the small community was about 100. All the families were Cherokee, but few were full-blooded. As had been the case for several decades, there had been mixing between the white settlers and the Cherokees. In fact, the current chief of the tribe, John Ross, was only part Cherokee, with one great-grandmother providing his linkage to the nation."

The destiny of the small village of Crossville sat on my shoulders alone. I still owned the land, having leased parts of it to anyone who wanted to become part of the community. He had also used some of the excess money from the ferry and mill to purchase more adjacent tracts, making mehim one of the largest landowners in this part of Lumpkin County.

It was still a trying time for us all, as surrounding this hamlet of tranquility was anything but peace. Pressure was continuing to mount on the Cherokees to leave, and federal troops were being moved in to help with any forced removal. The first great exodus was to take place in 1835 when a minority party of the nation signed a treaty on behalf of the nation with the US to cede all remaining land in Georgia, and move to Arkansas. This was met with much resistance, but the machinery was being put into place for the ultimate removal of all the Cherokees."

Also, people began to question just how much longer we could hold out. After all, since my family was still fairly young, what would happen to the community if I were to pass away suddenly? Or, even worse, cave to the pressure being put on me by the other settlers to get with the program and support the removal. After all, they reminded me often that there was far more money to be pocketed if he wasn't giving most of it away to help keep the school afloat.

The worst thing was, the more successful we became, the more Bryant became incensed at what we were doing. It was a powder keg, waiting for a match. And that's what happened next.

It was a cool night in mid-September. If there was trouble, it was going to be at some point over the next few nights when there was little or no moon. Last month, whoever it was that was doing this had set fire to the corn crib. Thankfully, with a recent rainy spell, the fire only did minor damage before they could get it extinguished. The month before that, all the livestock had been let out, leading them on a three-day hunt to find the animals.

They were being dubbed the "Pony Clubs." News had spread from several other villages and towns scattered throughout the foothills that these attacks were occurring. It was pretty much those who were intent on forcing them out who were leading this campaign of terror. Now, every bucket, bowl, and trough in the village had been filled with water, and they had even practiced a bucket brigade to get water from the river to put out any fire that might be set.

They had set up a rotating schedule to provide security during the hours of darkness when they always seemed to strike. Jacob had paired up with a young man named Josh, whose family had recently been burned out of their home and had sought refuge at the mission with the others.

They had also learned from previous months when there was no way to respond to an attack once it had happened. They had organized two-man patrols to be awake at all times and then alert the rest of the village if there was trouble. They had all agreed that their primary purpose was to protect the structures and livestock. Only if the sentries felt physically threatened were they to fight back.

There was one other thing about Josh that led to Ben assigning Jacob as a partner – Josh had taken quite a liking to Ben's daughter, Little Fawn, and he wanted Jacob to feel him out before he came asking for Little Fawn's hand in marriage. There was not much of a chance to get to know him, as they had to be quiet so as not to alert intruders.

Even by sitting there in the dark, senses attuned to any sign of an intruder, Jacob still couldn't help but let his mind wander. He still remembered that day over twenty years ago, when he had left home as a young boy not much different in age than Josh. He thought about the adventures, several nights, of sitting outside the barn, guarding the hen-house from whatever the peril of the moment happened to be. Then, there was Ben's "chance" meeting, the journey to Georgia, and now he was caught in a struggle for life and death. After all, he now owned this property. Everything they were doing here ran counter to what was happening throughout this part of the state. For most of the new property owners, they were in the process of removing the Cherokee from their property or charging them such exorbitant rent that they, in essence, became slaves on the very land that had been theirs for generations.

For Jacob, there was never any question of doing this once they had made the decision to make a deal for the land. Also, he believed in what Ben was doing – providing educational opportunities for these families and introducing them to the Christian faith. He also knew the pressure that they were facing – he had lost a few friends over his decision. For others, he could tell that he had put them in a very awkward position by asking them to defend him in the community.

Of course, he could do like the others, force the mission to shut down and order the Cherokee to leave, but deep down inside, that still small voice whispered to him that would not be the right thing to do.

The first two nights were quiet as he and Josh fought off the sleepiness that so easily invaded their minds. That all changed the third night. There were three of them – all with hoods on their heads, riding horses. Each of them had a lit torch in their hand, looking to toss it into whatever would burn. Fortunately, the men in the community had managed to relocate the corncrib to a more secure location, away from the road, and the rain earlier in the day had left the roofs all wet, thwarting any fire that might start. They rode quickly down the small road that ran through the village, but as they Fortune when, out of nowhere, two riders on horseback came crashing right in through the middle of the arbor. Their intent was to burn down the altar, but there was little other than a little straw on the floor that could catch fire quickly. Josh ran quickly to the small schoolhouse that had been built, and started ringing the bell sitting on the pole in front.

The riders broke free from the arbor and then rode right towards Josh. Whatever led to the next action will never be known, but Josh took it upon himself to take on the riders. He pulled the dagger out of its holster on his hip and took a swipe at one of the riders as he came by. The knife caught the rider along his calf, causing him to scream out in pain. The rider came to a stop, with blood dripping off the end of his boot and struck the ground.

"Why, you dirty little Indian," as he reached and pulled out a knife and drew back his hand to throw it at Josh. Jacob saw the glint of the blade as he screamed at Josh to duck. But it was too late, as he heard the muffled thud as the knife found its target, landing in the middle of Josh's gut. "What the hell were you thinking?" Jacob could hear one of the other riders exclaim. "Let's get out of here," as they took off into the night. Josh stood there for a moment, staring down at the knife, watching his life gushing out around the wound. Seconds later, he slumped to the ground, his life gone. Soon, a crowd of the villagers, all who were awake by now, gathered around the young man lying in his own blood. Jacob retrieved the knife. He recognized it almost immediately. It was the one he saw Jon Bryant a few months earlier at the tavern when he met with Zeke.

The mission had designated a plot on a hill not too far away from the arbor for a cemetery. They buried Josh there the next afternoon, the first to be interred there. Jacob helped carry his coffin to the burial site, watching the pain his mom and dad were going through and seeing the tears roll down the face of Little Fawn, who had lost the one she had hoped to spend the rest of her life with.

For the moment, the attacks seemed to die down, and an uneasy peace once again settled over the little village. But, for Jacob, he was still very uneasy about what could happen next. IT didn't long for that to happen.

As had been their habit, Jacob and Ben were sitting by the fireplace at Ben's one evening two weeks later when things got suddenly quiet between the two of them. Sensing that something was perhaps bothering Ben, Jacob asked, "Something is eating at you, my friend; what's wrong?"

"I need to tell you something – She's with child." He almost blurted it out, tears in his eyes.

"Pregnant? Who is pregnant? Is it Tayanita? Are you going to be a father again?" Jacob was getting excited.

“No, not her – it's Little Fawn.”

“Little Fawn?? How can that be? But she is - who is the father?” Jacob was silently thankful his oldest was not quite at the age to be the father, but he was concerned for his friend. Although bastard children had happened before, it complicated things that Ben was a minister, and one of the things he had preached to the teens and young adults about was the dangers of fornication.

Ben now seemed relieved he could tell someone the news. “Her mom and I have talked to her extensively. I was not aware, but she and Josh had often met in the middle of the night. They stopped their meetings a few weeks ago when we started putting out patrols at night.”

“My biggest hurt is for her and the child at this point in time is that the child will grow up without a father. Plus, with all this turmoil, it is just not the best time to be bringing a child into the world.”

“May God help us all.” Said Jacob, as he looked around at the small village that was so sturdy, yet so, so fragile.

“Yes, may God help us all.” Replied Ben, almost prayerfully.

Chapter 49

Crossville Mission Station, November 1837

"We will not leave!" The old man slammed his fist down on the small table that sat in the darkened room. "This is our place, our land! I don't care what old Ridge, Boudinot, or even ole Hickory thinks! We are staying put!"

Smith leaned back in the small wooden chair that looked to be close to cracking and crashing onto the floor. "Broom, there is really no choice. Whether you like it or not, the treaty has been signed, and the migration is already well underway."

"I suggest the best thing for you to do is to prepare for the move. The future of the Cherokees is not here in north Georgia."

The room grew quiet, except for the latest revelation from the slight, graying man who had been appointed as the federal agent to the nation 6 months earlier. His job was clear – go to small communities and villages throughout NW Georgia just like Crossville, convincing the natives that things would only get worse and that it was best to leave voluntarily before being rounded up like cattle.

There were about 25 people sitting under the arbor, mainly men, but also several of the women had joined them as well – considering that unlike their European "friends", women played an important role in determining policy within the nation.

A young man, Thomas, stood up toward the back of the room, "So, just how do they propose we do this?"

A nervous smile broke out on Smith's face. This is what I have been waiting for, he thought, an opening. Get them to consider the option – soon, they will be on board…

Smith, sensing the victory at hand, cleared his throat. "Arrangements have been made. You will be responsible for getting yourself and your family to Hightower in three days. Once you are there, you will be escorted to Ross's Landing. There, you will be put on a boat with your belongings and be transported by river to Arkansas and your new home."

Jacob was not convinced. He had been on the trip the agent was describing, having traveled on many occasions to Ross's Landing in his recent journeys. There, he had met some of the rivermen, that guided the boats down the river, first to the Cumberland, then into the Ohio, down the Mississippi, before finally making the journey up the Arkansas to Fort Smith. It was anything but an easy trip.

But, the whole world seemed to be divided. Those of the Ridge Party felt it best to leave now, while the terms were good, rather than wait until being forced out. The only reason that Crossville was even still a factor was due to the horse trading that Jacob had pulled off three years earlier. Without it, someone else would have owned this property, and they would not have been so gracious to what had once been the native sons of the land but now had become almost overnight "squatters" on their own land. In fact, some of the treaty bunch had even used him as an example of why they needed to get out now on more favorable terms.

Jacob stood up. "Men and women of Crossville. Hear me out. As some of you know, this land did not come cheap. I had a thriving business just across the river and traded it for this property – just for the purpose of providing a place for us to live in peace together."

He continued – "I have traveled the routes he is talking about. This will not be an easy journey. There are many perils along the way, not to mention some – not all - but some who will be waiting at every turn to harass and hamper your travels. Also, do not be deceived. Although we have mild winters here, the route you will be taking will not be as kind to you. If you feel you must leave now, you will be battling the winter, and it will not turn out good for you. I urge you – wait. Wait until Spring comes. It will be much easier then."

Smith stood up, obviously not happy with the upstart farmer who should have been on his side but had already shown his reputation of siding with the Cherokee. "Folks, this IS the best time to leave. Yes, you will face a tough journey with many risks involved. But waiting here only increases the chance of something bad happening… something that you do not want."

Murmurs broke out among the group. Jacob could tell the decision to leave was not unanimous.

"One week from today, we will be assembling a group at Hightower to begin the journey. I can't make you go, but I can promise you this – those coming later won't be as nice, and there won't be a choice."

With that, Smith put his hat on, walked over to the edge of the arbor, and turned around. "You're not getting many more warnings." And with those words, he disappeared into the darkness.

The darkness outside the cavernous arbor where they sat only matched the mood inside among the crew assembled there. They somehow all knew that this was it. The time had arrived for a decision.

"Do we need to vote?" came a voice from one of the crowd.

"Yeah, let's vote!" came another voice.

A basket was produced, along with some coal to be used as a makeshift pencil.

30 minutes later, Jacob stood up among the group. "Those wanting to leave – 20. Those voting to stay – 5".

He felt like he had failed. He had worked so hard to make this place a place of refuge and peace. Ben sat in the back of the arbor, looking dejected. As the men slowly got up to leave, soon Jacob and Ben were the only ones left. "I'm not sure what just happened, but I am not sure this was for the best."

Jacob could only nod in agreement, squelching the sob building up in his chest as tears stung his eyes. He looked around at the arbor and, in the flickering light of the lanterns hanging on the posts, the small schoolhouse a few hundred feet away. All of this would be gone.

When they left the arbor that evening, there was a begrudging acceptance by both men that the dream they brought to fruition over these past six years was coming to an end, and likewise, they would likely go different paths in the future and likely never see each other again. Beginning the next day, they, along with several others at the leadership core of the school and mission, began organizing for the long journey west.

The decision was made to leave much of the records and valuables behind. They kept a listing of everything collected, including heirlooms, jewelry, anything else that could be taken from them at any of the checkpoints along the way. Ben had pledged to stay until the end, as his daughter was due in to deliver their first grandchild in the spring, plus it was too dangerous for her to go right now.

After much prayer and discussion, it was felt best for Jacob to remain with his family. He had a good business going with the grist mill and ferry, and plus, someone would need to take care of what was left behind. Provisions were being packed, things were given away, and windows boarded up. There would be few goodbyes, as most of them would be traveling together. The exit started as a trickle, but by the end of the month, most of the families were either gone or getting ready to leave. The only ones left showing no signs of leaving were Ben, his wife and three sons, and Little Fawn. Jacob and Sissy had their two boys as well. The place had become a ghost town in a little over a month since the meeting at the arbor.

The winter passed, and both families went through the motions, as nothing was the same. Round-ups had started all through the hills. People were being herded like cattle into stockades, with little more than the clothes on their backs. In addition to the federal troops, local militia bands and vigilantes were also contracted to assist with the effort. The whole world was coming apart, or so it seemed. Jacob would often walk around the village at night, crying and asking God to intervene to restore peace and protect his and Ben's family. Every trip to town was met with angry glares. They knew where Jacob stood, and as time went along, he also found himself being shunned by many settlers who did not appreciate his position on the matter.

The time had come. Their families would have to make a decision. For Ben and his family, it was really not a decision. Ben and his family were already on the registry. The only choice they would have was to leave voluntarily or wait to be herded up at the point of a bayonet.

For Jacob, it was complicated. He had learned recently that there were several families like his – they had some sort of informal relationship with a Cherokee family and chose to leave on the journey as well. Even for these families, most of them were squatters wgi owned no property and could easily pick up and go. Jacob had too much invested in this place, and he felt the need to continue to protect the mission in the slim chance the circumstances changed, and they could begin again. Despite this, the desire to pick up everyone and go too made for a lot of sleepless nights as things began to sprout out in the spring – normally a time of hope and excitement, but not this year. Definitely not this year.

Chapter 50

Crossville Mission Station, May 1838

It was all coming to an end, in spite of what a lot of people hoped for. The events of the last few months was just too much for most to bear. I guess some were expecting the government to change its mind, to somehow let them stay, but it was not to be. One day in early May, they showed up. Ben's decision had been made for him. Our plan was already in place to execute. The matter of us leaving had been settled. We would stay put for the short term, and if things worked out, we would follow later. The most important issue we had to deal with was Little Fawn. There was no way she could make the journey, so we kept her here with us – and would hide her to protect her and her unborn child, who had remained behind, and we feared for her and her soon-to-be-born child... we had to do something to protect her...

The cave was lit with a single lantern, which sat on a small table near the entrance. They had been here for a week, waiting and hoping. Things were quiet for the moment. There were sleeping mats laid around in the small space. After moving the records into the cave that had been left behind from the mission, Jacob quietly began to move more of their stuff here in preparation for what might come next. There was no way they could keep Little Fawn in the open – so using the cave made the most logical sense.

If they come here again, we will be prepared this time to fight to the end, Jacob thought as he looked around at his wife and sons. He had hoped that when the troops showed up the collect the McDonalds, they would be the feds. At least they were halfway civil. However, that would not be the case as a small detachment of militia showed

285

up. Especially mustered just for this mission, these roving bands of "soldiers" were little more than the pony club that has wreaked havoc with its earlier attack. They had quickly moved Little Fawn to the cave as the band had swept through the village, going door to door, until Ben and [wife] walked out and gave themselves up, and were quickly ferried away.

That was a week ago. Tonight, Little Fawn was in the final stages of labor – there was no midwife – those that could tend to her had left, and he didn't trust letting anyone else know where she was at, as they would be on her in a moment to whisk her away. It was just too, too risky to do that.

Jacob's own son, Adam, lay on the other side of the cave, swaddled and looking around at everything, peaceful in his own little world. Jacob was worried – just how long would he be able to survive in this damp air? They had enough provisions to do them for a few days but would have to eventually come out to get more or to return home.

Jacob had sent Jesse and Caleb, his two older sons, out to provide security or warn when and if trouble arrived. Jacob's instructions had been clear – don't engage, don't try to fight. Run as fast as you can down to the river, take the ferry and head downriver, away from this place. He looked at them wondering how they would handle the turmoil they were witnessing. After what he had gone through at their age, he was hoping that they would avoid the same trauma. Right now, he wasn't sure if they would.

That had in face been their original plan - taking the dugout canoe that was sitting by the riverbank; *these goons wouldn't know one if it fell on them,* Jacob uttered under his breath.

But it was too late for that now. Little Fawn was too far into labor to risk it – not only for her sake but also for the sake of the entire family. Nothing like a woman in labor, screaming in pain, to alert all the troops within five miles of this place.

This would be the riskiest time for them all. Although they were in the cave, at least 100 feet from the entrance, there was no telling where air vents were dug, which would project any sounds all over the hill above. Sissy was doing her best to keep Little Fawn quiet, but there was only so much she could do.

"It won't be long now," Sissy said as she sat on the floor next to Little Wren. Little Fawn had been talkative for the first few hours as the labor started, but now she was quiet, except for the times when the contractions hit her. The excitement of a child being born had faded in her eyes and now was replaced with a rather ominous sense of dread.

"I can't… do… this," came the voice from the soon-to-be mom.

"Yes, you can – do it for me – you are about to have a beautiful baby," said Sissy.

Another contraction seized her. They were getting closer together.

Jacob began to feel a little queasy. Although he was there when all three of his boys were born, that was with a midwife, and there wasn't so much stress and worry.

God, not sure what you are doing here, but please, please help us. I don't know what we are going to do next, Jacob prayed silently.

Peace and quietness settled in the room once again as the contraction faded away. "I have to check on the boys," Jacob said as he dropped to his knees to begin to crawl up the small tunnel to the cave's entrance. It was obvious that this was not the main entrance to the mine – that was on the other end of the hill. He had thought about breaking in there, but it would be too easy to be discovered.

After a few minutes, Jacob popped out of the small hole next to the river. It was unclear how this had been used other than to provide a quick escape or a place to bring out ore and rocks directly to the river. Either way, it attracted much less attention and lessened the chances of the entrance to the cellar being discovered. Besides, it was at least a hundred or so yards away from the house and would attract little attention from anyone who would be prowling around there.

He had positioned his sons about twenty or so feet up the hill, just off the path. They were to lay quietly behind an old fallen tree, and if they saw any activity, were to provide warning. They had rigged a rope from their position, down the hill, and in through the tunnel to their place of refuge. If anything came along, three short tugs on the rope would warn them inside that danger was nearby. It also gave them the ability for Jacob to find them in the darkness.

As he climbed out of the gulch, he noticed the orange glow through the trees and could smell the smoke. They were burning down the houses. ***There were voices.*** He had warned the boys about talking – one voice traveled far in the night – but there was a third voice as well. Whoever was with them had a lantern, which lit up the top of the hillside. Jacob grew worried – he crept slowly from tree to tree, trying to stay in the shadows and to move as soundlessly as possible. *George would be proud of me*, he thought. When he got to a point to see better, he saw his oldest son Jesse, standing about 15 feet away, facing him. His other son, Caleb, was nowhere to be seen.

"So, I am going to ask you again – What are you doing out here?" When he spoke, Jacob recognized the voice immediately. He didn't want his son to see him, so he stayed extra still.

"I… told you we were just going to Gainesville, and we got lost. We decided to stop here and wait 'til daylight". Jesse was never a good liar, and sure enough, he didn't start being one here, either.

Where the heck is Caleb? Jacob began to look for signs of his younger son. Hopefully, he hadn't been caught and taken away.

"I don't believe you. Aren't you Jacob Childer's boy? Yes, I believe you are. All of you, Childers. Injun lovers. Where's your dad? I tell you what – one way to find him. I'll just have to take you with me; then, maybe we can flush out your dad." Joel spit out a long stream of tobacco juice. You can even be my helper."

Jacob, terrified, watched them walk slowly away, with Joel holding Jesse by his collar. He had to think quickly of what to do next.

He followed close behind, and as they approached the top of the hill, Jacob felt a hand touch him. It was Caleb.

"Where have you been?" Jacob whispered.

"I saw that man coming and was hiding. What are we going to do?"

They had reached the top of the hill. Jacob then saw the destruction.

All the cabins were burning at one stage or the other. The barn had already collapsed in a shower of sparks. It was as if Hell had descended on this little plot of land.

He then heard Joel tell his son, "We now get to save the best for last – you are going to help me burn down the rest of it."

Joel walked over, still holding on to Jesse, walked him over the arbor, where he proceeded to tie him to one of the support pillars.

"Let's see if this will get your daddy to show himself!"

He then walked over and grabbed a burning stick out of the nearest fire. He was going to set fire to the arbor.

To this point, Jacob had held his cool, but this was the last straw. He stepped out from behind the tree, hoping to be the distraction that would allow his boy to escape.

"Bryant, that won't be necessary. You have found me!" Jacob yelled as he charged the smaller man. He caught him totally off guard, and his shoulder caught him right square in the small of the back, knocking him to the ground. The burning stick went sailing well away from the arbor.

All of the frustration, all of the pent-up stress of the last few months came out. The two men rolled around, biting, gouging, and punching. John connected with a punch to Jacob's nose, splattering blood. Jacob countered with a punch that no doubt broke a rib or two. Jacob then followed up with a quick punch to the groin, which put John curled up in a ball on the ground, writhing in pain.

"Boys, quick, get out of here!" Jacob yelled at Jesse. By this time, Caleb had untied him, and they were standing there, gazing at their dad's newly discovered fighting skills. "Get to the cave!"

Suddenly, John came to his senses – "Cave? Did you say cave? Yes, take me there – I would be interested to see what you have!"

The boys took off down the hill, and despite his injuries, John started limping off after them. Jacob panicked. He had let out the secret. It would be just a matter of moments before they discovered the secret, and they all would hang for it.

His nose in pain and barely able to see through his tears, Jacob tore off after them, this time with a fairly large rock in his hand.

It only took a few yards to catch up with the ailing man in front of him, who had stopped as he gasped, trying to catch his breath. Jacob let out a yell and descended on him, coming across the side of his head with the rock. John hit with a thud, the puddle of blood growing ever bigger around his now smashed skull. Jacob collapsed on top of the dying man, and everything went black.

Daylight was starting to break when he awoke.

Chapter 51

Jacob slowly sat up, looking around at his surroundings. His nose ached from the blow he had taken the night before.

Devastation was everywhere, and what had happened when the militia, or better yet, mob had shown up the previous week was still evident. This time they finished what they had planned to do the first time - to make sure no one could return here. They had done a pretty good job. All the cabins were reduced to ash, including the one that housed the school. The barn that had corralled and stored so many of their harvests. Fortunately, the arbor had been saved, as well as their own house and the mill, which sat a few hundred yards away from the other places.

At the sight, Jacob could feel great sobs welling up inside of him, and he just sat down next to a soot-covered tree and cried.

After some time, he felt a hand on his shoulder. It was Caleb.

"Father, are you okay? Mom sent me to look for you. She needs you."

Jacob took his son's hand, and they walked down the hill together.

Upon entering the chamber that now was their makeshift home, , Sissy rushed over and hugged Jacob deeply. "I am so glad you are okay," she said as tears rolled down her face. "Come, see what has happened."

Jacob walked over, and lying contently in Little Fawn's arms was a very healthy baby boy.

In all the turmoil, destruction and death, a new life had begun.

"So, what are you going to name him, he asked little Fawn, as he sat down on the ground beside her mat.

"Hezekiah – just like the King in the Bible," she said, beaming at Jacob. Jacob could see that she was very weak. He was worried.

The baby laid there in his mothers arms, but after a little while, Sissy took him away to clean him up, then laid him next to Adam in make-shift crib they had made out of some pine branches.

Little Fawn had fallen asleep, or so it appeared to them. After a little while, they noticed she had not moved much.

"The labor was very hard on her," Sissy remarked. "Maybe she just needs a good night's sleep."

Sometime in the middle of the night, they were all awakened by the soft crying of the infant. Sissy arose and walked over to place Hezekiah on his mother's breast. Then, she screamed when she realized – Little Fawn was gone.

Chapter 52

We did the most honorable thing we felt we could do at the time. We stayed in the cave as long as we could. It was me, Sissy, Caleb, Aaron, the baby Adam, and of course, Little Fawn's lifeless form and Hezekiah. We fed him the best we could with what milk we had from Nellie, our goat, and Sissy, since Adam had not been weaned. Fortunately, we had been able to move some of our food into the cave beforehand, and spent the next few days rounding up the few chickens that were scattered in the woods. The boys had helped me drag the body of the man I had killed, Ezekial's son Jon, into the mine, so as not to attract attention on the outside. No doubt, Zeke would be poking around here, once he realized something had happened, and his son was missing. We could have buried them both, but it would have attracted too much attention. So we left them there and turned the cave into their tomb. Of course, we did prepare Lil' Fawn a little more than Bryant. We just sort of propped him up against the wall. That's the way we left them. To this day, I have not returned to the mine, hoping to wipe away all the memories of that fateful time…

Jacob

They had ridden for five days. The boys had stayed behind to keep a watch on and protect what was left of the mission station. Sissy rode on the back of the wagon with the two babies, protecting the most precious cargo that Jacob had ever hauled. Their mission was simple – find Ben. When the remaining Cherokees were rounded up, they put them in stockades at various places. They would simply go to each one, bribe the guards if necessary, then look for the McDonald's among those being held. No doubt, the joyous occasion of the birth of the child would be overshadowed by the death of their precious daughter.

Jacob knew of at least four camps in the area, but when arriving at them found them empty. Everyone had already been moved. Having traveled this route many times before, Jacob knew he had to get to the landing at Rossville.

He had not been here since they had traded away the business. What he expected is not what he saw now. The place was still bustling, but there were no longer any Cherokees to be seen. The settlers had taken over, and they had even started referring to the place with a new name - "Chattanooga".

Curious, Jacob asked around about any new groups of Cherokees expected to leave on boats any time soon. There was none, he was told. Instead of moving the Indians by boats, they had decided to take them north, across Tennessee. It was safer, they were told, as it eliminated the risk of a boat sinking or capsizing.

Dejected, getting no help from the local population, they knew they would never see their friends again. Turning around, they headed back home, arriving two days later in Crossville.

The baby thrived. They named him Hezekiah, and the local circuit rider that had been assigned to this newly settled area of the state christened him a month later. He was now their son.

Chapter 53

Dawson County – Present Day

"As for the Childers family, life began to slowly return to normal, as normal could be. They sat down with their other boys when they got back, making them swear an oath not to ever discuss what had gone on here to anyone. Thankfully, the gristmill, ferry, and most importantly, their home, had been spared the terror of that fateful night. As the years passed, the forest gradually overtook the ruins of the old village, the arbor became the centerpiece for the newly organized camp meeting grounds, and Jacob continued to build his new business literally on the ruins of what was Crossville. It was as if the whole chapter of his life involving the Cherokees had never taken place."

"There were also three daughters, so seven children in all. All the daughters married and moved west. 25 years later, Jesse would lose his life in the defense of Atlanta, and Adam would die at Gettysburg. Only Hezekiah and his older brother Caleb, my great-great-grandfather, would return alive, with Hezekiah having saved his life at Petersburg."

"The journal also contained some other important information - it appears that after returning, building the grist mill and settling down, the cave was sealed up. Jacob built a new cabin with a cellar that hid the upper entrance, and plugged up the lower entrance. It would have stayed sealed had it not been for the lake being built." Colin sat back, relaxing, and sipped on the cup of coffee in front of him, seeing the look of astonishment and wonder on his son's face. It was as if he now realized just how special this place was.

"So, Dad, what about Tom? Can you tell me his story, too? What did you find out about him? Was it connected in any way to Jacob?" Luke asked.

"No, not really. I have completed some more research on him, but still working on it. As I have already noted, we found a few personal belongings of his that were left behind, including a picture of him and his mom with Jacob, not long before Jacob's death. All I knew about him was from a few newspaper clippings and what Red had told me. Other than that, he went crazy in his later years. From talking to some of the older folks around here, so was able to piece together what I believe happened to him. It turns out he and his mom had a pretty tough life, not all of it of their own making."

Chapter 54

Gainesville

April 5, 1936

Clickety-click, clickety-click, clickety-click, the road sang to him as he drove along. The car glided along the road, as each joint lulled him into a rhythm, which helped to clear his mind. There was so much to sort out what he had discovered, and what he would do with it over the days and weeks to come.

It was surprisingly warm and muggy for early April. You could almost reach out and touch the air, it was so muggy. The final preparations had been made. Now it was just a matter of executing the plan. A plan that had only come together in the last few weeks, the fulfillment of a lifelong quest for justice and revenge…

He remembered that day well. The day Papa died. His death had set this whole thing into motion. As he drove along, he let his mind take him back again to that day over 30 years earlier, the moment that he had relived many times, especially over the last year...

The family dynamics had been tense as long as he could remember. After all, how many men marry someone 40 years younger? The family never liked her, and for that matter, Tom. Except for one – the old man. As long as he was alive, his mom Sophie and he had enjoyed a quiet, peaceable life. Her and Jacob, or Papa, as Tom would call him, had hit it off from the start, much to the chagrin of his grandchildren – after all, she was younger than some of them. His dad, Hezekiah, had brought her home, not long after he buried the mother of his other children, and disappeared for several months. She had nowhere to go, and he needed someone to take care of him. There were whispers, and of course, plenty of gossip. She herself had been born in the ashes of the war, literally. Born and raised in New Orleans, – the daughter of a prostitute, Either way, her skin tone and hair gave away her mixed heritage, created a lot o whispers in the community. Added to this, she was educated – at least more than most of the folks that lived around these parts. No one asked Hezekiah how he found her, but one thing was never in doubt – he loved her, and she loved him.. Soon after their arrival, she announced to the world she was pregnant. Nine months later, young Tom came into the world. Since Jacob and Sissy had long since raised their kids and grand-kids, having a young child around helped them to feel younger and virile in their old age. Added to this, Sissy passed away not long before Hezekiah brought Sophie back home to live. For what remained of the family, however, they were not happy with the scandalous nature of this whole arrangement, and the tension was felt every time the family would gather. Besides the rumors of her sordid upbringing, her dark skin tone and other features pointed to her heritage. With the tensions beginning to mount in the area, it was not good for the family to be seen as harboring a "negro," even if she was more white than not.

After the initial shock wore off, things settled into a sort of peace. Although Sophie would never be the same as the rest of the family that her predecessor had been, they were glad to see Hezekiah happy again, and of course, her nursing training would come in handy to help care for Jacob in his old age. Then, tragedy struck. While working with a friend to clear some timber, Hezekiah was impaled d by a falling limb from a tree – pretty much a freak accident. He was buried two days later, and whatever goodwill had built up was eclipsed once again by whispers, suspicion, and envy. The family felt sure she would leave and take the young Tom with her, but this was not to happen. She really had nowhere to go, and given the close relationship with Jacob, every time it was hinted that it was time to move on, the old man would put his foot down, and that was the end of that conversation.

Tom slowed to let a deer and fawn cross the road. *Good thing I was on this straight stretch, or I might have hit it,* Tom thought. Drops of rain began to pepper the windshield as he drove through the night.

He remembered the times well. Not long after Papa became ill, he and Momma would spend hours, first on the front porch, then as time progressed, in his room, sitting by his bedside. They weren't sure exactly what was going on, but the doctors had suspected cancer. Mainly, 90+ years of life had worn him out. One day, early on, while they were sitting on the porch, Papa had turned to Sophie and asked her to start writing down what he told her. He already had a journal he had kept in his younger years, but there was more to be told – and re-told.

Oh, the stories he heard. Papa told them of how he came to Georgia. He heard about how he almost drowned in the river. He heard how Papa came to own this place, how he lost an uncle at Antietam. When it seemed like he had almost finished telling all the stories he could tell, his mood became more somber – the stories became more scattered. He started talking about crazy things – like Indians and massacres and such… and gold. Although Tom was just a lad of eight, hearing these last stories was more than intriguing.

Soon, the end came. It was an end in more ways than one. The old man died late one October afternoon. They buried him at the church, right next to his wife Sissy and just a few graves away from where they had laid his son Hezekiah a few years before.

Within a few days after the his passing things began to change. Although Jacob had made his daughter, granddaughter Ola, promise to provide for Sophie and Tom, they did as little as was to be expected from the family that had begrudgingly accepted her to be with them – they could live in the old house out back that Jacob had built, or they could leave immediately. Sophie chose to stay in the old house, at least until they could find something else.

Times were changing, and with the road being improved into Gainesville, there were more opportunities there. Soon, Sophie found work as a nurse at the new hospital in town, and they found themselves leaving with almost everything they owned on the back of the wagon that took them to town.

They had rented a small house near where Sophie would work, and that had been home for the past 25 years or so. Tom was able to go to school on a regular basis and eventually took a job at a local store near where they lived.

For Tom, life took another strange turn two years ago, when his mom passed away after a short illness. He missed her terribly, but at the same time, she had been very protective of him, so he enjoyed the freedoms that came with being a young single man living in town. Things were prosperous in the small town that had become his home.

Tom had also found another passion that had been buried deep in his soul. He couldn't shake the memories and stories he would hear his papa tell during their times together before he died. Most pointedly, his Papa kept mentioning to him that "Some day you will understand; someday have your mother tell you…" He thought he knew – after all, he was a Childers. Or so he thought. He had asked his mom early on about it a couple of times, but she would either laugh it off or change the subject. It was as if she knew a secret he did not yet know, and wasn't yet able to handle. He soon was overwhelmed with all the fun of being a boy, then a teenager, and the desire to know faded into the recesses of his memory.

In going through his mother's things soon after her passing, Tom uncovered in reading his mother's diary a notation that sparked his interest once again.

There was a flash of movement, then the sickening crunching sound, which jolted Thomas back to the urgency of the moment. Pulling to the side of the road and grabbing a flashlight out of the glove compartment, Tom jumped out of the car to see what he had hit. He walked slowly along the shoulder, his heartbeat slowly returning to normal. The beam of light reflected off the young deer, lying halfway in a ditch. "Good," Tom muttered. There were lots of folks who walked this stretch of road, and he was glad he had not hit another person, as he still felt the buzz from the three drinks he had downed at the club before leaving for Gainesville. He knelt down next to the small deer, which was likely a young doe. He could see that she was suffering, but still alive.

Heading back to the car, Tom reached back in the glove box and pulled out the .38 revolver he had stashed there. He walked back to the deer, and one shot put it out of its misery. Of all the ways he could have used the gun he had bought just a couple of years ago, he never figured he would be using it for this. Although times were getting better, there were still some desperate people struggling to survive. Anyone perceived as having money or who looked wealthy could be a target. Also, he had enemies. Not many, but they were still there.

The new programs that the government started 2 years earlier had been goo to Tom. When FDR established the CCC, he was fortunate to get an administrative position, supporting several camps in the area. This also gave Tom the chance to take advantage of his position – he had developed a way to reward himself out of the funds allocated to the regional camps. He managed to do this quietly until one day, when one of the camp administrators assigned under him approached him about discrepancies he found in the books. Tom had to quickly cover his tracks, which resulted in the camp administrative clerk having to leave the camp and the CCC. For a short time, Tom felt bad about framing the young clerk, but it was for the best. Soon afterward, when a friend offered him a bookkeeping position at the local furniture plant in Gainesville, he jumped on it. Besides, he could get away from the situation he had created, at least until things settled down again. Also, the hours would be more stable, which would allow him more time to pursue his latest quest.

Although the seed had been planted many years earlier, sitting by the bedside of his Papa Jacob, it never sprouted until his discovery. His mom, Sophie, was a very detailed, organized person, and as such, had maintained a diary that she updated daily. In reading his mom's entries, most days involved the routine and mundane. There was, however, one section which captured Tom's attention, and had gotten his blood boiling again, of how they were treated by the rest of the family after his papa Jacob was gone. In particular, the entry from June 10, 1903, really drew his attention:

Jacob died today. Our conversations have been wonderful, although I feel as though he never quite got to finish his story. As he requested, I put the journal in the hiding place with his other things. There are many secrets there. Rest well, my friend...

Tom had been there that day, and although 32 years had passed, he was surprised at himself about how strong the memories of that day had been. When she wasn't attending to his needs, his mom had sat quietly by his bedside, as he poured out his life's story. Young Tom had heard tales of Indians, of perilous travel, of wild animals, and other things to excite a young boy's imagination. Especially intriguing was the word the old man kept muttering over and over as he lay dying – gold. Now, 30 years later, he had to find these things and the secrets they contained.

So, he had written a letter and paid a visit. By this time, generations had changed, and instead of dealing with the emotions – prejudice, anger and jealousy – that his mom had to deal with within the "family", he was greeted with a warm embrace by his cousin, who now lived in the house that his uncle had built. His cousin had pretty much given him free rein to explore the property, which he did. After a couple of months, his cousin opened up the old house again and let him move back in for a low amount of rent. His cousin thought he was just interested in the history of the place, but it was much more than that he was after. Now that he was back pretty much full-time, he could search better for what had been hidden away. After several weeks of searching, he noticed that one of the rocks seemed to have been removed and replaced in the chimney in the main room. Grabbing a chair, he was able to reach the stone, which easily slid out of his hand. In there, he found the book, which he recognized immediately. He sat down in a small chair by the window and gingerly handled the precious artifact he had in his hand. He didn't know what made him more nervous – handling the fragile treasure he had just found, or seeing his mother's beautiful handwriting in the document. He fought back tears as he read, the latent grief and even anger over how their lives took a change soon after this was written.

As Tom skimmed through the book, his eyes found what he was looking for.

For Tom, once he had read it, he had to get to the cave. It just had to have gold in it. Maybe this was the Cherokee gold everyone had been talking about. He would be a rich man. Stories had been told for decades about the lost Cherokee gold, and he only imagined what fame and fortune it would bring to him if he were the one to find it. His heart started beating faster with the thought of what fortune its discovery would bring.

Tom sat there for a moment. First of all, if the wrong person got hold of this, there would be trouble. He had himself tangled with these Bryants, and he wanted no part of them. Knowing that a Childers had killed one of their own, no matter how long ago, wouldn't sit well in the community. Like the pages he had removed the week before, he also carefully removed the pages of the journal, hopefully burying the secret forever. To make sure no one else found out about this, quickly removed the pages that might lead anyone to discover the secret that only he should know. He carefully folded them, then placed them in an envelope with all the other things he had gathered. Then, one final thing began to sink in - his heritage, his lineage, had been totally upended.

Instead of being an outcast, the son of a mulatto prostitute's daughter, he was a CHEROKEE. He read the story of his dad's birth again – better HIS story. This changed everything. Now, there was no question this was his gold to get. But he, and only he, now had this valuable knowledge that no one alive shared. By this time tomorrow, he would be a rich man. He carefully replaced the journal in the rocks of the chimney, then began to explore to find where these treasures were at.

It didn't take long to find the entrance. It was cleverly concealed in the floor of the cellar in the old cabin.

When he discovered the remains entombed in the cave, he was at first startled. She was just lying there, strangely mummified, lying just as she had been a century before. Although the journal entries told the whole story of her, it never said that the cave had, in fact, become her tomb as well. But, she wasn't the only one there – in a more crudely dug grave, half uncovered, were the remains of a young man – apparently the one that Jacob had killed when he was trying to protect his family. He sat there for a moment, taking it all in, but remembered, this was not what he was there for. They were gone, buried. The gold needed to be found.

The map was surprisingly accurate, and within 10 minutes, he had found the small vault carved out of the wall of the cave. Wiggling through it, he came to the three small boxes. All sitting together. They were partially buried, and there was no way he could get them out of the mine by himself. He had to have help. There was no way he or any of his friends would be able to lift the crates out of the hole. There had to have been another way in. Soon, he found the small tunnel that led away from the burial chamber and vault, and after 5 minutes of squirming through the tight space, he found himself popping out behind a rock near the riverbank. *This is perfect, he thought. We can bring a barge right up here, and load them on and be on our way…It will be the best way to get back at them…*

Chapter 55

Gainesville

April 6, 1936

Even the weather couldn't dampen his mood as he dressed for work. He hummed along with an old tune that was playing on the radio as he quickly shaved, then dressed by the dim light that hung from the ceiling in the small room in the house he and his mom had shared. He almost sold it when his mom died, but being located just a few blocks from downtown, it allowed Thomas the convenience of living close to work.

After eating a quick breakfast at the diner next door, he walked the rest of the way to the office. His mind wandered over the events of the last couple of weeks, the discoveries he had made. He had a hard time hiding the smile on his face when he realized how much his life was about to change for the better. Once he had discovered the notation in his mother's diary, all the pieces began to fall in place.

He had already arranged for three of his closest confidants from work to meet later that day. They were still skeptical, but now he had the journal entries for proof, and of course, what he had seen with his own eyes. The plan was relatively simple: they would take a small boat to access the riverside entrance. They would enter the cave quickly, then the three would drag the small trunks to the boat, and then disappear into the darkness of a moonless night. Of course, Tom had arranged to take his 80% off the top, with the other three splitting the remainder three ways. With times still bad throughout the country, the newfound wealth would keep him secure for years to come. They would all be rich.

Normally, early April mornings in Gainesville still had a bit of nip to them, but not today. The air was heavy, even more foreboding.than the night before. Although the sun was shining when he woke up, now it had been covered by clouds, and the western sky was growing ever darker, with an occasional distant roll of thunder. *Must be a storm coming,* Tom thought to himself. *I just hope the river stays low so we can reach the mine,* he thought anxiously.

By the time Tom arrived at work, two blocks from the square, he was nearly drenched with sweat. Reaching into his pocket, grasped a handkerchief and wiped his brow. Although he was in a bright mood from knowing what today would bring, he still felt uneasy deep down in his soul.

Just as every morning, he stopped at the time clock, which read 8:03 AM. Good, he thought to himself, plenty early. As was his habit, he sat down at his desk in the large room, which was soon to be filled with the hustle and bustle of the day. He looked around, as he knew within a couple of weeks, if not days, he would be able to pack his stuff up and move on. He allowed himself to daydream for a moment or two, just to linger on what distant lands he would travel to, away from this backwoods place that had been his home.

His desk, always clean and tidy, was sitting just as he left it the afternoon before. Of the five others that shared the large work area, where most of the plant's accounting and clerical work was performed, a couple had also arrived early. After taking a seat at his s desk, and in the few minutes he had before the large steam whistle on the roof of the plant sounded, Tom had a chance to look at the documents that had him in such a good mood, and coupled with the discovery he had made, would free him from ever wanting again.

Tom enjoyed a desk which sat near the windows, which provided a good view of the busy street the company sat on. In the distance, work was continuing on the new high school, and looking the other way, he could catch a glimpse of the town square, already getting busy at this time of the morning. As he sat there, his mind a thousand miles away, he noticed that the skies were getting darker and darker by the minute; in fact, cars that passed by were driving with their lights on. It looked as if it could start raining at any moment. The skies sounded almost a continuous roll of what sounded like thunder, or was it the 8:30 train that was pulling into the nearby depot? Large raindrops began to pelt the windows, as those walking down the street began to duck into doorways to escape the rain, which now became hard chunks of ice, as hail began to mix, then take over the rain. It was as if hell was being unleashed on the small town. The wind was now beginning to howl, as pieces of paper began to swirl around on the street.

Tom was now brought back to his senses as a distant door slammed. The low rumble was getting stronger, and a low vibration started that he felt deep down in his chest. Someone from outside screamed, and as the wind got fiercer, the windows near his desk began to shake. An awning across the street blew off its anchor, crashing into the middle of the street below. Suddenly, Jimmy Thompson, the plant manager, ran into the room.

"Everyone take cover!" he shouted, as everyone scurried to the back of the room to get away from the windows. Being furthest away, Tom hurried, stumbling over chairs and trash cans, to try and get to the conference room. Behind him, the large plate glass window in the front of the office bowed outward, as if pushed by an invisible hand, then burst into a thousand shards of glass.

Now unencumbered, the wind howled through the newly opened space. Tom was knocked to the floor by the force of the wind and pelted with debris and shrapnel. Something large hit his foot, and his own screaming joined the chorus of those who, like him, were fighting for survival. The whole building was now shaking, and as Tom curled into a fetal position, the worst of the storm hit. He heard the crashing of furniture as desks began to blow around. He realized, as he dared to peep, that the roof was missing. What he did not notice, however, was the missile that a few minutes later had adorned someone's desk as a paperweight, which caught him squarely on the side of the head.

Everything went black.

When he woke up, he was pinned underneath boards and bricks that a few minutes earlier had been his work home. He felt a wetness and looked down at where the blood had soaked his shirt. He felt, and where his ear should have been, there was nothing but a pulpy mess. He managed to free himself. He smelled smoke. It was also deathly quiet, as the hustle and bustle of the small town was now buried under tons of debris. Then, the screams. There seemed to be voices coming from everywhere. For a moment, he didn't know where he was or who he was. He tried to get up and walk, but his foot was twisted at an odd angle, and he was dazed and confused. The folder – it was gone. He had to find it. The treasure was his. No one else had a right to it. He tried to stand up, but his twisted leg wouldn't work. He sat back against the rubble he had just freed himself from. Time passed as he drifted in and out of consciousness. After a time, two young men showed up, helped him to his feet and gingerly onto a stretcher, and carried him to a nearby church that had now become a makeshift hospital.

As for the building, it was reduced to a pile of rubble. The plant, which sat behind the building, still smoldered from the fire that broke out soon after the storm subsided. The cloud of death hung in the air, and for those who had survived, the long journey to recovery had only begun. It was as if some giant hand had taken a shovel and scraped it through the downtown area. Destruction was everywhere. Cars were in buildings, parts of buildings in cars. Small fires burned. Columns of acrid smoke formed omnous columns reaching to the sky, which had a pasty white color.

A cool breeze blew gently down Washington Street, as if to apologize for the fit it had pitched earlier. The streets were strewn with paper, and with it, an envelope, now with its contents scattered throughout downtown. Some would be burned, others would simply rot away. As for his buddies, they became M-301, M-307, and M-312 in the makeshift morgue set up in that vacant lot three blocks away. The plans for riches had perished with them.

Within a week, the injured had been tended to, some to be patched up and sent away, to whatever was left of their homes. Along with others, Tom found himself in faraway Atlanta to be treated for his wounds, some of which would never heal. As the wreckage and debris were cleared, bodies were recovered, and funerals held. Some just simply disappeared, with only a photo or a diary left behind. Crews of young cadets from the nearby military academy and even from the college in nearby Dahlonega joined in the cleanup and recovery efforts. President Roosevelt himself would stop by to provide comfort. Even with the chaos, in the weeks and months that followed, things slowly returned to normal for the small town nestled in the north Georgia hills.

Tom Childers was the only survivor in the office of Thompson Chair Works that day. It would take about six months before he could walk again, although the limp would remain for the rest of his life. The greatest loss that day for Tom was his mind. Although he would appear healthy, deep down in his brain, something just wasn't the same again. He never really knew what hit him.

Near Anderson, South Carolina

April 7, 1936

"One hell of a storm. Thought we may need to go to the shelter," Randall told his wife, as he put on his coat to go out and check on things in the barn. His family had lived on this land for over 100 years, tucked away in a small place not far from Anderson. Walking around the small yard next to the house, he noted that besides the few small limbs strewn about the yard and some tin missing from the roof of the old barn, it looked like someone had dumped a wastebasket out in the yard. Scraps and even whole sheets of paper littered the place. Mixed in were even some old photos, and he even found an old shoe that the storm had blown. "That must have been some humdinger," he thought as he picked up and straightened the mess. Most of it was a soggy mess and ended up in the trash pile, but one piece was quite the mystery – it was in some papers in an envelope. He started throwing them away, too, but something stopped him. He folded the envelope in half, sticking it inside his coat pocket. "Somebody might come looking for these someday," he said as he turned and walked back to the house.

Chapter 56

Northeast Oklahoma

Five Years Later

The rain was relentless. He found himself glancing often at the display on the dashboard, hoping the rain would let up soon so he could find the way that he was seeking. As soon as he relaxed, the car would hit a puddle, causing the car to jerk toward the shoulder. The radio belted out a country song that was a hit many years ago. The joints in the old concrete road matched the rhythm of the wipers in the rain. He was headed to a place he had never been before. In fact, the little town of Talala was almost in Kansas.

Unfortunately, the weather was not cooperating. The night before, the flight had arrived just in the nick of time, as the airport had been shut down soon after his landing due to severe weather in the area. He was happy he had decided to land in Oklahoma City, and not try the connection to Tulsa, even though he would be going that way. He stopped for the night just outside of town. Today had turned out to be no different. Mid-May seemed to be prime for storms, and as he drove, his weather app on his phone kept breaking the silence of the road with its blare of storm warnings.

Colin had tossed and turned most of the night as he was trying to imagine what today's meeting would be like. He had no idea what to expect; all he had was a small package lying on the seat next to him and a large cup of steaming coffee sitting in the cup holder. Caffeine was his best friend this morning, as it took all he could do to negotiate the puddles standing on the roadway. *Good thing I upsized*, he thought, as the windshield wipers beat out a rhythm that kept him alert to the road ahead.

Soon after leaving Tulsa, the weather cleared and the rain slowed to a drizzle, as he outran the storms for the moment. After a quick stop for a refill, he was on his way again. I'll be there soon, he thought, as he looked for his exit.

Suddenly, as if out of nowhere, there it was. The deer. It had already been wounded, halfway out on the road. He swerved, but not soon enough. The dull thud resonated through the car, and he felt the car beginning to pull toward the shoulder, as the dashboard lights lit up like a Christmas tree. Once the car rolled to a stop, he got out and walked around the car, observing the grotesque scene. The deer's carcass had wedged itself under the car, causing the front rim to rim to be bent, and there was a stream of oil and antifreeze running out from under the car. Obviously, the car was undrivable.

He just shook his head. This is just one more crazy thing in this adventure he had been a part of…

The news was not what he wanted to hear when he called the rental company. The storm had wreaked havoc after he left Tulsa that morning, and it would be at least an hour before they could get anyone out to him.

"Hey – there's a storm comin. You okay? You need any help?" The voice seemed to come from nowhere, but when he looked up, Colin could see an old pickup sitting a hundred feet up the road. Standing on the other side of the car was the driver, a rather weathered elderly man, wearing bib overalls.

Colin paused for a moment. He looked strangely familiar. "Yeah, seems like I hit a deer. Tried calling the rental company, but it's going to be at least an hour, maybe more, before they can get here." Colin responded as he tried to wipe the dirt from his hands.

"Well, this is no place to ride this thing out – hop in, and I will give you a ride. There's a place we can get away from this storm. We can wait things out there." The man jumped in the truck and, reaching over to the passenger side, popped open the door/

"One of these days, I'm gonna get that handle fixed," he said with a grin. The door squeaked as Colin pulled it open. It was obvious no one had been a passenger for a while, as he found himself fighting for space with the empty drink bottles lying on the floor.

Colin was thankful for the ride. So many things had happened these past five years, and even though he was frustrated over not being able to get there just yet, a sense of peace and patience washed over him, replacing the frustrations of just moments before.

Ten minutes later, they were seated at a booth in the restaurant at the travel plaza where the car would be towed. After speaking again with the rental company, they arranged to have the car repaired. Clarence must have been a regular, as it seemed as though everyone knew him.

"So, my friend, it's obvious from your driving a rental car that you are not from around here. So what brings you out here to our part of the state?" He said that as the lightning flashed outside and the storm began to blow.

"Well, I'm looking for someone. There is some unfinished business I need to take care of." Colin was guarded in his response, but it came out wrong, like he was looking for trouble.

Clarence sat back in his seat. "Well, you can see we ain't going anywhere anytime soon, so why don't you tell me your story?"

Colin smiled ever slow slightly. "I don't really know where to start".

"Well, the beginning usually works pretty well."

By this time, the storm had really caught up with them, and Colin was thankful for his ride and the way everything had worked out. Had this all happened 10 minutes later, he would have been caught outside in the mess.

Colin began, "Well, it all started a long time ago…"

For the next two hours, Colin told of how he ended up back in Georgia, his coming to terms with his past, about Jacob and his adventures, and the enduring mystery of Tom Childers. Clarence just sat there most of the time, with a slight smile on his face, at least looking like he was interested in Colin's practical life story.

"Mr. Childers, we finally got you taken care of." The young lady who had taken care of him earlier was standing by the table. "You can pay whenever you are ready." She smiled at Colin, then turned and walked away.

Colin continued, although puzzled at the interruption. "As I was saying, once everything had been confirmed as authentic, as well as other circumstances, it completely changed the direction on what I decided to do with the property. I did end up building a couple of homes there, but I have also worked with the local universities in Dahlonega and Athens to do archeological research on the place. We are actually going to try and recreate the village of Crossville as it was before the removal. I get the feeling there is much more to discover there."

Colin looked outside and noticed the storm had now completely cleared, and the sun was beginning to peep through the clouds.

"Colin, what a way to spend a rainy Saturday morning. Glad you and I got a chance to meet, so you could share it with me. But, you never did quite tell me what brought you to our part of Oklahoma."

"The more I have read, and re-read the journal, I was just impressed with the work that was done there by Ben McDonald, and the relationship He had with Jacob. In fact, the impact on me has been tremendous. Their courage has been an inspiration, and for the first time in many, many years, I feel at peace. God has been good to me."

"It has become a passion of mine to find if he has any living descendants. During the time I have been piecing together Jacob's life after the removal, I have also spent time researching Ben, including finding any living descendants. The only one I could find was a descendant by the name of Samuel. Sam Anderson. His grandmother was a McDonald, descended from Ben. He lives in a veterans' home not far from here. I have some things I want to give to him that I think are his."

"Sam Anderson?? Wow – he is well known around these parts. Real war hero. Medal of Honor winner. I'm surprised you didn't learn that when you were researching."

"Wow – that's interesting – I don't know how I missed it." Colin reached over and picked up the tab left by the waitress. "I've got this. You were more than gracious to sit and be bored with my story over this morning."

"Trust me – it was my pleasure," Clarence said, with a slight grin on his face.

Colin handed the clerk the bill. "That will be $6.50." The waitress said.

"$6.50? Are you sure? I mean, there were two of us. The gentleman with me is sitting right over the…"

"Sir, I don't follow you. There was no one else with you. You ordered the two eggs, hashbrowns, and bacon. Most of the last two hours, you just sat there, staring out the window."

"But – Clarence…"

"I know. Do you think you might need some help?" The waitress was growing concerned.

"No, I will be fine. I guess I am tired from the trip, and anxious to get on my journey. That is all." Colin turned and walked out the door to his waiting car.

Surprisingly, the trip to Talala only took about 15 minutes, and soon he found himself turning into the driveway of the Northeast Oklahoma Veterans Home. The building was an aging brick structure that had begun to show its age.

Colin found a parking spot, and as he walked up to the front door, his heart pounding in his chest…When he had contacted the home last month, they had put him in touch with Sam's daughter, who, after listening to his explanation, was more than happy to help make this whole thing happen.

After introducing himself at the front desk, Colin was shown to a small parlor down the hall. Colin looked around the room – there were various pictures of what he assumed were the residents, many of them from times gone by. He quickly realized that this was a tribute to all those who had spent their final years together here as a band of brothers.

"You must be Colin." The voice behind him jolted him back to the present. Colin turned to see an older gentleman sitting in a wheelchair, wearing a plain polo shirt and slacks. Colin could help but notice an empty leg where his left foot should have been. But what really stood out was the wide blue ribbon around his neck, from which a bronze-colored, five-pointed star hung. The Medal of Honor.

"I, I am." Colin was awestruck, not so much with the aura of having never met a Medal of Honor bearer, but more that he was looking at the very person whom he had been seeking for the past two years.

"I was looking for you to be here earlier, but I guess this storm delayed everything. My daughter is also expected to be here; hopefully, she will be here in a few minutes. Susan, will you bring her in here when she arrives? I know Colin would like to meet her as well." Sam seemed very at ease, almost as if he knew this day was coming.

Colin began. "As I explained in my letter, I inherited this property, and initially, I thought I would just develop and sell it, but things worked out a little differently, I suppose." Colin's heart was beating through his chest, as he began to relate to Sam what he had discovered, to include about Ben McDonald, and the discovered friendship with his ancestor, Jacob.

Tears welled up in both of their eyes as Colin related how the mission was destroyed, and Little Fawn had died in the act of giving birth. When he finished, the old man sat up straight, wiped a tear from his eye, and began to tell Colin the rest of the story.

"This came from my grandmother, who was Ben's granddaughter. There are very few stories of the Trail of Tears. For most, it was as if we wanted to blot it out completely." The old man paused as he collected his next thoughts.

"Ben was one of several ministers who accompanied our people on the journey here. Ben and his family arrived in one of the first groups, but he wasn't content just to be here. He would go back two more times, meeting more groups as they crossed the river from Kentucky. On one of the trips back to help, he became ill and passed away somewhere in Missouri. His dying wish was to be buried in a simple grave, alongside others who perished on the journey."

"Wow, that is very interesting. In my searching, I had found other ministers who had traveled with the parties to Oklahoma."

Sam then started again. "But, I have to admit, getting this letter from you was a bit of a surprise."

"I see. So you didn't know about Ben's past before?"

"I knew a little, as I had done some research as well, but couldn't place exactly where Ben had lived. But there is something else I need to tell you about…"

"Morning, Dad! Sorry, I was late. Storm was a beast." Came the voice of Sam's daughter as she entered the room.

"Morning, Sweety. Yes, that's what the nurse told me, after you called." Sam replied with a big smile on his face.

"Colin, I would like you to meet my daughter Amanda."

Colin was suddenly and completely confused. She looked extremely familiar. He sat there, staring at her. "I'm sorry, you look very familiar. Haven't we met before? Where are you from? What do you do?" He was immediately curious.

"Oh, I live in Kansas City. I am a professional musician. I play the violin in the orchestra there. But that's not where we met."

Suddenly, it clicked in Colin's mind. She had been there. She was the one in the woods. At the meeting. Standing on the lakeshore. Playing the violin. Why was she in Georgia? Now Colin was really getting confused.

Sam spoke up. "By a strange twist of fate or providence, we were brought here today. You see, I had something I had to do. I had made a promise a long time ago to an old friend, just like Ben and Jacob."

He continued. "You see, this goes back to our war. Colin, I made a promise to a friend one day that I intended to keep. He had saved my life, and unfortunately, he was severely injured and would not survive.

Everyone in the room became silent. "You see this medal around my neck? It was for actions I took two days later that ended up saving an entire platoon. I would not have been there to do what I did had it not been for the sacrifice he made two days before."

Colin sat there for a moment, wondering why he was hearing this story.

Sam continued. "We went through officer training at Benning together, and shipped out the same day to Vietnam. Two weeks before I was wounded in battle, I received this medal. It was your dad who saved my life, but in the process, lost his." Sam sat there quietly, his chin quivering, tears in his eyes, while the room got silent.

"We were on a patrol together when we came under fire. I would have been killed, but your buddy put himself in harm's way, killed the sniper, but in the process, exposed himself to enemy fire and was shot himself."

Colin was confused by what appeared to be an old war story that the old man had likely told many times before. He tried to say something, but didn't know quite how to reply, and get the story steered back to Ben and Jacob.

"I called for a medic on the radio, but soon learned he wasn't going to make it. One of his last requests was for me to find his son and give this to him."

The old soldier held out his hand. It was the other half of the medallion that had been hidden away by his mom, but which he now wore around his neck. His dad's half. "That friend was your dad, William Childers, Jr."

Colin almost passed out. He sat back in the chair, staring at the medal, as huge sobs began to well up from deep in his soul. Finally, he was able to choke out – "This is almost too incredible to believe. Are you sure this is my dad's? I mean, these things are all over the place. Do you have anything else?"

"In fact, I do. Here is a photo we took, not long after arriving in country." He handed Colin the photo he had been holding.

Colin glanced at the photo, hardly able to see the photo from the tears. He was staring at a copy of the same photo he had seen many times before. Now, he knew who the other person was in the photo. Sam Anderson.

"This is absolutely incredible, how all this time, I was looking for something, not quite knowing what it was, but in the end, it was you really looking for ME??"

Both men hugged, cried, and by this time, some of the other residents and staff had gathered.

"You are right. Fate, providence, whatever, made this moment real." Colin said as he was finally able to collect himself.

"So, Amanda – your daughter? She was part of this, too?"

"Yes, she was." Colin jerked around to see Linda standing in the doorway.

"What are you doing here?" Colin asked. "How did you know about this?"

"Oh, Amanda and I talked a couple of times –"

"Now. Time to listen. Sit down, while I tell you more about your dad."

Chapter 57

Dawson County

Present Day

"That's crazy how all of this was connected." Luke sat there with a look of amazement on his face. "So you are saying that there is a lot more to be learned about this place? This answers some of my questions, but I guess there is more to be discovered?" Luke said, showing about as much excitement as one would expect from a 13-year-old boy who had just sat through a two-hour history lesson. "What about the gold?"

"Yep, much more," Colin replied. They could have talked about anything, and it would have been good to spend the time together. "You better go ahead and get those fish cleaned, then freshen up. It will be time to go before long." Free from his history lesson, Luke grabbed the cooler and disappeared around the corner to the sink in the garage.

Colin had picked up Sam and Amanda at the airport two days ago. They talked all the way back. Of course, after they had found each other a few weeks before, they really hadn't stopped talking. Colin had spent the next day showing him around town. They went and sat for a long time at the arbor. It was the only time they didn't really talk a lot, as Sam was left speechless as he took it all in. They finished the day at the lake shore, near where the ruins of a small village of Crossville lay. After an archeological team had cleared most of the area, they worked with painstaking care to recover any artifacts that might remain. Colin thought he could see a tear in Sam's eye as he shared with him the plans to reconstruct the village as a memorial to the small band of Cherokees and their families that lived here, most of all Ben McDonald. Exhausted, they headed back to his place for the evening.

That's when Colin showed him all his dad's stuff. They both cried again. They talked late into the night.

Alone again in his reflections, he was startled by Sam.

"Good Morning, Colin," Sam said in a voice that brimmed with enthusiasm and renewed vigor, as he guided his wheelchair across the wide patio. Are you ready to go?

The drive to the cemetery was a short one, but Colin's heart was beating out of his chest, as he had never imagined this day. Linda, along with Junior and Cindy, was waiting. He guided everyone from the car as Amanda pushed her dad's wheelchair. As they walked through the early morning, the sun began to peep through the trees and reflect off the markers in front of them. He had wondered over the years if he would ever get to see it. The place took on even more special significance, now that he knew how fate had brought their families together.

For Colin, the healing was sweet. He was at peace with himself and with his God. He walked beside Sam as they approached the hallowed place. He saw his grandparents' names on the headstones, and he knew they had arrived.

Right next to them was a simple marker:

William Childers, Jr.
1LT, 75th Ranger Regiment
1936-1971
KIA - Republic of Vietnam

They stood there for a moment, each in their own thoughts. Colin placed his hand on Sam's shoulder, who motioned for Colin and Amanda to help him to his feet. Then, as if on cue, they both slowly raised their hands in a salute, standing there for several moments, frozen in time, with tears streaming down their cheeks.

Somewhere in the distance, that perhaps only heard by the two of them, Taps slowly played, as the sun rose overhead.

The End

Acknowledgements

When you spend more than a decade doing anything, let alone writing a book, it is almost impossible to recognize all the people who were there to encourage, strengthen, and push me to help get this work across the finish line.

The seeds for On the Banks of the Chestatee were planted long before the story was put on paper. As a young man, I heard many stories from my grandmother, Annie Lou "Tish" Moore, and cousin Henry Lewis Carruth that ignited a desire to dig deeper into my own family's story. In addition to this, two of our family historians, Peggy Taylor Hulsey and Barbara Parks Kerby, through their lifelong interest and efforts, created a treasure trove of source material and models for several of the characters in the book. I tried to stay true to the historical events and actual locations portrayed in the story.

My initial readers were valuable parts of the journey, taking a rough manuscript and providing input on how to make it better. I knew that Michael Kelly and Frances Steedley were both to be ferocious readers and were able to validate the whole premise of this work. My own son, Ben Carruth, provided great insight into areas that needed tweaking and challenged me to continue the editing process, even after I thought I was finished.

My sister and fellow genealogy sojourner Sheila Burtz was also a help, not only in telling me when I needed to set aside my genealogy quests to write, but also to read and provide insight from a historical perspective. Finally, my cousin Melissa Hulsey Sheriff was a valuable member of the reading team to help me portray an accurate picture of the community that is the setting for this work.

There were two special people who made a valuable contribution. My brother Jeff Carruth provided the original drawing that graces the cover – his contributions to help preserve the landscape of northeast Georgia through his immeasurable talent to paint and sketch will have an impact for generations. My cousin Linda Maurer, through her career as an English teacher and librarian, was my greatest reviewer and contributor – her single comment – "You need an ending!" helped me to look again at the story's flow and helped to bring it to its final form.

I also want to recognize those many people who provided the continued encouragement at different points to keep moving forward, often listened to me explain something I was trying to put into words, then offered insight, or helped me overcome obstacles to get things moving. My friends, such as John Shepherd, Amber Harris, and Kay Draughn, come to mind, but many others have also been there.

The most important one I want to recognize: that person was my greatest encourager, supporter, and even critic throughout these years of crafting this story. Besides reading the book herself and providing valuable insight, she was the sounding board when I got stuck on some detail, put up with me spending many hours pounding away on a keyboard, or staring quietly out the window, with the details pinging back and forth in my head. My wife, my life partner, the peas to my carrots, Lydia Carruth, has been my strength and inspiration through this whole process. She has put a boot in my butt when I needed, put up with my occasional grumpiness when I felt like giving up, and celebrated when I would reach my goals through the process. (By the way, she hates peas...)

Last, but most importantly, I want to give credit to my Lord Jesus Christ. He gave me the ability to complete such a project, and it is through Him that I have life. I pray that this work is true to what He would have me communicate.

Robert Carruth